THE WOLF AT MY DOOR

SAM HALL

DESCRIPTION

All Jules wants is to get a job. The drought is causing work to dry up along with the land and she and her dog, Buddy are starting to get desperate. Then she spies an ad for an all-rounder at a remote place called Sanctuary, whatever that is.

Somehow Jules is the only applicant and it appears all her prayers have been answered. She now has food, board, a job and a whole lot more. It appears Sanctuary is the home of a huge pool of ridiculously good looking men who are 1. All vying for her attention and 2, expect her to choose to have relationships with multiples of them.

Just as Jules thinks she's Alice and she's fallen down the hole into Dickland, she starts to look past the guys who read romance novels to better understand women and the HR manuals written by kink practitioners and starts to wonder. What is behind the huge fence at the centre of Sanctuary? Why is everyone waiting for the full moon? What secrets are the staff hiding? Join Jules as she finds her answers to these questions and those she never thought to ask.

The Wolf At My Door

The Wolf At My Door © Sam Hall 2019

Cover art and design by Mibl Art

This one is dedicated to my alpha and beta readers. I was a bit leery of this one, feeling like it was all just thinly veiled porn, but with their support I ended up with something I was proud of. Couldn't do it without you guys!

IF YOU'RE IN ANY WAY RELATED TO ME

Don't read this one. Seriously, Christmas dinners are already awkward and weird without imagining me writing werewolf orgies. Just delete the book, put the Kindle down and sidle away. It'll be better for all of us.

AUTHOR NOTE

This book is written in Australian English, which is a weird lovechild of British and American English. We tend to spell things the way the Brits do (expect a lot more u's), yet also use American slang and swear more than both combined. I've included a list of what I think are Australianisms used in the book at the back in a glossary.

While many people have gone over this book, trying to find all the typos and other mistakes, they just keep on popping up like bloody rabbits. If you spot one, don't report it to Amazon, drop me an email at the below address so I can fix the issue.

samhall.author@gmail.com

1

Please, please, God. Buddha. Hecate... whatever, I thought furiously as I waited, *let me get this job.* There I was, in the very nice air-conditioned head office of the vaguely named Sanctuary, my legs neatly crossed, my foot bouncing up and down at a million miles a minute. The only other person in the reception area was one of the staff, dressed in what looked like the uniform for this place, a khaki shirt and pants. *I wonder what they do here? Maybe work with animals? A lot of people who work with animals wear khaki,* I mused as my eyes flicked around the room. *Zookeepers, rangers, why is that? Surely black or grey would hide more dirt. Or camouflage, with those weird blobs. Is that why soldiers wear camo? So the blood doesn't show, and they look invulnerable? Maybe animal workers should develop their own pattern that hides dirt.*

I watched the girl sitting at the desk, her fingers flickering over the keys of her keyboard. She'd smiled when I came in, offered me a glass of water, let the interviewer know I was here, and then turned back to her work. Of course she did, she had purpose, a job. I'm not sure if I'd ever noticed that unconscious smugness the employed had. They were insulated from the fears I faced on a daily basis, they knew where their next meal was coming from, that they could make their

I

next car payment, they could even splurge a little. I tamped down an irrational flare of jealousy. It wasn't her fault I wanted to feel that smugness and never, ever take having a job for granted again.

I needed this job. I had driven for five hours out into the middle of nowhere, and was waiting for an interview for a position I knew nothing about and had no previous experience in, my car sitting outside with all of my worldly belongings. My dog, Buddy, was tied up to the porch railing with a bowl of water, with me hoping that wouldn't piss them off. The job was supposed to come with food and board, but I still didn't know if that extended to one occasionally neurotic Husky. I was banking on them seeing his baby blues and opening their arms wide to let him join the family in response to his sheer beauty. I shifted on my seat as I felt my stomach roil and squirm. I'd had him as a puppy, fallen in love with this little black and white ball of fluff. Back then, I'd been full of that same unconscious smugness, thinking I would have no problems looking after him. Now we were both on reduced rations. I'd blown most of my severance check on petrol and caravan parks, driving around trying to find work in a country that was in a downturn. Despite the fact I am an atheist, I started sending up those prayers again, to any divine being that would listen. Right now, I'd sell my soul to the Devil to get out of this mess.

I'd seen the job in the paper the other day, advertising for an all-rounder. It was a total long shot. I had no idea what an all-rounder would do, but I was prepared to give anything a go. I'd spoken to the manager, Kelly, over the phone, and when she'd asked me to come in for an interview, I'd almost burst into tears. I'd taken a breath, steadied myself, and replied that I'd be delighted in what I hoped was a professional voice, waiting until the call ended to have that cry. Then I'd dried my eyes, had a cold shower in the caravan park ablution block, and picked out the most appropriate outfit I had left.

What are you going to do if they don't want you? I thought, eyes flicking from the receptionist to the door of Kelly's office and back again. *What are you going to do for Buddy?* I'd grown up in a small town, Melville, that I'd loved. My mum and dad had been born there,

Dad had always proudly told us seven generations of Bronsons had lived and died in Melville. I knew almost everyone by name, lived in the same pretty white clapboard house, until my brother Daryl sold it in a fit of foresight. He'd packed up after Mum and Dad died, and was now making a living as an accountant in the big city.

Me, I'd done alright at school but didn't want to leave to go to uni, so I'd had a range of jobs to keep a roof over my head, the last one was working at a diner. I'd gotten an arts degree by correspondence, but having a good understanding of world wars and cultural geography had proved not especially useful. Problem was, with the drought that seemed to be stretching out for decades, and with the salt rising on what used to be A-grade farmland, jobs were drying up and towns were getting smaller and smaller as a result. I'd stuck my head in the sand when people tried to talk to me about it. Pa used to talk about the big droughts from his day, and Melville had survived them, but this was not that time. Everyone was living in cities, unless it was little towns on the coast for rich people's sea changes. Cute farming villages hadn't been identified as hot spots yet, so slowly trucks, trains and tourists all stopped coming.

Gary, my boss at the diner, could barely look me in the eyes when he let me go. He'd given me my pay, said he'd give me a glowing reference, and sent me on my way.

The manager's door opened and I jerked upright in my chair, startled by the sound. I swallowed the small gasp I'd almost made and smoothed my face into a professional polite mask. A woman with long brown hair and wearing khakis came out, going over something on a clipboard with a tall man standing beside her.

"OK, I'll get right on that," he said.

"Can you send Finn in for me? I've got that interview for the offsider."

"Yep, he should be in the shed." I watched the guy take off for the door with a wave. My heart started to race as she turned. *Was she ready for me? Was it go time? Now?*

She looked up and smiled at me. "Miss Bronson? Come on through."

3

I followed at a polite distance, walking into a conference room. A large map covered most of one wall, a whiteboard on the other. "Kelly Dwyer, we spoke on the phone?" the woman said, holding out a hand. I wiped mine on my skirt, then cursing myself internally for making it so obvious that I was nervous, I took it and gave it a firm shake. "Have a seat." She grabbed the chair at the head of the table, in front of the large window that showed a panoramic view of the park. The forest beyond the buildings of the Sanctuary was beautiful, the kind of cool, green stillness I needed right now.

"So, you're interested in the all-rounder position?" she asked, looking down at some notes.

"Ah, yes."

"Do you know what the position entails?"

"As I said on the phone, not really. I assume you need someone who'll gofer, do, pick up, get whatever you want."

"That's pretty much it, though what that means in Sanctuary can be a bit different than the city. Where are you from?" I told her. "Ah, it's lovely down there. The drought is driving people out though, right?" I nodded, not trusting myself to speak at that moment. For most people, this was idle dinnertime discussion or a short news clip in the evening. For me, it was watching the town I loved die. "So you're keen for work, then?"

I looked up at Kelly, really looked at her for the first time. When I'd come in, I know I'd smiled and met her gaze, but it was all a bit of a blur. With my heart pounding and sweat prickling on my skin despite the artificial cool, I'd sat down as quickly and gracefully as possible. She looked back with equanimity, like she could see past my neatly pressed white shirt and black pencil skirt I'd only ever worn to job interviews, through that to what lay beneath: I was homeless and desperate. Social security payments wouldn't be coming through for a few weeks, and I was broke.

"I am very keen," I said, and I was proud to hear my voice come out strong and clear, "but I think I can also be an asset to your company. I'm hoping it will be a win-win situation. You want someone who's prepared to live on site, who can do a range of tasks without having to be asked twice. I can do that. I mainly served customers and cooked at my previous job, but I've cleaned the diner from top to bottom, dealt with difficult clients, made deliveries, and even repaired door hinges on some cupboards. While I'm not exactly a DIY queen, my dad taught me the right end of a hammer, and I can change my own tires. I've worked in shops selling goods, helped out the local vet when they were still in town, and done same basic car maintenance. You could obviously get someone who has more skills than me, that knows the running of... whatever it is you do here better than me. Maybe someone who's studying business management..." I trailed off for a moment, seeing in my mind a legion of smarter, cuter, stronger MBA students, lining up for the same job against little old me. I swallowed down the lump in my throat and then looked back at Kelly. "You could easily find someone more qualified than me, but I don't think many people would be more motivated. Seriously, I'm ready and willing to learn."

"Well, she certainly sounds eager." My head whipped around to see a guy walk in through the conference room door. Oh. My. God. Up until now, my brain had been a teeming mess of anxiety, complete with a slideshow of what life would be like without a job: Buddy dying from starvation, and me giving hand jobs in alleyways for money. I was struggling to pay much attention to my surroundings or Kelly's expressions as my heart pounded. That all paused. It was like the world had stopped spinning, my heart had stopped thumping and instead, I experienced the most perfect moment of quietness. He came inside, giving me a brief nod and a smile, but I just stared. I'm sure with my mouth hanging open. Holy crap, this guy was gorgeous.

He was tall and on him, the ubiquitous uniform seemed to have been solely designed to stretch provocatively across his broad shoulders and chest. He had long, reddish brown hair that was tied back loosely at the nape, and his eyes were a pale grey that almost glowed in contrast to his warm brown skin. He moved with an easy confidence, pulling out a chair and taking a seat. My heart lurched in my chest, like it had all of a sudden realised it needed to beat to keep me alive. I blinked several times.

Get it together! I hissed internally. *This is an interview, not a bar!*

He didn't seem to have noticed, just slouched down into his chair, resting his elbows on the arms and bringing his fingers into a steeple. Then, those eyes turned on me. He seemed to look me over, impersonally, then with greater interest. His eyes flared wider, his gaze raking over my body from head to toe, though I had no idea why. I wasn't terrible looking, but I was well-aware I was the same middle of the road, mildly pretty that most women were.

"Ah, Finn. Was wondering where you got to." He didn't respond as he continued his inspection. "We don't actually have a long line of post grad students, Miss Bronson," Kelly said, with a smile. "We've found that university students are full of excellent ideas, but can lack the..."

"Common sense? Practical skills? Ability to follow even the simplest order?" Finn added, finally snapping out of whatever brain fart had him spinning his wheels.

"Quite. We are looking for someone with your sort of real-world experience, someone who has a proven track record of working hard. We've found locals from around the country tend to be the best fit for us." I fought down the surge of hope I felt in my chest. My brain was running ahead, seeing me in company housing, being able to feed Buddy decent quality food... *Keep it together*, I snapped at myself, *that doesn't necessarily mean you personally.* "So, Julie, if you're happy to take the position...?"

"Oh god, yes," I said, my breath coming out in a rush. Finn's eyebrows shot up.

"You're OK with this, Finn? She'll be your employee."

Fuck! Working for the hot guy? I knew this job was too good to be true! Seriously, could women be accused of sexual harassment as well? Because I didn't know if I could stay professional around this guy. He looked me over one more time, then nodded. "Sure, it'd be nice to have someone who actually wants the job for a change."

"Well, there'll be a trial period, it's all written into your contract, paid of course. We'll set you up with some uniforms and one of the bungalows, and you're welcome to move in when ready."

6

"I could start now, if that works," I said, trying to sound calm and failing. "I've been staying in caravan parks, so everything is in the car."

"Along with your dog? That was your beast out on the porch?" Finn asked.

"Uh, yeah, that's Buddy. Is that going to be a problem? I meant to ask over the phone..."

"He will need to stay this side of the fence, for his safety as much as anything," Kelly said. "There is a risk, keeping him here. This far out, we do have issues with wild animals."

"I know he's a Husky, and they're bad for escaping, but Buddy's never been an issue. But yes, I understand. I brought him here, he's my responsibility."

"OK, I'll get Finn to set you up with uniforms and a place to stay. Drop back in the morning. Karen will have some tax file forms to fill out, and I'll need to do a little induction." Finn got to his feet, so I followed suit. "This is a largely male-dominated workplace," Kelly said, "but we have had very few incidents. I keep it that way by making certain all employees are aware of the processes." God, was she talking to me? Was my interest in my boss that obvious? It was hard to tell as her gaze shifted slightly, so I wasn't sure if me or Finn was the intended recipient.

"Of course, what would be a good time for you?" I asked.

"Come see me around 9 am, and welcome aboard."

"OUT THIS WAY, JULIE," Finn said, opening the front door of the reception building. As we walked out, I saw the receptionist's eyes jerk up and follow us, or rather Finn. I empathised with her. My eyes wandered over to a strand of hair that had gotten free from its tie, falling down the side of his face, and felt a completely irrational desire to smooth it behind his ear. Instead, I clenched my hands into fists. He turned and smiled, probably wondering why I was just standing there. He took a deep breath, nostrils flaring a little, the smile widening then smoothing away, as if he was trying to stop from laughing. "You coming?"

"Sorry," I said, attempting to cover for my complete lapse in professionalism. "I'm a bit tired and overwhelmed. I'll be much better tomorrow, I promise." *Get it together girl!* I thought. *Go to town, bone some guy who isn't your boss. You got this, you have to.*

"Don't worry about it," he said, placing a hand on my shoulder. I stiffened slightly but don't think he noticed. I didn't want to be that girl, but I just stumbled along, not really taking in what he was saying, the warm weight of his hand getting all of my focus. "So, this is your Buddy?"

"Uh, yes. Hey, baby," I said, dropping down beside my dog and giving him a scratch. I hadn't noticed because I was too busy trying to be cool as the boss steered me down the porch, but he was whining now he'd seen me, wanting off the lead and to be walking wherever I was going. "I'll be back soon and then we'll get you settled."

"You can bring him with us, if you like. I'll leave the proper orientation for when we're both fresh and dressed appropriately."

"Yeah, I guess pencil skirts aren't real practical."

"No..." his eyes slid down to look at the offending garment, seeming to linger on my legs, before he looked away quickly.

Dude, is this guy into me? I thought. I could not deal with this, no way, no matter how gorgeous he is. I needed a job, not a boyfriend.

"All the women here wear pants, so it makes for a change. Anyway, let's head to the shed, and I'll get us a cart. I'll show you around the facilities and then get you settled."

I busied myself with unhooking Buddy's leash. The moment he was free, he started pulling me with his entire weight, wanting to walk, sniff, pee on everything. "Buddy!" I snapped and gave his lead a jerk. He looked back at me, shamefaced, but then went right back to sniffing around wildly, though not straining as hard. Finn led the way, which was OK by me. I'm not really into guys arses, but even I could tell that this was a particularly fine specimen, showcased in perfect fitting pants. I almost stumbled into him when he stopped suddenly, a smile slowly spreading across his face.

"So..." he scratched at his neck, "the shed is where we keep all of our vehicles. We sign them in or out, depending on who needs them. The mech crew service them, so they're in tip top condition. So if you have any issues, talk to them."

"Okay," I said, not really getting what was amusing.

"The guys...well, there's Stevie, but she can be just as bad. The guys are a bit...old school."

"What? They'll want to open car doors for me?"

"No, they'll probably stare at your tits the whole time you're talking to them. They'll probably even make comments."

"Oh!" I said, and then burst out laughing. "Hey, I worked in a diner whose main clientele were truckers. Trust me, I've had customers describe what they'd like to do to pretty much every part of my body. I'm good at busting heads if needs be."

"Yeah? Look, Kelly's going to go over this with you, but the long and the short of it is we have a lot of guys, straight guys mostly, working here and women...well, sometimes they can be seen as fresh meat. We used to not worry too much about fraternising, and then we had a few incidents. This place is too remote for us to think about ruling out office relationships, but..." He looked me square in the eyes, like this was really important for me to remember. "Never feel like you have to do anything. If you feel hassled or pressured in anyway, just let me or Kelly know, yeah?"

"Of course." My eyes flicked over to the big green shed in front of us. All I could see was a range of vehicles lined up outside and a big, dark entranceway. "I'm a little nervous about going in there now."

"Yeah, I think I built this up a bit. Let's... grab a cart and go."

"OK." I looked down at Bud, who was wondering why the hell we were standing around. "C'mon boy."

2

Finn disappeared into the shed before me. The first thing I noticed as I followed, was the strong smell of motor oil. The second, once my eyes adjusted to the change of brightness, was that there was a guy with no shirt on, bent over the engine bay of a car, and not just any guy. This was no pasty-skinned bloke in his 50s with a sagging paunch, promising to give you a lube job. This was a body that would have made Brad Pitt circa Fight Club go and hide in the corner and have a little cry. Every muscle was clearly delineated. I know, because I watched the mesmeric bunch and shift of them as whoever it was under the bonnet tightened a something-or-other with a hooziwhatsit.

This is just ridiculous, I thought dimly, *do they only employ hot guys in this place?*

"Hey Ethan!" someone shouted. I turned to see another guy in the more usual overalls, though they were unbuttoned to the waist to reveal an equally well-muscled chest, standing there with a smirk. He had obviously caught me looking. He nodded his head, indicating something behind me, and when I swung back, I was face to face with the owner of that body.

Buddy let out a growl, then a bark. "Shut up, Bud," I said, and when I looked up, Ethan had come even closer. I could smell the sharp scent of fresh sweat, oil and cedarwood, and I could feel that heat of his body, he was so close. I put up a hand with a frown, putting it square in the middle of that perfectly formed chest, and shoved him back when he seemed inclined to just keep coming. He was tall (weren't they all?) with brown hair that had probably been cut all layered and spiky, but he'd let it grow to that in-between length. He had a little stubble across his chin and a smear of grease down one side of his cheek, pointing to his shit-eating grin. True to Finn's words, his eyes dropped to the neckline of my shirt, and his stare was so intent, I could almost imagine his eyes boring straight through the fabric to my body beneath it. "And who do we have here?" he asked with a smile. "That's a nice dog."

"Thanks," I said, not bothering to conceal the irritation in my voice. He was good looking, but I was never keen on blokes who acted like a dick about it. Ethan just kept on staring. "Does this..." I gestured to the bare chest and the penetrating gaze, "usually work on women, or is this something new you're trying out on me?"

"Don't mind him." I turned to see a tall woman with long red hair, also in overalls, come out from between a couple of cars. She wiped her hands on a rag, then held one out to shake. "He's got a banging bod, and he still thinks that's all it takes. I'm Stevie, you've met Ethan and this is Derek. You must be Finn's new offsider."

"Yeah, I'm Julie and this is Buddy. Finn said he was going to..."

"Get the keys to one of the carts," he said, appearing at the doorway, shaking a set of them. "Well, you have your clothes on, and none of the guys look like they've been slapped. I'd say this was a good day so far."

"Give them time," Stevie said. "There's a couple of other guys who work here, Nick and Sonny. I'll introduce you next time you come through. You have any issues, you let me know."

It was then that I realised I was still holding her hand. She smiled nice and slow at this, watching me let it go. Then she just went back to what she was doing, tossing a smile at me over her shoulder. What had just happened? This place had a seriously weird vibe about it. It was kind of like one of those bad sexual harassment training videos, where the characters are all stereotypes of sleazy work mates, yet because the actors were totally hot, you ended it feeling strangely conflicted about the message.

"You ready?" Finn asked, and I nodded and followed him outside. I got in the passenger seat, Buddy jumping into the back. "The fenced area here is strictly for authorised personnel." He pointed to the high reinforced fences at the rear of the compound. "Ever shoot a gun?"

"Yeah, like years ago, when I was a kid. Will I need to here?"

"No, not really, but it can be handy." He pulled up to a massive steel door in the side of the 20 ft fence. "You have to swipe in to get inside the sanctuary itself, so we know who's in and who's out. For now, as your job's with me, you won't have a card. Unless you're with someone who knows what they're doing, you're not going in."

"That's a bit of a relief," I said. "So, what will I be doing? Kelly was kinda vague, and the not knowing is making me a bit anxious."

"Don't be." He turned and gave me what I'm sure he thought was a reassuring smile. All I saw was those eyes and those cute little crinkles... *Get your head in the game!* I snapped at myself. "Mostly it's boring stuff, like paperwork and running around, getting things signed. You'll be fine. Sanctuary is a self-sustaining community, more or less. It has its own farms, shops, clubs, but most of the focus is on the mines, which are behind the fence. This is the animal shed. We keep all the supplies for our dogs there. The building next to it is the vet surgery, and Doc Hobbes is our in-house vet. If there's anything she doesn't know about biology, it's not worth knowing. You can take Buddy in there if he has any issues, and she'll see him if she has the time. You'll need to do stock rotation and check supply levels inside. Anyway, let's jump out and see if anyone's around."

He parked the cart over near the big door of the animals shed, and we walked in. "Hello? Anyone home?"

"Hey!" I heard a female voice, which was followed quickly by its owner. "Hey, I'm Nerida! You must be the new girl." Nerida was gorgeous, all shining, dark brown hair, big brown eyes and long tanned legs only partially covered by a short pair of khakis.

"Julie."

"And who's this gorgeous little man?" she said, dropping down in front of Buddy. He could be a bit standoffish with strangers, but he seemed to relish the tummy rub she was giving him.

"That's Buddy."

"Well, Julie, Buddy, come in and meet Lou and Aidan."

Nerida beckoned me with a huge smile, slinging an arm around my shoulders when I drew close and steering me into a small office. "Guys, this is Julie. She's going to be helping Finn out." The guys I assumed were the man and the woman sitting on the couches. They didn't move or react as Nerida swept in, just took me in with two pairs of the oddest coloured eyes. They looked almost like a washed out amber, or a yellowy green. I was guessing they were brother and sister, as they had the same lean bodies and ash blonde hair. "So, you'll come and slop up with us sometimes, you know that, right? Don't mind getting your hands dirty?" Nerida asked.

"Don't know what slopping up is, but sure, I'm used to pitching in."

"Oh, it's making up the food bowls for the guard dogs. Finn has been promising me a hand for ages now, and he said you could come in for a couple of hours in the morning."

I turned to look at Finn for confirmation. "Do you really need her or are you just looking for someone to gossip with?" he said.

"Well, you could hardly blame me for the latter. Women are hard to come by here." Finn was unmoved by this, crossing his arms across his chest. I looked away quickly, not wanting my ovaries to spontaneously combust.

"Do you really need her?"

"Lou and Aidan often need to go inside the fence..."

"Do you really need her? There's plenty of things I'll need her for."

Nerida's eyes narrowed, and she cocked her hip. "I just bet you will. Seriously, Finn, are you telling me you can't spare her from whatever you're planning for an hour or two in the morning? I'm getting snowed under here. Either that, or give me more staff from the outside..."

He shrugged at this. "If it's not Julie, I'll check with the guys. One of them can do it."

"Yeah, but will they? I'm..."

"I said I'll get on it. Julie needs to be settled and into a bungalow before the evening meal. We'll talk later."

For a moment, Nerida's full lips thinned down to a hard line, but she didn't seem capable of staying that way for long. Her bright brown eyes swivelled to me, and her smile quickly reinstated itself.

"Well, I for one am glad to see more of a female presence around here. The guys... they think they can have it all their way, if you know what I mean. Look, meet me outside the mess hall at 6. You're going to want someone in your corner when you go in there for the first time, trust me."

My eyes widened. What the hell? I was desperate for money but...

"Stop scaring my employee away," Finn said. "C'mon, I'll introduce you to the doc." Nerida gave me a cheery wave, Lou and Aidan just watching without reacting. I fought back the urge to shiver and followed Finn.

I wasn't sure why they were saying this was a male-dominated environment, when we walked into the small surgery and an older woman with soft brown hair looked up and smiled. She had a bunch of glass slides out, with a vial of blood she was applying with a pipette. "Ah, this must be Julie. I'm Bree Hobbes," she said with a smile.

"Wow, news really travels fast around here," I said, and held out a hand. She shook it warmly and then looked down at Buddy.

"No, no, they just do a background check before they employ anyone. They often get me in to take a look. So, a Melville girl, huh? Any relation to the Donohues?"

"On my mother's side, three generations back. Really? I only rang about the job this morning."

She shrugged, "We have access to some pretty high-end databases. So, who is this handsome gentleman?"

I made introductions, and Buddy again seemed happy to take the fussing. He was usually better with women, but still, this was unusual for him. And a background check? Was that even legal? I'd definitely not signed anything to say that was OK. The vet talked about how healthy Buddy was, which was a relief considering the slim pickings of the last few weeks, and her thoughts on what to feed him to keep him in good condition.

Dr Bree straightened up and then seemed intent on looking me over.

"A Melville Donohue, hmm? Do you mind if I take a photo of your eyes? There's a lot of genetic quirks in that neck of the woods, due to a largely static population. I find some of them manifest in some interesting iris formations. It's a pet project of mine."

"Uh, I guess. Though I'd assume I'd be more Bronson than Donohue. That was my great grandfather, so a bit of a distant connection."

"Bronson and Donohue? Fascinating, yes, must take a photo. I can take your headshot straight afterwards, for your ID, and get that out of the way." She picked up a DSLR with an odd lens attachment, whose purpose soon became apparent. It came to rest on my eye socket, blocking my vision. "Just focus on the green light for a moment..." she said, then I was blinded by a bright flash. I jerked away, reeling a little, only to be caught by a couple of strong hands.

"Oh, sorry," I said when I saw it was Finn. Slowly, my sight returned without the big white spots.

"Excellent, excellent," the doctor said, looking on her computer screen at what looked like a large image of my eye. "You've got the golden flare here," she said, gesturing to the yellowish coloured fibres around my pupil. "And these little dots here... This is quite a common iris pattern in this county , though not so much outside of it. Have a look at Finn's eyes."

I glanced up almost shyly. There was nothing awkward about staring into the new boss's eyes, up close and personal, nothing at all. I was handed something that looked like an oversized jeweller's loupe, and I put it to my eye, testing out the magnification on it around me.

"Take a look," she urged. He met my gaze with a slight smile, and with a bit of manoeuvring with the loupe in place, I could see his eye in full technicolour glory. "Can you see that same flare of yellow around the centre?" I could, kind of. His eyes went from yellow to green to grey, all the colours blending in together. I put the loupe down. "Whereas if you look at mine," she brought up another image of a hazel iris, "you'll see that my iris is relatively uniform. I haven't noticed anything significant about it yet, but it's an interesting pattern. Now, let's do your ID photo." Finn steered me outside as soon as was practical.

It was about now that I really started to wonder what I'd gotten myself into. This place was weird, people were acting weirdly. I considered briefly the idea that I might go to the city and try my luck, but I knew what my answer was. Right now, I didn't have the money for petrol, accommodation or food, so it wasn't an option. I looked around at the green buildings and figured, I only had to stick it out long enough to earn some money, and then I could get out of here if it turned out too weird. I took a deep breath, I could do this.

"Look, you've probably got a lot to do before you feel comfortable in your accommodation. Why don't we cut the tour short for today and go and get you settled?"

Oh, fuck yes, I said internally. Instead, I nodded and tried hard not to sigh with relief. The names, the workplaces were all starting to blend together in my head. After overcoming the mountain of anxiety before the interview, I was now feeling really flat. I just wanted to have a shower, put some jammies on, and go to sleep. Once we were in the cart, Finn drove us up a road that peeled away from the sheds and out to a slight rise, where a series of cabins were situated. It looked like mine was one of the ones at the back.

As we pulled up, I could see it was cute. I had visions of dilapidated caravans or sagging demountables, but this was a nice little cottage with a porch that ran around the whole thing. Finn got up and walked up the steps, fishing some keys out of his pocket. He unlocked it and opened the door with a flourish.

"Wow, this is lovely!" I said. "I thought it might be a bit musty, but it looks ready to move in."

"Yeah, Kelly had a good feeling about you on the phone, so she had some of the guys give it a clean before you arrived, just in case."

"Did I need to be worried about the interview at all?" I asked.

This got me a slow smile. "You met a lot of the criteria we had for the job, so we were hopeful, but we wouldn't have taken you on if we didn't think you were up to it."

"I wish I'd known. I was panicking."

"Yeah, I know."

"You could tell? It was that obvious?"

"No," his smile broadened a little, "I'm just really good at picking those kinds of things up."

"Yeah? You're not like a mind reader or anything, because that would be super embarrassing."

"Oh?" An eyebrow arched slowly. "Why's that?"

"Oh, you know…" *Because I checked out your arse. Because I was struck momentarily dumb when you walked into the room. Because you smelled so good when I was sitting next to you in the cart.* "Because if I'm getting pissed at you, I don't want to get sacked for mental insubordination."

"Right, well, feel free to call me whatever you like in the sanctity of your own mind. Hey, chuck me your car keys, and I'll give you a hand moving in."

"You don't have to…"

"I don't want you to have to carry those boxes all by yourself. It's fine, it'll go faster if I help."

3

————

Which is how I ended up with Finn running boxes up the stairs and inside the house, my car parked round the back. I went to try and carry some of it, but he wouldn't hear of it. Instead, I was left to start unpacking my meagre possessions while Finn worked up a sweat. I tried not to look as his shirt began to stick to his chest, though I did nearly drop some plates because I was so busy 'not looking'. The final straw came when he stopped, whipped off his shirt and closed his eyes, standing underneath the ceiling fan to cool down.

Y'know in the old cartoons, where you see the wolf's eyes bug out and his tongue roll out like a carpet? Pretty sure that was an accurate representation of me, because he was everything his clothes had hinted at. He wore a white wife-beater singlet but still, the taut muscles of his arms caught my gaze as they followed the vein that ran down the inner side of his bicep to his forearm. I could see the slight shift and bunch of his abs under the thin, damp fabric. He opened his eyes a slit, smiling slightly at me as I tried to jerk mine back to something more appropriate.

"There any water in the fridge?" he asked.

Did I imagine a husky rasp to his voice? No, must be wishful thinking. He walked into the tiny little kitchenette, close enough to brush me, and I fought back a shiver. I could feel the cool air of the fridge and the sound of a cap being twisted. I was thirsty, I thought, real thirsty. I turned around and tried to squirm past him and see if there was any more water. "Here," he said, passing a half empty bottle.

"Oh, it's OK, you must be hot..."

"Here."

"No really."

"Take it." This was delivered as a gentle command. He pushed the bottle into my hand, his fingers brushing mine. I felt that familiar, low down shiver in my body. Parts of it twitched in response to this little gesture.

"You're the boss," I said.

His smile widened at this. I swallowed a mouthful of water, the moment becoming too loaded for me to do anything else. He seemed to watch every movement. I pushed the bottle back into his hand and then stepped around him, leaving the kitchen. "Look, this feels... really awkward and probably premature, but I feel like I need to clear the air. Are you...?"

I couldn't bring myself to say it. He was gorgeous and I was ...me.

"Attracted to you?" he said. "I thought that was obvious."

"I wouldn't go assuming that. Clarifying is probably a good idea. I... well, look at you. You're smoking hot, but I need a job, like really need a job. I was on my last little stash of cash, which might have gotten me to the next town over and that's it. I can't afford to fuck about with the boss." His eyebrows shot up. "Not like that! Though I guess eventually like that... Fuck, I'm not doing this very well."

"You're worried about the job if you have anything other than a professional relationship with your supervisor."

"Yeah."

"Talk to Kelly. She'll talk about this in detail tomorrow."

"OK."

"I've gotten everything out of the car, so I should go anyway. I think I'm about ready for a really long shower."

"Oh." I knew he was inferring something, but I didn't get far enough to try and work out why. All of a sudden, my mental slideshow was flashing up its estimations of what that would look like, water sliding lower and...

"Head over to the mess shed at 6, it's the first one on the right down this road. Don't be late, or you risk going hungry. Nerida will probably find you, though."

"Uh huh..." I jerked my attention back to the Finn standing in front of me, rather than soapy, naked dream one in my head. "Thank you for everything today."

"No problems. See you at dinner."

"Hey, you made it! And you brought Buddy!" I'd gotten to the mess shed a bit before 6, worried I'd miss meal time. I hadn't had lunch and was starving. Nerida popped out from inside, a big smile on her face.

"That'll be OK, right?"

"Sure, sure. C'mon, we've got a table at the back. Us chicks need to stick together."

"Ah, right... So remind me, why do us chicks need to stick together?"

"Oh, no reason. This is a good place to work. People are fair, pay's good..."

"Great."

"Come and have a seat, Jamie and Dex are already here. They'll fix you up with a drink. I totally want to see your face when they get here. You look pretty too, that's a really cute top, with the embroidery and everything."

"Yeah, I wasn't sure... Uniform, casuals..."

"It won't matter much, but I know what it's like, wanting to look your best."

"Pretty sure you don't need to work at it," I said. She was amazing looking, rocking that fresh faced, super happy look that men ate up with a spoon. It was never something I was able to imitate, I just came across as unmedicated.

"Naww, listen to you. You're sweet. Well, here we are, best seat in the house. This is Jamie..."

"Hi," a petite blonde gave me a wave.

"And Dex."

"Take a load off, sweet thing," an older woman with the growl of a long-term smoker gestured to the bench beside her. Her hair was a fall of harshly dyed burgundy, but she had good bones, though she looked like she knew she still had it. "What a gorgeous dog. Husky?"

"Yeah, he's about two years old."

"Just a pup then. So, you'll be gofering for our Finn. You excited?"

"I don't know what to think, to tell you the truth. One minute I was broke, no job, no place to stay, now I'm employed and have accommodation. My brain's still trying to catch up."

"Well, while it's trying to do that, have one of these," Dex picked up. "I call them Long Island iced teas, but I have no idea if they have the right ingredients. Drink up, love, it'll put hairs on your chest."

"So this won't be an issue...?"

"For Finn? He's had enough of them at meal times himself, so I can't see why not. Anyway, you're going to need some liquid courage, trust me."

Nerida giggled and poured one for all of us, and then called, "Cheers!"

"Guys, you're starting to freak me out. If this is some kind of hazing thing or something, just lay it on me, I can take it. Not knowing? Not so much."

"Don't worry. Here they come," Jamie said with a wide smile. She watched the front entrance to the hall, her eyes seeming to grow to twice their size, looking much like a kid at Christmas. I turned, and it all made sense. They seemed to walk in in waves, row after row of guys, filling the considerable doorway and filing in to take seats at the many picnic tables in the middle of the room. That wasn't all that unusual, blokes piling into a mess hall at knock off time no doubt happened all across the country. No, it was the guys themselves. My mouth dropped open, and I didn't bother to shut it because every damn one of them was at the very least good looking. Tall or short, you had guys with long hair, short hair, in between or dreads. Blue eyes, brown eyes, hazel or green, every skin and every hair colour, including a bloke with a purple mohawk. But that wasn't what had me sitting there like a fool. Every single one of them had well defined physiques, from long and lean, to full on body builder types, shown to advantage in shirts with the sleeves ripped out and thin white wife-beaters. Every single one of them had the kind of dramatic facial structure with high cheekbones that you saw in fashion mags or on male strippers.

"What the actual fuck?" I said, my head whipping around to confront the girls. My eyes narrowed, "Is this a joke? Am I being punked?"

They all started laughing, assumably at my stupid expression. "Oh, no," Dex said, "this is all real."

"A porn set then? Seriously? You can't tell me all of these gorgeous guys happen to work at a mine in the middle of nowhere. That makes no sense, whatsoever! How is that even possible?"

Nerida shrugged. "We've all asked those questions, and no one's really come up with an answer, though maybe Doc Hobbes has a theory. After a while, you just learn to accept and enjoy."

"Enjoy!" I hissed. "I can't work with that. Is there a sex shop anywhere near, because I am going to need an industrial strength vibrator."

"You won't," Dex said, a rapt grin on her face as she gestured to the benches. "Trust me, there's plenty who are willing to go above and beyond whatever a battery-operated appliance would do."

"Well, they can't all be straight," I spluttered.

"That is true," Jamie said. "Greg is gay, so is Neil."

"Vance is," Nerida said.

"Yep, and Nick. So's Stevie, but that's a whole other ball game," Dex said with a grin. "Some are bi, or willing to give it a go though, if that floats your boat."

"Floats my boat?" I hissed. I picked up my glass and took a long, deep swallow. This got a few low cheers from the girls, and they misread me and followed suit. I wiped my mouth with the back of my hand and then leaned over the table. "How the hell do you know the sexual preferences of your work mates?"

"Have you had the talk with Kelly yet?" Jamie asked.

"No! What is this talk? People keep telling me to wait for the talk. If you know something, spill!" I said.

"Well, Sanctuary's less a workplace, and more one big family," Nerida said with a broad smile.

"A not very closely related family where a lot of the members fuck each other, if they so desire," Dex said. "That's what Kelly's going to talk to you about, consent and boundaries, how to negotiate a sexual or romantic relationship in the workplace, and what to do if things start turning ugly. That doesn't really happen though..."

"No, everyone's clear on the rules," Nerida said. "Sometimes it all gets a bit heated, passion and all that, but the management team are pretty good at settling people down."

"So you've..." I gestured at the other tables.

She blushed prettily, "Well, a lady never kisses and tells..."

"Seriously? You're going to go with coy now?" I asked.

"Don't worry about who Nerida's slept with, think about yourself," Dex said. "You're gonna get some offers tonight, if you want them."

Gulp. I turned away from the women, almost afraid of what I might see, and sure enough there were plenty of guys checking out our table, some even looking directly at me. I grabbed my drink reflexively, feeling much safer taking a long, slow drink than looking out at the combined workforce of my new place of employment. Buddy shifted at my feet, sitting up and giving out a low growl. I twisted to see a tall guy in a pair of worn blue jeans, workbooks and a white singlet had appeared at my side of the table, waiting for me to notice. His long, dirty blond hair fell over his shoulders in a messy wave, and he regarded me with a small smile. "I'm Shaun," he said, holding out a hand. I looked at it dumbly, seeing the long thick fingers, the callouses on the palm, the grime that had collected under

SAM HALL

the nails, before realising he wanted me to shake it. I didn't want to touch him at all, afraid I was going to dissolve into a little puddle of goo and then my dog would be put up for adoption, hopefully to find a new owner who could keep her cool around hot guys. Buddy gave another sharp bark which helped me snap out of it.

"Buddy, chill! I'm sorry, I'm Julie," I said, shaking his hand.

"I know."

"Word's got out, huh? So, what do you do, Shaun?"

Keep it light and professional, I told myself, *and you'll be fine. You can do this.*

"Whatever you want me to," he said with a purr, "and for as long as you want me to."

"Oh."

I'd heard people's voices described as a purr in books before, but never really known what that meant. I now knew. His voice was a low, sexy rasp, his words coming out with complete confidence that I would drop trou and let him fuck me, right here, right now. I understood why he would come across like that, as I felt like I was barely restraining myself from doing so. Vaginas are funny things, much harder to sense than I assume a dick would be, but mine was awake and paying attention. All of a sudden, I felt...slippery, like everything was slick and ready to have something very large pushed inside me without any resistance.

"Everything OK here?"

My awareness jerked away from my nether regions, and my eyes flicked up to see Finn watching me still holding Shaun's hand, a smile on both of their faces. Finn was professionally polite, but Shaun? He looked very pleased with himself, his nose working as he seemed to be taking in deep breaths as he observed my embarrassing lapse in manners.

"I'm sorry..." I stuttered out.

"Don't be. You can hold any part of my body you like," Shaun said.

"Shaun, mate, this is Julie, a new employee," Finn said. "She's

24

only just been given a contract, hasn't even signed it yet, and Kelly hasn't had a chance to go over the terms and conditions yet."

Shaun nodded to show he understood, but those pale blue eyes still held mine. "Come and see me when she's spoken to you," he said, capturing my fingers again and brushing his lips across my knuckles, "anytime, anywhere you choose. You just let me know."

And that was apparently the end of that conversation. My hand was released, and I was treated to the view of yet another A-grade butt as he returned to his seat.

"You OK, Julie? Is there anything you need to help you settle in?" Finn asked.

Dick and lots of it, my brain supplied helpfully. *Naked muscly bodies overlapping themselves into some kind of super horny carpet that I could roll myself all over and then fuck myself to death on. Shaun naked, on his knees using his tongue to...* Shit, I'd settle for just one dick right now. I last got laid over a year ago. A hot young truck driver had rolled into town for a 'good time, not a long time' and I'd made use of him, but since then... Most of the young people had left before me, looking for better opportunities, which meant it was me and the menopausal set.

"I'm fine," I said and forced a smile, "but I'd kill for a coffee. Dex's brew is going to put me on my arse." Finn faltered at this for a second, then pointed to a bar over on the back wall.

"Come this way, and I'll show you the bar," he said.

He showed me the expensive looking coffee machine and was going to demonstrate how to use it, but I'd dealt with more temperamental beasts at my old job. I felt a little less flustered, going through the familiar motions of making a coffee, pouring myself a double strength mug and handing him the other.

"Milk with one. Just the way I like it," he said, a little shocked.

"Most people do," I said with a shrug and sipped my own dark brew, feeling a little bit more settled now there was some distance between me and the masculine smorgasbord in front of me.

"So, you remember what I said, right? No one here is going to try anything if you're not into it. There are a lot of guys here, and they are always keen to see new female staff, but no definitely means no. Anyone who pushes that is out on their ear, no questions asked."

"What about women? What if one of us was trying to push ourselves onto a guy who didn't want it?"

It took Finn a while to answer, like maybe he had never thought of it before. Finally, he nodded, "I think the same rule applies. We want people to feel safe here, and they can't if their wishes aren't respected. No one's going to come and try and break into your house or anything, if that's what you're worried about."

"I don't know if worried is what I'm feeling," I muttered. "Hey, where are the other women? Like Kelly and Doc Hobbes?"

"Kelly's over there at the management table, Doc Hobbes has her meal in the clinic most days, Stevie's with the guys, and who else...? Yeah, Karen the receptionist is with her partner, Burt, over there." My eyes swivelled over to the table the girls were sitting at. There were several guys hanging around it, talking to the women. With the smiling and touching going on, I was pretty sure they were flirting. "That's the single women's table. Nerida was probably playing a joke on you, getting you to sit there, as usually women only do that..."

"If they are looking to get laid. Got it. Look, I'm going to grab Buddy before someone starts chatting him up. Do you mind if I sit with you guys?"

"Ah...sure." He didn't sound too pleased with this, but I didn't care. I walked through the gaps between the tables, ignoring the comments and looks and called to my dog.

"The single table? Really ladies?" I said as the girls turned around to me. "I'm going to go and sit with Finn, but thanks for the heads up."

"Sit with Finn?" Nerida said. "But then everyone will think..."

"It's all good. Enjoy your meal, and I'll catch you tomorrow," I said, and then I marched off to where Finn was sitting.

He just stared down at his empty plate as I arrived, but all the other guys looked from me, to him, and back again, quickly shuffling to make room for me and Buddy, who hopped up on the bench seat with a little growl.

"You locked that down quick, Masters," the sandy haired guy sitting in front of Finn said.

"Yeah, I'm happy to play by the rules, if we get a chance to compete, but if the minute new blood gets here, she's marked? Well, that requires a response," the darker haired guy next to him added.

I frowned, looking at them, then Finn, and back again. The boys were locked into some kind of staring contest, like maybe they could use a Care Bear Stare to resolve whatever they were talking about. The thing was, and I didn't want to assume and come across as a self-absorbed twat, but it seemed they were talking about me.

"What's new blood?" I asked. All eyes up and down the table swivelled over to me. I met the hazel ones of the sandy haired guy sitting across from Finn head on. "Well?"

Finn started to say something but the guy just replied, "You, love, you're the new blood. New girl, new chick...." his eyes trailed down to take in no doubt the intricate embroidery on the neckline of my top, "new woman."

"So you were talking about me, whilst I was sitting right next to you, to Finn? And how am I marked?" I looked down at my blouse, my arms. "Pretty sure I don't see any marks, unless you count this scar here, when I cut the top of my finger off a few years ago." I was kind of joking, kind of mad, yet every eye strained to see the small circle of white scar tissue.

"I'd be happy to count whatever part of your body you like," the darker haired guy said.

"Well, as exciting as that sounds, I learned to count all my fingers and toes when I was a little girl. Right now, I really need something to eat..." Three hands instantly went out to grab my plate, the sandy haired guy able to wrest it away from the others with a grin. Finn watched him with a dark look as he got to his feet, his own plate in his other hand.

"Anything you prefer, my lady?" one of the other guys said.

Seriously? This place was fucking bonkers. It needed a whole lot more women to dilute what seemed like a ridiculous amount of seething testosterone. Stupid thing was, they could easily have run tours for single women through the place and made a lot of money and settled these guys down. "No seafood, no eggs," I said with a sigh, "they make me ill."

"But plenty of protein to keep your strength up? I'll be right back."

"Really, I can't fill my own plate?" I said with exasperation, watching as he joined the line of workers getting food from the bain-maries. "What if I don't like what he brings me?"

Finn looked down the table and back to me, "Don't worry, you'll have plenty of choice." Was that a double-entendre? I didn't get a chance to ask, he got up to get himself some food as well. I leaned into Buddy and gave his lovely soft fur a pat.

"It's alright, Bud," I said, "leftovers are for you."

Finn was right. Sandy haired guy, whose named turned out to be Brett, put a huge plate groaning with food in front of me, with some of the other guys putting other plates around me. It was kind of sweet in a way. I smiled nervously under the attention and picked up my cutlery, "I'm sure it's lovely." I moved to spear a chunk of potato salad on my fork and put it in my mouth, but everyone was still watching with rapt interest. I put my cutlery down and stared point-edly until the guys started eating as well. It was still weird, and I was getting plenty of surreptitious looks, but still, I could eat in some peace. Finn came back to the table without a word, but that seemed to stop the observations for a while. All except for Buddy, who sat there patiently salivating, waiting for me to find stuff I didn't like, which I moved to a bread plate and put down on the ground for him to eat.

"What are those?" I asked the guy who was sitting beside me now that Buddy was on the floor. He had a bunch of what looked like long skinless sausages on his plate, served with some kind of salad. He was a big guy, which was saying something in this place. Most blokes seemed taller than me, but this guy towered over the rest. I got a slow smile as he turned to face me, swinging one leg over the bench seat so that I could see just how big he was. It wasn't the super bulky bodybuilder look, more man as big as a mountain.

"Have a taste," he said, spearing one on his fork and holding it out for me to take.

"Julie, don't..." Finn said but the other guys hissed him quiet.

"Fair's fair," Brett said, and Finn fell silent with a frown. My eyes flicked between the three of them, and I went to take the fork from mountain guy's hand. No dice, he grinned as he held it firm against my grip. Buddy looked up from his food, I could almost imagine a frown on his face as he watched the two of us, so I let go and plucked the sausage off the fork and took a bite.

"Wow!" I said, it was a meaty, spicy blend that burst with flavour in my mouth. A groan went down the table as I took another bite, so I stopped. "Seriously? Are you guys that hard up that a girl eating a sausage gets you going? You're all gorgeous, you'd have no problems finding someone to...ease your load with if you went to the pub."

"Pub's five hours away from here," darker haired guy said, "and women usually aren't turned on by the prospect of a roll in the backseat of the car." Privately, I thought they were underestimating the lengths a woman would go to for a pretty face, but that was just me.

"Well, tonight I'm going home to bed, to sleep, by myself," I said, "so why don't we all chill." That seemed to do the trick. Big guy went back to his meal, and so did the others.

Finn gave me a sidelong smile. "Well done." He started eating, but it took me a little longer. That smile, it took my breath away, and it wasn't until Bud was pushing his head against my leg for more food that I realised I was staring, open mouthed. I dropped him something off the many plates and turned back to my own food, only noticing now that some of the spicy sausages had been put onto mine. I scanned the faces of those closest, and only got a few quick smiles from the other guys to indicate where they had come from.

"GOD, I'm stuffed, and so is Buddy," I said. Some people were still eating, most were having a beer or a smoke, sitting and chatting. I got to my feet and picked up Bud's plate. He wouldn't need kibble when we got home. Hopefully after a short walk up the hill, we could both just roll into bed. I was dead tired. "I've got to see Kelly at 9 am, where and when did you want me to meet you afterwards?"

"Kelly will give you a walkie talkie. Just let me know when you're done, and I'll come by to get you. You OK to get home? I'm finished here, I can take you up on the cart."

"It's OK, I need the walk to work off some of this food baby," I said, patting my stomach. A few of the guys' eyes flicked up at this, but everyone seemed to have calmed down a bit.

He looked a little disappointed, but nodded and said, "Well, sleep well."

"You too. C'mon, Bud."

It was easier to ignore the looks when I was tired. I just floated out the door, feeling that bone deep satisfaction from having a full stomach, coupled with the knowledge I wouldn't have to scrape together money for food anymore. With the money they were paying me, and the free food, clothes, accommodation and utilities, I was going to be set. I walked out of the warm shed out into the cool night air and looked up at the moon. It hung there, bright enough to light my way, almost completely full, beautiful and silver.

"Can I walk you home?" A voice came from the darkness. I saw the red glowing end of his cigarette before he emerged out into the semicircle of artificial light from the lamp over the doorway. It was the guy with the long blond hair. What was his name?

"Shaun," he said, seeing my expression, "we met before."

"Oh, yeah," I said.

Oh, yeah! my body said. It remembered all too well how slick and swollen I'd felt when he was coming on to me. The novelty of a hot guy cracking onto me had dulled a little, but still, he was a pretty amazing specimen. I jerked my eyes away from my unconscious inspection of his chest and arms and shook my head, "I'm heading to bed."

"That's OK. So am I."

With us? With us! My body was like some kind of incredibly perky yet horny cheerleader, giving her most enthusiastic cheer for this idea. I clamped down on it, while things seemed laid back here, I was pretty sure becoming the office slut wasn't a great way to secure my job. And anyway, I was tired. *No, we're not! No, we're not!* Yes, I was, and so was Buddy. I knew the dog would sleep anywhere, anyhow if he wanted to, so I needn't have worried, but I had a lame excuse and I was sticking to it.

"By myself, unless something else comes up," he said, obviously taking my inner dialogue time as reluctance. I guess it was probably more plausible to him than me having an argument with my vagina about having sex.

"Look, if you're cool with just walking me up to my bungalow, that'd be great. I didn't take the car because it's not far, and Bud needed a walk, but I should have brought a torch with me."

"My pleasure," he said, and flicked the cigarette away. "This way." I walked beside him along the track that looped behind the mess hall and back up to the accommodations. The night smelled of pine resin, bracken ferns and a peculiar warm, woody scent that I think was all Shaun's. "So, how's your first day gone?" he asked.

"Nerve-racking, weird, awkward, then weird again. Fuck it, I'm going with this has been a bloody weird day."

He chuckled at this. "It will get easier once you've had a chat with Kelly."

"The girls filled me in. You can nail whoever is willing, just don't let it interfere with work."

"Sort of. It's a bit more complicated than that. Plenty of people are in relationships, have kids, they just tend to hang in the married quarters on the other side of the compound. Things can get a little... intense in the mess hall." As if to support what he said, I heard a high shriek that dissolved into a giggle as we passed the back end of the hall. "It's up to you."

I stopped walking and turned to face him. Maybe because in the darkness Shaun just became some dark anonymous figure, but now I felt much more comfortable talking about the whole situation. I was too tired to bullshit. I'd maintained a veneer of sanity over my over-whelming free-floating anxiety all day, so I hit him with it. "Y'see that's what weirds me out. Like, where I was from, small town, small gene pool, finding someone who wasn't your cousin who you were attracted to was hard work. When I got laid, it was like I'd climbed a mountain or achieved something momentous beside an orgasm, y'know."

"OK."

"You don't get it, you can't, I guess. But it's like I went from that to here, where every kind of guy I could possibly want is on display, and so many of them act like they'd be grateful for the chance to explore whatever sexual fantasy I can think of. I mean, you were like that within ten seconds of me getting there."

He took a step closer but stayed shrouded in darkness, the moon casting shadows on his face. "I was."

"And y'know, instead of checking your family tree for possible incest, I just see the body and the hair and…"

"And…?" His voice came out in the low rasp that he'd used before.

I shivered and backed up. "And I'm going to bed."

"Julie," he caught my wrist, stopping me from walking off, but letting go the moment I stopped. "Look, I'm not going to try and get into your pants tonight, you've made it clear that's off the table. But if you stay here, this is kind of important."

"What's important? That I feel like I'm punching above my weight here? Seriously, if insecurities are important, I'm a fucking VIP."

"Julie." He slowly reached out, then ran a hand through my hair, tangling his fingers in it. He didn't move any closer, like this was enough for now. "If I have what you're saying right, you are feeling a bit weirded out by finding so many guys attractive? The fellas would be stoked to hear that…" I gasped at that, thinking about the consequences of opening my big mouth finally. "But don't worry, your secret is safe with me. Working in a very male-dominated environment, we don't hear that a lot. Maybe if we were a bit more sensitive and New Age, we might compliment a bloke's six pack or whatever, but usually we're too elbow deep in mud and grease and shit to worry too much about that. Trust me, that's a shed full of blokes who'd step over their mothers to hear a woman praise their looks, anything. I mean, Jack's told me I have a nice arse…"

"Yeah, you do. Totally do."

"Good to know, but it's different coming from someone you'd like to see naked. Very, very different, and something we don't have a lot of opportunity to hear. Something that most of us would go to great lengths to have."

"Which is like, no pressure at all. God, I am too tired to deal with this weirdness…" I strode off, just wanting to be home.

"Julie." He caught me around the waist, pulling me close, but not enough that our bodies would touch. "Julie, there's no pressure, not unless that's what you want. You're not seeing it right, love. You're in control, totally and utterly, right up until the point you don't want to be. Those guys in there, me, Finn, we have no say unless you say so. With one word, you can tell us not to touch, say or pursue you ever, and it will happen. Every other guy here will make it so, so don't feel pressured."

"That's probably the strangest thing anyone's ever said," I said, almost in a whisper. It was so different to my previous experiences with men that I found it virtually impossible to believe. I looked over his shoulder, where I could dimly hear the party going on in the hall. In Melville, girls weren't raised with that kind of freedom. We were the ones who could get pregnant from teenage indiscretions, so it was up to us to make sure we went out with the 'right' guys. Guys who wouldn't push us, force us, or take what they wanted and leave us to deal with the aftermath.

Parents formed a strange surveillance society, both obsessed with what we were doing and endlessly lecturing their daughters about their responsibilities, whereas sons floated by without constraint, while having no clue what we actually did when they weren't around. My teenage sexual experiences happened in a totalitarian state. Don't let guys go too far, don't lead them on, don't say no at the last minute, even if you were no longer into what was happening. Good girls didn't. That loosened up with adulthood obviously, but still, I was bloody discreet when I slept with my trucker. Being grist for the rumour mill in Melville meant severe consequences, until the next person stepped out of line. I looked at Shaun's dark outline, he seemed to honestly believe what he was saying. If he hadn't, there wasn't much to stop him from taking what he wanted here. Would anyone hear me scream? I realised I wasn't being as careful as I thought I was.

"C'mon," he said, slinging an arm around my shoulders. "Let's get you home. You don't have to listen to me, you don't know me from a bar of soap, but Julie..." He turned to look at me in the darkness as we walked up the rise, Buddy gambolling off in the grass. "I'd like the opportunity to change that."

We arrived at my front porch, my shoulders and left-hand side warm from his contact. I climbed the steps, suddenly shy. What was this? Had this become a date? He followed behind me, slow, watching me the whole time, carefully picking his way towards me and giving me every opportunity to flee inside if that's what I wanted, something that hadn't occurred to me until now. He stopped just in front of me, grabbing my hand with his, holding it up, fingers loosely tangled in mine, dropping a brief kiss where our palms met.

"Can I see you again?" he asked in his low husk.

"You'll see me at work..."

"You know what I mean," he said, coming closer. I could feel his breath, a mix of mint and tobacco smoke on my skin.

"What do you want to do?" I asked, half in a whisper.

He drew me against him, his groan tickling my ear, his body twisting, almost in a slow, freeform dance. I could feel the hard shift of his muscles against mine as we moved. "Don't ask me that right now." His hands ran down my back and up again, restive and shifting, like he didn't know where to put them. "Julie..." he whispered as his lips trailed along my neck, not quite kissing.

My lungs felt tight in my chest, as if no matter how deeply I breathed, I couldn't pull in enough air. My heart thundered in my ears, an erratic crashing sound, but none of that mattered. Every sense was attuned to the points where our bodies intersected, the pressure, the caresses all a maelstrom of sensation that held me captive. He said I was in control, but I couldn't have felt less in control right now. Maybe that's what spurred me to act. I reached out for his face as if in a daze, almost startled when my hand connected with his neck, my fingers sinking into the raw silk of his hair, thumb resting along the steel curve of his jaw. I felt the muscles flex and shift as my mouth drew closer, as I drew in his breath, so close my lips tingled in response.

I let out a little whimper as I closed the distance between us, brushing my lips against his, evading his attempts to deepen the kiss. I bestowed brief, glancing caresses, until he began to groan in frustration. His hands tightened over my lower back, jerking me hard against him so I could feel how much he wanted this. Him and me both. It felt a bit like losing consciousness when I kissed him properly, as everything but him dropped out of my awareness. His hands shifted to fist into my hair as I opened my mouth against his, and his tongue was flickering out the moment I did so. His lips felt like steel and satin, soft enough for me to sink my teeth into, pillowy and pliable, then hard and brutal. Finally, he pulled away, gasping, his forehead resting against mine.

"We've...we've only just met," he said.

"I know..." I said, taking little nips at his mouth, running a tongue against his lower lip.

"Julie, Julie, we need to stop or...." I didn't want to stop. My body had given up cheering and was now ready to lie down on the nearest available flat surface, spread my legs and take him inside me. Seriously, we needed to fuck. "Just tell me..." he said.

Thinking about saying those thoughts out loud kind of jerked me out of my fever. I pulled away, smoothed my hair back and blinked. Yep, he was still smoking hot, and as I looked down, I got a clear outline in his jeans of what he had been thrusting against me. I reached out a shaking hand and found my fingers partially wrapping around something big. "Uh," I cried. My brain rather helpfully supplied me with a 3D and full Technicolour recreation of what they thought this dick would feel like going into me.

He pushed my hand away and said, "Not unless you say you want this."

Which of course gave my pre-frontal cortex time to kick in. I had no idea who this guy was, what the consequences would be for sleeping with a colleague before the much-lauded talk with Kelly. What would Finn think? I needed a job, not a boyfriend, I reminded myself. Buddy whined to be let in, and I turned and unlocked the front door, leaving it open.

Part of me wanted him to take the need for consent away, to shove me against the wall and show me how good it would be between us, to bamboozle me with a flood of sensation that would overwhelm all my doubts. Trouble was, that had happened before, and when I woke up those doubts were still there, even if he wasn't. *Oh, god*, I groaned internally. I was going to say no, for now at least, and I couldn't quite believe it.

He smiled, part disappointed, part hopeful. "It's ok, I knew you'd say no. Can we pick this up tomorrow? After you've talked to Kelly, if you still want to hang out after work, I'll come by. I'll grab some food from the mess crew. I know a great spot for a picnic."

"I'd like that," I said. "I haven't had much of a chance to see the sights around here."

"I've got something I'd like to show you," he said in a growl, then gave me the kind of long, slow, sweet kiss you give someone you don't want to leave. We pulled apart finally when Bud came to the door and barked. "Cock blocked by a dog," he said. "First time in my life. So, tomorrow?"

"Tomorrow."

4

fter he'd loped off into the darkness, I realised what I'd done. Mentally, it seemed like a sane thing to do, not sleep with a colleague within hours of getting a new job. But who knew right hurt so good? My nipples were tight little beads, feeling every rasp and shift of my bra as I moved. My clit actually ached, throbbing in time with my heartbeat and leaving me wondering if I should call Shaun back. I shook my head and plodded over to the bathroom to have a long, long shower.

WHEN I WOKE up in the morning, I realised three things: I didn't need to worry about money anymore, I had somewhere to live, and I worked with a virtual herd of hot guys. I had slept badly, thrashing around in bed through a string of dreams where a variety of sexy partners got me all hot and bothered, only to have to take off for some reason before clinching the deal. My clit still throbbed sulkily, despite me doing my damndest to appease myself, but today was a new day. I bounced out of bed, freaking out Buddy and sending him skittering across the floor, wondering where the fire was. I just swept past him and into the bathroom. By 8:45 I was showered and dressed in the

SAM HALL

khakis someone had left last night for me, and ready to head down to have 'the talk'.

My dog got excited when I locked up the bungalow, racing down the hill and back again. Where he found the energy, I don't know. "Morning." I turned and saw the three blokes who'd sat next to me at dinnertime walking towards the compound as well. Jesus! Mountain guy really was huge. He'd have to be six foot seven or more of solid but not bulky muscle, which unfortunately led to my gaze dropping lower, wondering if he was big everywhere. It was like visiting Loch Ness. You had to look into the depths just to see if the monster was lurking there. Something shifted beneath the khaki fabric. *Whoa, was that real?* I thought as I stared at the considerable bulge. Visibility was compromised, but what was hinted at was massive. I jerked my eyes up, stumbling away. Holy shit! "Have a great day," I said before walking quickly away, the guys' laughter ringing in my ears.

I arrived at the admin building well before 9 and set Buddy up with a bowl of water on the porch. "Hi," Karen the receptionist said. "Can you fill out these forms for me? I'll let Kelly know you're here."

"Come through, Julie," Kelly said. I dropped the completed paperwork on Karen's desk and walked into her office. She smiled once we were both seated. "I have your contract. The trial period is for a month. If at the end of that time we find you are not a good fit for the job, the contract will be terminated." I swallowed hard, glad I hadn't slept with Shaun. I still had to win this job, and trying to do so with a sex hangover wasn't helpful. "You will have several performance reviews though, so there should be no surprises for anyone. You look worried."

"I'm not sure what the position entails, so I guess I don't know if I can even do this job."

She smiled at this. "I was going to get Finn to go over that, but to reassure you, it's basically doing whatever he needs. From menial things like getting coffee, to helping with paperwork. In some ways, you'll be a personal assistant, though the work won't be restricted to

38

administrative stuff. I tend to look after the overall organisation, keep the books in the black and make the big decisions. The day to day running is down to Finn, so your job is to make that easier for him."

"Ok, I guess all I can do is do my best, and hope I meet your standards."

"You'll be fine. Now, from Finn's comments about the mess hall, it's beyond time for me to chat about the HR issues of working here."

"News gets around fast, huh?"

"You've lived in a small town, you know what it's like. Don't worry or anything, he said you dealt with the attentions of the male staff confidently and appropriately, but the reality must be faced. We are hours from civilisation and have few female staff. Sexual and romantic relationships happen. We accept and support that, but everyone needs to be clear how this works. Your sex and love life is none of our business, except when it creates potential risk for the company. The risk lies with sexual harassment, obviously. Female staff often find our views on workplace relationships comparatively permissive when starting work here, sometimes shockingly so. Some, even many, male employees will make plain they are interested in a sexual or romantic relationship. They may do this during or after work, though this can't take away from the tasks they have to do that day. If this gets oppressive, or makes you uncomfortable in any way, let me or Finn know, and we will deal with it. All parties involved will be notified when a formal warning is in place, and any offensive actions beyond that point will result in an immediate termination of employment for the offender. Please, feel confident that we will support you. I know many workplaces pay lip service to the idea of zero tolerance for sexual harassment, but I assure you, that is not the case here. We are too far away from anything, so we must police ourselves for the wellbeing of our organisation. Now, did you have any questions?"

I frowned as I tried to get my head around it. "So, you're telling me it would be OK to flirt with some guy when I'm supposed to be work-ing, as long as I get my work done?"

"We expect our employees to be self-directed and show initiative.

If you're looking for a boss to micromanage you, this won't be a good fit for you. The expectation is that you can manage your time wisely and complete all tasks set. If you think you can fit some flirting in while doing this, feel free, but realise that this will be frowned on during time sensitive tasks."

"So, sleeping with the entire male workforce, as long as I get my work done, is OK?" I asked with an incredulous laugh.

"We have over four hundred male staff, so that would be a considerable feat of endurance. Some staff are in relationships, so causing distress by trying to break up happy couples would definitely be frowned upon. Creating discord in a functioning workplace would be grounds for a negative performance review, and if you were attempting to force yourself on a man in or out of a relationship, he could bring a sexual harassment case against you. But other than that, my question would be, would it interfere with your work? Were you getting all your tasks done? That's actually a good question. I'll make a note to add that to the next group training session."

I let out a laugh that sounded almost more like a bark. This had to be a joke. What kind of crazy place was this? My boss was coolly telling me how to have gang bangs without messing with my work performance! I scrubbed at my face with my fingers, hoping maybe to wake myself up from the weirdest dream my id could have thrown at me. "You're struggling to take this in," Kelly said. "That's common. Would you like me to give you some time? We can continue this later?"

"No, I...." I shook my head. "What you're suggesting would have me fired, feathered and tarred for being an unrepentant slut at my previous jobs. It's just hard to hear my new boss say, sure, go for it, sleep with whoever you like."

Kelly shrugged, "Well, I can tell you from experience, we tried it the other way too, of course, and it didn't end well. We had major issues with interpersonal conflict, good qualified people leaving the organisation to pursue the relationships we were banning, not to mention sexual harassment. We spent considerable time with a team of mediators and psychologists, and came up with an alternative way to manage the situation. This was reviewed by consultants from industries with high incidents of sexual interaction in the workforce and refined. So far, it's worked well for us. We've even had articles written about our HR practices in some esteemed journals on business management, if you want to read them."

"Ah, no. I'll take your word on it. Wait, what industries? Like porn?"

"Some were from the adult entertainment industry, others from the BDSM community, and some representing sex workers. It was incredibly illuminating, once we move beyond our enculturated view of sex to a more pragmatic one, job satisfaction increased..."

I just bet it did, I thought.

"Staff retention, productivity, any metric you'd like to apply improved. We've worked this way for ten years, with an incident rate most companies would die for. It's a social experiment, but so far, it's been a successful one."

I sat there, trying to look all keen and professional, but seriously, my brain went straight back to when the guys walked in the door to the mess hall. It played back in super detail the many, many details I hadn't noticed the first time, perhaps exaggerated for my benefit. Then it was a slideshow of Shaun's kisses and his sandalwood scent, the guys bringing me food, the bloke with the monster dick, and Finn... I shook my head, and said, "What about when there's an unequal working relationship? Like a leading hand and a subordinate?"

"Thinking about Finn, are you?" My eyes went wide, but she just laughed. "It's OK, I noticed a bit of a frisson during the interview. That can be more difficult to negotiate, due to the power imbalance. Irrespective of who wears the pants at home, during working hours, it's important that assigned roles are respected. If you are adept at shifting gears, from your work persona to your domestic one, I can't see there being an issue. It's been awhile since Finn has had a significant other, and it would probably be good for him. But if you found it too hard, I would suggest you either terminated the relationship or asked for a transfer within the organisation."

"I didn't mean... It doesn't matter." I'd bounced in here full of energy, and now felt like I'd somehow gone through the ringer. The anxious part of my brain was screaming, "It's a trap!" and was sure the moment I stepped out of line, I'd be sacked on the spot. I also couldn't see a bunch of red-blooded straight guys being OK with all of this. If anyone was going to police a woman's sexual interactions, it was guys. Incredibly sexually responsive to him equals ideal mate, incredibly sexually responsive to a few guys equals slut. I seriously had no mental models to make sense of what she was proposing. It was always one guy, one girl, married until someone strayed, and then the condemnation of the whole town came down on their head in Melville. I swallowed, my throat suddenly dry. I felt like a kid let loose in a candy store, but some of the candy would end up with me out of a job, again giving hand jobs in alleyways if I wasn't careful. Well, fuck.

"I'm sorry this conversation has been so focussed on sexual inter-actions. I've told our instructional designer it doesn't really send the right message. Sex first, job second, but the complex nature of this workplace means it's something that has to be addressed from the start. Finn has mentioned you have been approached already by some of the men?"

"Uh, yeah."

"Then please don't feel pressured in any way to respond. Find your feet, if that's what makes you feel comfortable. You're in control here, do what works for you." I nodded, just wanting this conversation to end. This was like getting the sex talk from Mum, but worse. I had to impress Kelly to keep my job. I needed some time to get my head around this and work out what I thought, and I didn't want to do that in front of the boss.

"Ok, thanks," I said. "Should I go find Finn now?"

SHE GAVE him a call on her walkie talkie and then asked Karen to set me up with my own, a utility belt with a dizzying array of attach-ments, and an ID badge that also worked as a key to the areas I was allowed into. I went outside and sat down next to Buddy in a daze, my fingers burying themselves into his fur. A cart pulled up in front of me, and I started to get to my feet, but saw it was Shaun. He was smiling, but then noticed my expression. He climbed out and took a seat beside me, placing a big hand on my leg and giving it a pat. "How'd it go?"

"I..."

"It's a lot to get your head around, huh?"

"You could say that again." I let out a long sigh. Life had been so much simpler in Melville. Stupid drought, stupid downturn. I turned to look at Shaun, really looking at him for the first time in the morning. Yup, my brain hadn't been making it up. He was fucking gorgeous, and I both wanted to see exactly how those fingers on my leg would feel up inside me with a bit of a curl, and jump in my car and drive and drive and never come back. I don't know if he could see all that in my face, but his expression became sympathetic, and he pushed a strand of my hair behind my ear.

"Don't worry too much about all of this. Just find your feet, there's no rush. Just let things happen organically, if they're going to."

"I just... I've got a million questions. Like, how do you choose?"

"What? A guy? The same way you always did. Find someone you're into and are attracted to."

"But what if you're attracted to a lot of them?"

He chuckled at that. "God, don't tell the guys that. You'll have a stampede on your hands. Look, I don't know if you're ready for this, but the women here, they often...end up with more than one guy."

My head jerked up at this. "No fucking way."

"Well, yeah. There's too many blokes and not enough women. Some people really get off on it, especially women. Y'know how you girls can keep on coming, you have us at a disadvantage there, so..."

"OK, stop. You're right, I'm not ready for this. Fuck, couldn't they have told me this was some kind of swinger club before I drove all the way out here..." I put my head in my hands. A warm hand came to rest on the back of my neck, making small circles on the skin.

"Look, you want out of here? I'll give you the petrol money to get to the next town. Don't feel pressured or trapped. If you choose to stay, if you choose to give any of us the time of day, you do so because that's what you want to do, OK?"

"Why are you being so nice?" I asked. "Last night you were all 'anytime, any place baby'."

"You wanna know the truth?" I nodded. "I read romance novels."

"No way!"

"Yeah, you can keep that quiet, but I wanted to work out how women's minds tick. So I figured it'd be a good place to start, and a lot of blokes in those books are really sexually aggressive. I gave it a go, but it seemed to put you off a bit. It's why I waited outside, figured I better take another tack, see if that worked."

"Well, in the name of market research, they both kind of worked, but I think I prefer nice guy."

"Nice guy it is, then. So, you still up for a picnic, or do you need a bit of time?"

I tried to think about it but struggled. My brain was mush right now, but I looked at him and remembered what they kept telling me. I was in control, I didn't have to do anything I didn't want to. I could hang out with him this afternoon, see how I felt about it, and then go from there. "Yeah, I'd like that."

"Cool. Well, here comes Finn. I'll be at your place at 5:30, OK?"

5

"Julie, I'm going to get you to work with Nerida today, if that's OK. I've got some dramas beyond the gate I need to look after, and we've got to do your training before you go in there. She'll be ecstatic, just let her know this is not long term. Ask her to show you how to do stock control in the animal shed and the veterinary clinic," Finn said. He was looking a bit flustered, sweat already beading on his forehead.

"Yeah, sure."

"I'll be back with some of the animals for Doc Hobbes, but if I'm not by lunchtime, go to the mess shed with Nerida."

"Ok."

"And stop worrying so much, you'll be fine." He stopped the cart outside the animal shed and let me get out before taking off at a rapid clip. I shook my head and wandered in.

"Girlfriend!" Nerida said, running over when she saw me. "So, what happened to you last night? Sneaking off with Shaun, you naughty minx."

"Nothing happened. He just walked me home."

"Treat 'em mean, keep 'em keen. Used to be my motto too, until I came here. Now it's kind of redundant. Well, you ready to learn how to slop up?"

"Sure, it sounds delightful."

"Ah, it's not that bad. C'mon."

It turned out that slopping up wasn't really sloppy at all. It was weighing and portioning a combination of raw meat, bone meal, fish oil, eggs and some other stuff to keep the dogs healthy. I hadn't heard or seen one yet, so I was dead curious as to what they looked like. I thought maybe I'd get a chance to see them through the fence, but no dice. Buddy sat there drooling as we divvied up a bit over a hundred meals, the meat coming from a massive walk in fridge, and the other ingredients in big bins along the walls. "Oh, look at you," Nerida said, putting a half serve in front of my dog.

"Sit, Bud," I said as he went to devour it. He sat alright, but made that growling/yodeling sound Huskies make when they are unimpressed. I just cocked an eyebrow at him and waited for him to settle. "OK, now you can eat."

"Oh, honey," Nerida said. "With that kind of attitude, you'll have no problems with the guys here."

"What, you make them sit and stay before they..." I said as a joke.

"Before they eat me out? Sure, honey, gotta show them who's boss. Then they take their fill, and keep on taking right up until I tell them to stop..." The bubbly brunette had instantly transformed into some kind of languid, khaki clad dominatrix. She laughed and went back to normal when she saw my face. "I get it, you're probably wondering what the fuck you've done, landing in a hotbed of sexual deviants. But seriously, it's pretty boring most of the time. People work, sleep, get laid, just like everywhere else."

"Right, so Finn said ask you to show me the stock control system?"

She gave me a cheeky smile, seeming to see through my transparent attempt at changing the subject. I really, really needed people to stop talking to me about sex for a moment. I'd had plenty of conversations with girlfriends back in the day, but they were in the circle of trust. Complete strangers? Not so much. She started showing me what to do, pulling up the stock order on the animal shed computer, and how to fill out the forms and get proper authorisation. She pulled some clipboards off the wall and demonstrated how to monitor stock levels, ticking off what we had and writing down amounts, when a couple of carts arrived.

"Looks like its feeding time!" Nerida said. "Use your swipe key to get into my office, the one you were in the other day. Ask Lou and Aidan to come out, they always go on the feed run."

Ah, the freaky couple I'd seen yesterday. I wandered up the hall-way, looking at the various doors, until I saw the one with a light on. I swiped open the door and there they sat, almost in identical positions as before. The only thing that betrayed the fact they were alive was their eyes moving to take me in as I arrived.

"Hey, Nerida said you guys were going on the food run?" No response. "Did you want to come out...and get on the cart?" Nothing. "Guys? Hello?" I waved a hand in front of the closest one's face, but got no reaction other than a flutter of eyelashes "OK, guys. If this is some kind of taunt the noob thing, can we cut the crap? This day has been confusing and weird already without the Village of the Damned vibe you got going on. Guys?" I looked at the two of them in frustra-tion, then moved to try and take the arm of the one I was standing next to. I could drag them out if I had to.

Yeah, no I couldn't. Eyes slowly swivelled to look at my hand wrapped around what I thought was an arm but was apparently really a block of cement. Lou or Aidan had the kind of wiry build that often proved to be stronger than someone puffed up by body build-ing, but seriously, I couldn't move his or her arm an inch. They just sat there, regarding me with those yellowy green eyes. "Hey." I'd taken a step backwards, looking at the two of them warily, when another person appeared in the doorway. I turned and saw a guy with a long and lean build, a mop of black hair and grey eyes standing there. "Can't get 'em to move?"

"No, Nerida seemed to think I would just have to ask them. I'm Julie, by the way."

"Brandon. She would, she's pretty good at getting almost anyone to do her bidding, that's why she gets lumped with these guys." He gave a low raspy whistle and then gestured to the hallway. "C'mon, it's feeding time. Time to sort out those hungry dogs." Slowly, the two of them got up at the same time, moving to the door as one.

"Thanks for your help. I would have been here all day trying to move them. What's the deal anyway? Is there some kind of disability?"

"Not really my story to tell, but Lou and Aidan are siblings, and they got hurt a while back, never been the same. They can function, sort of. Look, next time, tell Nerida to do it. You don't have to put up with her shit."

"OK…" I said, detecting an undercurrent.

"You'll be at the mess hall for dinner?" he asked.

"Maybe not tonight."

"Someone got to you already, huh? Lucky bastard. Well, maybe I'll catch you around."

"Uh, sure…" and I watched him lope back down the hall. I returned to the slopping up table to see a group of blokes loading the meal containers we'd made up into the cart. A couple stopped mid delivery when I appeared, causing the men behind them to stumble and curse, but they seemed to recover quickly enough and got back to the job. That was something I was never going to get used to. Being the invisible waitress was more my speed, seamlessly taking and delivering orders, only noticed if the kitchen screwed up the order. I squared my shoulders and decided to ignore the attention, heading over to the storeroom where we had been doing a stock check and opening the door.

"Oh yeah, honey, you can ride me hard tonight…"

"Oh, shit! Sorry!" I said as I walked into Nerida in a clinch with some tall, dark and handsome guy. His eyes opened first, and he regarded me with a sly smile as I beat a hasty retreat.

"You OK?"

I blinked a few times, searching around mentally for the brain bleach, to see Brandon looking concerned.

"Stop chasing skirt and help us get these containers," one of the guys shouted.

"Blow it out your arse, Sam!" he called back. "You want me to get someone?"

I shook my head. "It's just taking me a bit to adjust here, is all."

"Don't worry about it," he said. "Same thing happens to most girls who come here." He had a look at his watch, and said, "It's nearly lunchtime. Why don't you wander over to the mess hall and grab a bite? Nerida and Sonny will be up to whatever they are doing for a while, and Finn's stuck with something behind the fence, so..."

"Yeah, sure, sounds good. Are you coming?"

He shook his head ruefully. "Animals eat before we do. Anyway, go on, these guys are gonna take forever if you don't." I looked around him and saw the blokes had slowed down to a snail's pace, watching what was going on.

I WALKED PAST THE LINE, Bud at my heels, and over to the Mess Hall. Being outside in the fresh air instantly made me feel a bit better. I looked at Bud, and said, "C'mon!" taking off at a jog, him running between my legs and barking as we went. I nearly tripped twice, but he was grinning and I was laughing by the end of it. I wandered inside and saw the place was half empty, thankfully. People looked up, but I just swept past, grabbing a plate and the makings of a huge sandwich and some juice, before scanning the tables for one where the guys on it didn't look up to see what I was doing. I found one towards the back, with three blokes sitting a fair way apart, not talking to each other and not looking around either, and made a beeline for it. "Do you mind if I sit here?" I asked.

The three of them looked up with a start, one guy's eyes flicking to the other, but the third nodding and gesturing for me to take a seat. I sat down at the other end, giving the guys their space if they wanted it, no sound other than the clink of utensils or the sound of people chewing. Finally, I said, "I'm Julie, the new girl."

"I know," the guy closest to me said. He had short greying hair and intense blue eyes. "Mack," he said, pointing to himself. "George and Al." The other guys gave me a nod and went back to eating. *Well, thank fuck for that,* I thought, *not everyone here was gagging for it.*

"So, what do you guys do?" I asked, relieved to treat them like any other person I'd meet on the job. Getting people talking about themselves was always an easy way to start a conversation.

"Construction, on the married quarters side," Mack said, apparently the spokesperson for the group.

"So, do you have partners? What's your wife's name? Have I met her?"

Mack smiled slightly and seemed to relax a little. A girl would have to be a bit weird to try and use questions about your girlfriend or wife as a way to crack onto you. "Louise, and I don't think so. She works in the married mess, running the kitchen."

"So, there's two different messes? You guys don't eat with the single blokes?"

He shook his head, "Not normally, we just needed to grab a quick bite today. Too many hot heads, and I've got a daughter. Not old enough to date any of these idiots, but some of them don't seem to get that message."

"Are single women allowed in? I mean, if they aren't looking to... you know."

The guys all looked at each other, as if considering it, then shrugged. George, an older guy with thinning blond hair, said, "I guess so. I admit, you'd want to run it past the women first. They get a bit...protective at times, but we've had some come over if the crap that goes on here gets a bit much. If you're not a troublemaker, people shouldn't take issue with it."

"God, no. I just want a bit of peace and quiet and normality."

"Hello there, Miss Julie." As if summoned by the devil to contradict my words, I looked up to see Brett and his buddies, the three blokes from this morning, coming and taking a seat in front of or beside me. Mountain dude boxed me, blocking my view of the people I had been talking to.

"How's your day going?" the darker haired guy asked, picking up a sandwich and biting into it.

"I'll talk to the missus," Mack said, getting to his feet, his mates following suit, "and get back to you."

"That'd be awesome," I said as they filed out. I turned to dark haired guy and said, "I'm Julie, and you are?"

"Darren, Brett and Monster."

"Monster? He's a big bloke, but why...." and then it occurred to me why he had that name. I looked down at my plate, studying the other half of my sandwich with rapt attention.

"Don't worry about it," Monster rumbled. "Most girls want to know if I'm big all over."

"Right, well, your mother didn't name you Monster. What's your real name?" I asked, wanting to change the subject to something, anything else.

"Peter," he said, almost shyly.

"Right, well, Pete, what do you do around here?"

"Well..." Darren said with a smile.

"Seriously, what's your job."

"Some construction, some mine work," he said.

"Mining? The place behind the fence?"

"It's the cash cow that keeps all this ticking along," Brett said. "No mine, no Sanctuary."

"So, what do you two do?"

"Drive trucks, haul out the ore and take it to the export site. So has Kelly had the chat with you?"

"Yep, and it was seriously awkward, and then I walked in on my colleagues making out in the storeroom of the shed. So if we could get off the sex topic, that'd be great."

"Nerida huh?" Darren said. "She on with Sonny now?" I nodded. "She likes her variety, does Ms Nerida. We had a bit of fun with her there for a while."

My eyes flicked to Pete, who was eating from his full plate with gusto, to a smirking Darren, to Brett who was watching me closely for my reaction. "What?" I asked, knowing I didn't want to know the answer, but unable to stop myself from asking, "All three of you?"

Brett nodded slowly, his light hazel eyes, a weird mix of green and amber, held mine. "See we grew up together here. Been mates since we were little kids. Girls, they think they want the Monster there, but when push comes to shove..." Darren grinned at the clumsy joke. "They need us if they want to climb the Mountain, or they will be very sad and sorry for themselves the day after. We help to...broaden their horizons, in preparation."

"So what? This is like Goldilocks and the three bears? This one is too small..." I pointed to the grinning Darren, whose smile was wiped away. "This one is too big and will rupture my cervix." I pointed to Pete. "But this one is what? Just right?"

"You cheeky bitch..." Darren muttered, but Brett held up a hand, silencing him.

"Only one way to find out," Brett said.

I looked sideways at Pete to see his fork had been put down, and he watched me as well with hooded chocolate brown eyes. Now, I'm not too prissy to admit I was in some ways curious. I lived in the age of the internet, so I'd seen a bunch of monster dicks going into places it seemed physically impossible to fit them, and seen girls moaning like it was the greatest fuck they'd ever had. Finding a partner similarly blessed and looking forward to a long life of painful sex and possible prolapse didn't seem like the most awesome thing in the world, but as a once off... He was like the sexual equivalent of bungee jumping or parasailing. I looked back into Pete's eyes and then said, "So you've been quiet during all of this. Is every sexual encounter you have a foursome? Do you like always sharing with your mates?"

His eyes dropped to his plate, then flicked to Brett and Darren before coming back to me, meeting them head on. "A lot of girls, when they're horny, think it's gonna be the greatest thing in the world, so the expectations are sky high. But when it comes down to it... Hearing a girl yelp in pain doesn't do it for me, not even a little bit. Watching them freak out and pull away, trying to put as much distance between you and them..." He turned back to his food and picked up his fork, methodically putting food in his mouth and chewing.

Don't look at his pants, don't look at his pants, I told myself over and over. The part of me that wasn't an arsehole recognised that his story made me sad. I couldn't imagine the majority of my sexual relationships ending with my partner shrinking away in horror. The other part wondered just how big was big.

"OK, I get that I asked, but seriously, enough. You call him Monster?" I shook my head. "Look you guys, you all talk amongst yourselves, right?"

"Yeah."

"Then you can circulate something for me. I had a chat with a couple of the married guys here, and they're going to ask if I can get permission to take meals over in their mess."

"Fuck, you wouldn't," Darren said.

"Yes, I will disappear into the married quarters. Fuck, I'll ask for my accommodation to be over there if needs be."

"Or..." Brett said, jaw flexed tight.

"Or you can circulate that I want everyone to back off a bit. I'm in a new job, a new place, and I'm trying to adjust. I'd like to get to know my workmates, not be told about the size of their dicks within five minutes of a conversation. I get that I started this, and I'm sorry Pete. I shouldn't have checked you out."

"It's OK," he said with a small smile. "I checked out your arse when you took off for the admin building."

"OK, then we're all even here. But going forward, I want everyone to chill. No more getting food for me, or offering to stretch my vagina enough to take your friend's dick, are we clear?"

"That go for Shaun as well?"

"It goes for everyone."

"Yet he gets to take you out this afternoon."

"Because he was nice to me."

"You can't blame us," Brett said, seemingly the leader of this little crew. "Some guys, they do the nice and supportive thing well. Some guys, their skills are elsewhere. Every guy that's interested is gonna want to offer what they have, no matter how you might react, just in case it gets them a picnic in the afternoon sun." He got to his feet, Darren following hard on his heels. I turned to Pete, putting a hand on the broad expanse of his arm as he went to go as well.

"Y'know a woman that wants you for you, she's going to find a way to deal with whatever you've got going on there. Women have babies, some even stick fists up their twats. There has to be at least one who'd be able to deal with what you're packing."

"Yeah, maybe," he said, and then followed his mates out of the hall.

"Hey Finn, you want me back at the shed, over?" I said into the walkie talkie.

"Yeah, we are en route. Get the doc and tell her we have some injured incoming. You might need to broaden your skill set and act as a nurse."

"Um..." *Was he fucking serious? Can do attitude, Jules, can do.* "OK, will do."

I made my way over the vet at a rapid clip, Buddy getting tangled in my feet, thinking I was playing again. "Settle down, dog!" I snapped. "Stay here," I said, and he settled down by the surgery door. I opened it to find the vet working at her computer, a sandwich sitting uneaten beside her. "Doc, I just got off the comms with Finn, and he said they are bringing in some injured people?"

"More?" She sighed and got to her feet. "Help me get the kit out, then scrub up using that soap over there. Do not touch anything once you've washed your hands." Several guys came in not long afterwards, carrying the limp body of a man. "On the table," the doc said. "What do we have? Contusions and lacerations?"

Whoa. When I turned around, I saw the man was covered in blood, long shallow slashes having cut through his clothes and skin. I swallowed, then blinked. I'd seen stuff like this on TV, but never in real life. I knew I should do something, anything, as the man moaned in pain, but I found myself frozen to the spot.

"Yep. Billy will be fine for now, it's Neil I need you to look at. We've applied a tourniquet," Finn said, striding into the surgery.

"This is happening with greater frequency. It's just getting worse as we get closer to the full moon."

Finn seemed to see me for the first time. "Julie, can I get you to go to the mess hall and grab us some coffees? We missed lunch and are running on empty."

That was what I needed to reanimate me. I shook my head, trying to clear it, and said, "Sure, of course. I'll bring some food as well."

He just nodded, and I took off at a run. Fifteen minutes later, I'd loaded up a trolley I'd borrowed from the kitchen staff with jugs of hot tea and coffee and a tray of sandwiches, and was pushing it over to the surgery. I left the trolley outside, as there was a bit of a step in front of the side door, and I couldn't lift it over without dislodging some stuff. I grabbed the jug of coffee and some mugs, and pushed my way through the first swinging door.

"You're going to have to watch the girl. With her heritage, she's going to be one of you, and uninitiated is vulnerable. They are getting more aggressive, looking for any vulnerability. They obviously think they can get through..." that sounded like the doc.

"Not if I can help it." That was definitely Finn.

"That's Sharlene's son. David's went last week, and Arlen's," another voice said. "They're doing what they can, but seriously, they need help. We need to go through the gate with some reinforcements."

"Not with new blood around."

"Those guys know how to mind their manners."

"And if she goes into heat?"

"Yeah, alright, but you're going to have to pull everyone back. Right now, we can't protect the whole area."

"That means we cede the land to them."

"I don't know what else you want me to do."

I made a bunch of scuffling noises in the airlock and then pushed my way through, letting the doors bang behind me.

"Got the coffee," I said. "There's mugs and tea and milk and sandwiches outside. I'll bring them in."

"Thanks, Jules," Finn said, looking exhausted. "Slade, give her a hand, will ya?"

Slade was a well-muscled guy with short, reddish hair and a scruff of a beard across his chin. "Alright." He didn't wait for me, striding out the way I'd come as I set down the jug and mugs. When I went outside, he was looking at Buddy with a slight smile. "You got him well trained. Most dogs would have scoffed the lot while we were inside."

"Nah, not Buddy. Good boy!" I said, and tossed him half an egg sandwich.

"He thinks you're the alpha," Slade said.

"Maybe. Animal behaviourists are revising their thoughts on that now."

Slade shrugged and then put me to shame, picking the trolley up with little effort and placing it inside the entrance.

"Looks like you have no problem calling the shots with the dog."

Inside, I made everyone their drinks and handed out the food. They seemed grateful, though distracted.

"Look, I'll be stuck here for a while with the doc," Finn said. "Training's not going to happen today. It's two o'clock, why don't you call it a day?"

"You sure?"

"Yeah, go home. You haven't had much of a chance to settle in, and we can try again tomorrow. It looks like we have a security problem, and I'll need to focus on that. Until you get your full training, I won't be able to take you with me."

"Oh, OK."

"I'll come by your bungalow at 9 am, and hopefully we'll have a better day."

"No problems," I said. Slade watched me stand up, his tea cup frozen midway between the saucer and his mouth. I waved goodbye awkwardly and walked out. *They want to get rid of me*, I thought as I left, *why?*

6

I had initially felt relieved to finish what was a confusing day, but once I entered my new home, I realised I had no internet and no TV. No books or magazines, either. I looked around the almost empty living room. It had a couple of slightly worn but comfortable couches, and a dining table and chairs, but not much else. I checked my watch and saw Shaun wasn't due for hours, so I got changed into some old training gear and went for a run.

Buddy was no longer nipping at my heels. Instead, the two of us ran full pelt along the back road that went past all the singles accommodations until I reached the last of them, then we flew down the rise. There was a lot more housing down this way, further away from the shed, the bungalows fanning out. My breath was coming in hard as I pulled up just near the bottom boundary fence, Buddy and I walking in small circles slowly to catch it. Beyond the fence was a small creek and a bunch of trees, growing thick along the bank. As I moved, I could see where the trees began to thin and a field of grass was revealed, turned golden by the low hanging sun. I walked parallel to the boundary, the field popping in and out of view, until I saw a group of guys working on the fence on the side furthest from me. I stopped, dropping back behind a tree trunk. The men were stripped down to their singlets or without shirts at all, digging holes, manoeuvring posts and then cementing them in, their bodies exactly what had been hinted at in the mess hall last night: well-muscled, the cleanly defined shapes apparent even this far away, moving together like a well-oiled machine.

You could have something like that under you tonight, my body prompted sneakily. Yeah, I could, and right now I could see no reason not to. They were over there, a safe distance away, completely oblivious to the golden sunlight that caressed their bodies and my gaze. It must have just gone break time as the guys moved from their tasks, taking seats on stumps of wood or prone logs, drinking down water or lighting cigarettes. One guy, his hair was long and brown, partially tied back, and a full beard, laughed at something one of his mates said before looking up. I don't know how, but his eyes immediately met mine. He didn't say a word, but the change in the group was almost instant, with every head swivelling around to look my way.

I gasped, there was no way they could see me, as far away as I was and partially hidden, yet somehow, I knew they did. I laughed, a short abrupt bark, jerking back from the tree. Not knowing why, I turned and ran off up the hill, past the other bungalows and blokes heading home for the day, only to leap onto my porch, hand on the door. There was no reason for it, they were metres away and unlikely to catch me if they decided to give chase, and why would they? My chest felt tight as I panted. I was fit, I was strong and I was in my domain. There was nothing anyone here could do to challenge that, yet I remained torn between worrying that one of them might and wishing they would. No one had followed, of course they didn't, I stood on my porch gasping and alone, but for Buddy. Yet when I looked down over the fence, creek and trees from my vantage point on the hill, I saw at least three guys standing in the middle of the far field, looking back.

GOING for a run had done the trick. I'd taken a hot shower, the fractious anxiety of the day wrenched from my body by a good workout.

By the time Shaun rolled up, I was feeling much more relaxed, lying on the couch. "Well, hey," he said from inside the door frame, looking down at me like he'd like to eat me up with a spoon. I got to my feet in a fluid slide and bestowed a long, slow kiss on his mouth. "You seem more chilled than before."

"Right now, I am in the 'this place is crazy but I may as well make it work for me' stage. Though fair warning, this could change at any moment," I said, winding my arms around him.

"Sorry I didn't get a chance to clean-up, I got held up with this last job. I was trying to fix the wiring in one of the sheds..."

"If you knew how horny guys in work gear made me..." I said, drawing in closer. His scent was driving me nuts, a weird combination of fresh male sweat, sweet sandalwood and something else... My nose ran down the side of his neck, clouding my senses.

"Darlin', you gotta watch yourself," he said in a low voice. "You say stuff like that in the mess shed, and you'll have a riot on your hands."

"Mmm..." I murmured as I moved closer, winding my arms around him. "You smell so good I want to..."

He grabbed my hand and shoved it against his rigid length. "And you make me hard just by breathing. Right now, it's taking everything I've got not to bend you over that couch, rip down your jeans and shove myself inside you over and over." I whimpered as a sharp twinge in my groin told me how good that would be. "I like accepting Julie a great deal, but I think the rest of you is still catching up, and I don't want her regretting anything. How about we pack up you and the dog, and go for that picnic?"

"Why am I like this?" I asked, pulling back slightly, feeling like my brain was made of mush. Sexy, sexy mush.

"It's just lust, darlin'. Now, come on."

I frowned at that, that couldn't be it. I had plenty of experience with lust before, and it was nothing like this.

"WOW, THIS PLACE IS BEAUTIFUL!" I said as we pulled off a dirt track and drove down a wildflower covered slope. Down the bottom, I could see there was a large rock outcropping, a waterfall and a pool of crystal-clear water.

"Milady," Shaun said, opening the SUV door with a flourish and offering me an arm. He held an honest to goodness picnic basket in the other. Buddy bounded out unassisted, immediately taking off to sniff around, and we followed at a more leisurely pace. We stopped just before the bank of the waterfall, Shaun flicking out a checkered blanket for us to sit on.

"You've got great attention to detail," I said.

"You ain't seen nothing yet," he said, pulling out a bottle of white wine. I admit I was more transfixed by his strong hands popping the cork than anything, but I took the brimming glass he poured me, grateful to have something for my hands to do.

SERIOUSLY, this place was turning me into a basket case. I felt like I'd run the whole emotional gamut today, from happy to horny, to freaked out to paranoid. And right now? I watched Shaun recline on the blanket, the buttons of his wash worn shirt straining across his chest, his jeans shifting to show just how well he filled them.

"So, what's your pleasure?" Shaun asked.

"Sorry?" My eyes jerked up to his face, only to realise he was talking about food. He seemed to note my distracted state, smiling to himself, but pulling out the various delicacies he'd been able to scrounge up and spreading them out on the blanket. "Buddy!" I said when he came over at a run, stopping at the edge, sitting and drooling.

"I come prepared," Shaun said, and pulled out a big meaty bone covered in cling film. He peeled it off, Buddy watching him with rapt attention, and then tossed it away in the grass.

"You really have thought of everything," I said. Those cool blue eyes flicked up to meet mine, holding my gaze steady until they dropped down to my mouth and lower.

"Here's hoping."

I clenched my teeth, not wanting to dash my drink to the ground and give in to the siren's call of his husky voice, and I didn't know why. If he'd walked into the diner, even if he was a jerk, I'd have slept with him if it was on the table. Maybe that was part of the problem, guys who looked like him usually ignored me, and I couldn't help but feel weird that that wasn't the case here.

"Penny for your thoughts?" he asked, probably wondering why I was being such a bloody freak.

I sat up straight and placed the glass on the ground and took a deep breath. "I'm thinking you're too pretty for me, and that the only reason you'd look at me twice is because you live in a place with no women." His eyes went wide, seeming to study mine, as if looking for confirmation I was serious. Then when this was confirmed non-verbally, he burst out laughing. *I guess I have been punked*, I thought. I got to my feet in a rush, wanting to put some distance between us before my face went from red to neon scarlet. I got one step away before he caught me around the knees, yanking me down to fall heavily beside him. I growled in response, clambering to get free, but he covered my body with his much heavier one, pinning me down.

"Get off me!" I snapped.

"So you can take off, thinking that this is some kind of pity fuck in the making? No fucking way. Jules! Jules! I'm fucking serious, calm down!"

I ended up on my back, his hips pressing mine down to the ground, my wrists held fast in his iron grip. I forced my eyes to stay on his chest as I panted, trying to catch my breath. Fuck he was strong! I didn't want to look at him. If I didn't meet his gaze, he'd eventually get tired of this, and then I could go home to bed, alone. I just had to wait him out. "Jules," he said, seeming to cotton on to my evil plan. "Jules?" My name came out now as a low, almost plaintive plea. Not whiny, I don't know if he could sound it with that raspy voice of his, just heartfelt somehow.

"Fuck it," he said, jerking back. For a moment, I thought he was letting me go free. Instead, he fell back into a seated position, with me across his knees. I'm not short myself, but for some reason, I felt tiny right now. He let go of my wrists, his hands going to curl around me and tangle in my hair. "You don't fucking know me, you've got nothing at stake here. Just talk to me, talk to me like I was a girlfriend or something."

"If you were my girlfriend, I'd be gay as fuck," I said with a grumble.

He laughed a little at that but seemed wary now, like it might set me off again. He rested his chin on the top of my head and curled his arms around me tighter. I should have felt caged in, trapped. Instead, I felt a kind of stillness settle over me. I was overreacting, I realised, and being a complete dick. This place, losing my job, everything had really thrown me for six. This was not how I'd thought my life would turn out, but it had, so what was I going to do about it?

"Jules, we're guys. If you ever want to find out if a guy's interested in you sexually, you don't think there's one simple way to check?"

"Yeah, but..."

"No buts. Relationships, whether a guy really likes you, that's probably trickier, but attraction?" He pulled back to look down at me, and this time, I met his gaze for at least a moment. "I don't know what the guys where you're from see, but I can't get past all this wild brown hair, this big beautiful smile and..." His eyes trailed down my body. "I better stop while I'm ahead." He swallowed. "You fight like the devil."

"Take off your shirt," I said, starting to shift from his lap.

"What?"

"Take off your shirt. You guys are incredibly intimidating, maybe if I..."

"What? You want to...confront your fears?"

"Maybe. Take it off, if you want me to touch you, that is." The buttons were undone at lightning speed, and he started to pull it off, pausing to look me over, as if he wasn't totally sure this was all right. Finally, he pulled it off, and I took a swig from his wine glass when all was revealed. Well, shit. It was as bad as I thought.

I ran a finger down the satiny brown skin of his shoulder, tracing down a winding abstract tattoo there, letting my hand curl against his collarbone and then further down. His abs jumped as I touched, as if he were a skittish animal and might shy away in a moment. I spread my fingers wide, resting my palm on the warmth of his chest. "Jules..." His breath was coming in short bursts, his eyes almost wild. I just took another mouthful of the wine, really noticing the curious mixture of sweet and sour before descending on him.

Now that I was the one making the moves, I felt more in control. This place was a dizzying kaleidoscope of sexually attractive male flesh, and it was really disorientating being bombarded constantly with visual stimuli, offers and overtures. Everyone was telling me what they wanted, and it made it difficult to know what I did. I acknowledged that I still didn't, but I had an idea as I listened to Shaun hiss at my fingers grazing his waistband. As weird and sleazy as the three guys at lunchtime had been, I was in some ways curious. Maybe not a curiosity I was ever going to indulge, but something I could think about in the sanctity of my own mind if offers weren't being thrust in my face all the time. I looked up at Shaun as I touched the button of his jeans, asking for permission. He blinked and then nodded quickly, holding a breath as I undid it with a flick and then slid his zipper down.

He's right, I realised, as I peeled his clothes back as far as I could without moving him. It was a lot simpler than I had been making it. I could have clear evidence of whether or not he wanted me, and here it was. I slipped my hand inside his jeans, and his hips shifted slightly, an almost involuntary buck as my palm rubbed against the rigid length of his erection. "Jules..." he rasped as I moved my hand against him, prevented from skin to skin contact by a pair of turquoise blue undies but for the moment, content to feel his rigidity.

Of course, it's fucking huge, I thought. Somehow, I had landed a job in an erotica writer's fantasyland, full of gorgeous guys with big dicks. I bet he didn't even take that long to get hard again. I peeled back his undies, watching him slowly become revealed. Well fuck, I know exactly how he'd feel going in. Comparatively smaller in the head, his dick flared out thick down the shaft, and I knew I'd feel that delicious pinch from being filled just slightly past capacity. I'd been so focussed on what I was doing, I hadn't really tuned into my own body. The throb between my legs drew my attention back. My nipples ached and my thighs were damp. Freed from all this thinking, I now knew what I wanted. I wanted to fuck.

I jerked at his jeans so he would move his butt, not wanting to be slow and careful anymore. I pulled them down his legs and then shifted to take my rightful place above him. "Jules, Jules…" he hissed, pushing me back, moving into a crouched position. "Not yet, darlin'. I might only get one shot at this, and I want to do it right."

"Shove your dick into me, that's what I want."

"Jules," he murmured, manoeuvring me down on the blanket and dropping his lips to my neck. "I'll make it good for you, I promise. If we do it your way, it's gonna hurt."

"No, it'll be fine…" I whined, but he didn't listen. His mouth crashed down upon mine, his tongue forcing its way past my lips, his hand scraping up my side and curling around my breast. He wasted no time in pulling my nipple between his fingers, my back arching, and incoherent whimpers coming from my mouth as I felt his caress right in my clit. His mouth soon shifted, freeing his hand to move downwards, his lips closing around my nipple and drawing me in deep.

"Oh, fuck…" I gasped as I felt his fingers slip under my skirt and over my damp thighs, pulling the saturated fabric of my underwear to one side, and then I yelped as he speared them into me. "Oh, god… oh, god…!" I cried, feeling a terrible pressure build in the base of my spine, the glancing touches to my clit as he thrust inside me making me claw at the ground.

"Let me taste you," he said, hissing in my ear.

I moaned, unable to lie still under his ministrations, but wanting something more. "Yes!" I yelped as he dropped hurried kisses and pulled his fingers free, leaving me crying out from their loss, only to flip up my skirt and skim my underwear down my body. "Shaun, please…" I said. I could feel his breath on my overheated skin for a few heartbeats, and then he ran his tongue along my seam.

My moans were coming in weird, animalistic bursts, but I couldn't care. Along the most tender of my flesh, a slippery mobile spear flick-ered, tantalising in its firmness, hinting that it could provide the hard, rough friction I was craving before slipping away. His fingers returned home, sheathing themselves inside me, and he rode my jerking hips right up until his lips closed around my clit.

Oh, fuck. It was a little like an out of body experience. My mind went white as the most incredible sensation burst through my body. I was coming, pleasure radiating out in waves, my cunt twitching around his fingers, feeling almost overpowered by his punishing strokes. When it finally stopped, I opened my eyes a crack, saw him panting and crouched over me, dick rigid. "How about now?" he asked.

"Oh, fuck yes," I said.

He had a condom out of his wallet in one moment, smoothing it on and adding a small sachet of lube. I raised an eyebrow at this, and he said, "A little trick someone told me. Trust me, it will help." Then he covered me with his body, I pulled his hips in close and arched my back to help the process. He was right, I soon realised. He was slow and careful about pushing himself inside me, pausing to let my body adjust. I needed it. I could feel a slight burn already, and I was pretty sure he was only half way in. "You OK?" he grated.

"Yeah."

He took that as wholesale approval and shoved the rest in, wrenching a cry from me. I didn't get a chance to adjust either, the control he had been using had apparently run out. His fingers dug into me as he thrust hard. It was both too much and not enough, my cunt sensitive, my nerve endings swirling with pleasure at the long-awaited friction, but I also longed to curl up in a corner and have a nice lie down. I was never great at coming more than once, so I didn't quite know what to make of this until he shifted slightly. "Oh, fuck," I yelped. It felt like he was fucking my clit from the inside, and instead of fingers and tongues, this massive heavy weight was pushing against it, never letting up. "Uh...uh..." My whine ratcheted up. His hand instantly went down between us, flicking over my clit. "Oh no..." I cried.

It was harder this time. I almost wanted to scrabble away, the wave rising and rising until... My body went limp, unable to do anything else, other than twitch under him. Seriously, I wasn't wowing anyone with my sexual performance right now, but fuck. I was seeing colours behind my lids, felt like I was tripping balls, my cunt snapping around his hardness. "Jules!" he cried, and jerked inside me, so hard I could feel the pulsations of his cum.

It took a while for us to move. It felt like having a house land on you or surviving a plane crash. You knew something momentous had just happened, and you had to pause for a moment to collect your-self. He pulled free of me, almost painfully, and then flopped down on the blanket. I looked across at him, and he looked back at me and...we laughed. It was stupid and ridiculous, but seriously, there was no other appropriate response. In that laughter was wonder and awe and self-congratulation and gratitude and secretly, relief that the kind of sexual experience you'd always dreamed about actually happened. It was weird, because it was just missionary with some oral, but fuck me, it did it for me.

"I think my vagina's broken," I said.

"No, it's not," he said, rolling into me with a smile. "I won't let it be."

"No seriously, I can't ever have sex again. It'll all be downhill from now. I'm going to swear off for life, go out on top."

"You can have a go on top anytime you like," he said with a grin, "and I promise, if your vagina is broken, I'll kiss it better."

"Oh, stop it," I cried, wriggling back. "I'm usually one and done, so this is all a bit of shock to me. Let's just...cool it for a sec, until I am sure my clit won't fall off. And we didn't get anything to eat."

"Well, you didn't," he said with a chuckle.

"I was going to but you were all, no, no, ladies first."

"Are you complaining?"

"Not at all, but I'm happy to give you a rain check on knob polishing."

He laughed at this, then rolled closer, "Really?"

"Sure," I said, trying to keep the smile on my face, but struggling as his eyes bore into mine. There was something fragile here, I thought, I needed to be careful with it. "I always pay my debts."

7

"We're going to be late for work," Shaun murmured into my hair. I didn't respond, just arched my back, pushing my butt against his hips, and he groaned. "You better stop that or I'll call in sick, tie you to the bed and fuck you till you're raw."

"That may be mission accomplished," I said, feeling a twinge as I moved. "I am now thoroughly glad you bought lube."

"Perils of sleeping with a guy with a big dick, babe."

"Having sex five times in the one night might have been a contributing factor."

"Mmm," he moaned as my hips shifted. "Once more could hardly make a difference..." He went to roll me over, but instead, I flipped him back, straddling him before dropping kisses lower and lower down his body.

"I'm sure I owe you a favour," I said, mouth hovering over the head of his dick. "What could it be?" He watched me, wide-eyed and hopeful, as I moved closer, grabbing him around the base and then bestowing one long lick from root to tip.

"Swing your hips this way," he hissed as my tongue made a leisurely swipe of the crown. I looked up quizzically. "We need to multitask, or we'll be late," he said with a grin. I shrugged and did as he asked, gasping around his cock as his tongue flicked out...

"I'M GOING to get you to go with Slade today," Finn said when I came outside.

By the time we had finished, had a shower and got ready, Finn was waiting on the porch. He smiled politely when he saw us, greeting Shaun with a nod of his head. "See you tonight?" Shaun said, dropping a kiss on my cheek.

"Sure."

"So," Finn said, "have you ever ridden a quad bike?"

"Ah, once or twice."

"Well, you'll be doing a perimeter check, so I'll get you to ride with him until he can do some bike training with you."

I looked over to where Slade lounged against the cart, arms crossed over his chest. He regarded me silently with a steady gaze.

"We check the fence each day. It'll be something I get you to do most mornings, so getting your head around it would be good. Be alert for signs of intrusion, footprints near the boundary, broken tree branches, holes under fences, etc. Slade will show you what to do. Show her around the rest of the site while you're at it. I barely got through the admin buildings."

"Got it, boss. You ready, princess?" Princess? I looked him over with a frown. He just chuckled and walked over the quad. "You getting on?" Finn had gotten into his cart, taking off to deal with the problem at the mine again, and I was now realising what I would have to do. I would have to get on the back of the olive green quad bike and wrap my arms and legs around a strange man. A very big, strange man.

While many men on the Sanctuary were taller than me, for some reason it was more apparent on Slade. He had scruffy, reddish hair with a bit of a beard going, and flat hazel eyes that seemed to take in everything without reaction. He lit a cigarette in a few abrupt motions, then turned around with a frown to me. "What's the hold up?" he asked, then followed my gaze as I watched Shaun's back grow smaller and smaller in the distance. "What are you worried about? That Shaunie will get jealous?" His tone was filled with that entirely male disdain that was able to turn you from a confident woman to a little girl in moments.

"Look, I..."

"What, you stressing about spreading your legs and letting me between them? Think your boyfriend will get jealous? Worried I might get all hot and bothered about it?" I swallowed the huge lump in my throat. He voiced my fears pretty accurately, but I sounded like a conceited dickhead when he said it. "Too late, honey," he said with a growl, taking a few steps closer, a small smile on his lips. "You breeze out here smelling of flowers, soap and sex, and I'm already half-hard. Can't say if that will get better or worse." He ran a finger along my jawline quickly, dropping his hand before I could jerk away. "But whatever you got going with Shaun can't be too strong if all it takes is a bike ride to turn your head."

"That wasn't what I was worried about," I said, finally finding my voice. "It just feels...bad to be touching another guy two moments after I was having sex with the first one."

He cracked up at that, his teeth stark white against his bronzed skin. "Ah, god save me from small-town girls. Look, I get that back in whatever backwater town you come from you have jealous, over-bearing dicks who feel like they have to growl and posture over their girls to warn off possible competitors, but I'd like to think we've evolved past that here. Will Shaun like you coming home tonight smelling of me? No. Will I enjoy it? Probably more than is polite to say. Will it be the latest entry in my spank bank? I don't know, but am happy to update you once this has become clear to me. What I do want to do is my job, and according to Finn that entails driving you around, Miss Daisy. So will you do me a favour, and get on the fucking bike?"

I gritted my teeth, taking a long whistling breath in between them, and then nodding. "I'm sorry, I do come from a backwater town, and I guess seeing a string of guys acting like possessive jerks made me think all of you had the potential to be possessive jerks. I also like him and don't want to upset him, because hurting people's feelings without a reason seems like shitty behaviour, but maybe that's just me. Get on the damn bike, I promise to ignore any and all erections, semi or full, and let's go to work."

He grinned at me, taking one last drag from his cigarette before crushing it under his boot. "Well, c'mon."

I threw my leg over the back of the quad once he was on and slid behind him, forcing myself to put my arms around his waist without being weird about it. *This is a job, I'm being professional*, I told myself. I swear I heard him laugh as he started the bike, taking us flying down the hill.

We stopped down at the shed to leave Buddy with Nerida and the crew for the day. She just smiled and looked over me and Slade with a lascivious eye.

"What you've seen so far is what we call the admin sector," Slade said as we rode out. "This is the married quarters." He pointed to a cluster of larger bungalows that spread out over a rise on the other side of the admin buildings. "There's more facilities here, creche, bakery, store... The queens need more stuff I guess, raising kids."

"Queens?" I asked.

"Mothers. Most workers here were born and bred, so this is kind of a village in a way. Now, the area we need to check starts here," he said, taking us down the path furthest away from the accommodations, where the land devolved into forest. He pulled up at the corner of a 20ft fence, covered in cyclone mesh and made from sturdy metal supports, and grabbed a clipboard from a saddlebag. "Basically, we go along the fence-line and make a sight check. There's sensors on the wire so that if there's a break, they pick it up early. What we're looking for is signs of activity outside it."

"What would want to break into a mine site?"

He shrugged, "What we dig up in there, its valuable, so there's that. There's also the dogs we keep roaming in there. Good for keeping intruders out, bad for being around little kids, if you catch my drift. We're checking as much to make sure none of them are getting out, as keeping other things from getting in. Now if you find anything, you write it up in this report form and then file it with the fencers."

Were they the guys I'd spied on yesterday? I imagined walking into their shed and submitting the reports, it probably would go as well as going to the mechanics on the first day. Fuck, I was never working in a male-dominated environment again. It was too damn embarrassing.

We walked and rode along the fence line for hours, Slade passing me a bottle of water and prompting me to drink at each interval. I was just filling in the form about some loose wire at one section, when Slade held up a hand to me. I looked up, curious as he bent down, staring into the mesh, then he gestured for me to come over slowly. I crept up to him, still getting a glare when I stepped on a twig with a snap. He crouched down and drew me with him, pointing at the wire.

It took me a while to see them, tawny coats blending in with the brown leaf litter and tree trunks, but I had to slap a hand over my mouth to stifle a gasp when I did. There they were, two huge dogs. Not the usual German Shepherds or Rottweilers, they looked a lot like Buddy, though with a pale grey and white coat and so much bigger. "They're so beautiful," I whispered. Slade glanced back at me, a lazy smile spreading across his face as he took in my expression.

"Check them out," he hissed, and then gestured to our left. I looked hard and then fell back onto my heels. There, timidly clustered around a wide tree trunk was three puppies, each a dull brown colour with some dark ticking around the ears.

"Oh my god!" I squeaked. I regretted it instantly as the animals started and took off.

"You'll see them again," he said, and got to his feet, dusting dried grass off his pants. "C'mon, I know a nice place for lunch." With the sun overhead, he headed for the forest, parking at the edge and pulling out a styrofoam Esky cooler, and then beckoning for me to follow him. Once past the first few trees the space opened up, and we could walk easily under a shady canopy. He gestured to a few logs which had fallen almost at right angles. He handed me a sandwich and another bottle of water and sat down, legs outstretched on the ground, his back against his log.

"This is nice, thanks," I said.

"Not quite a picnic basket at Old Man Falls, but it'll do," he said with a wink.

"So, I'm guessing everyone knows about that by now."

"You weren't at mess, neither was Shaunie. People put two and two together. Then Dylan, who works in the kitchens, let the cat out of the bag."

"Oh bugger, this is tuna. Here, you have it. I can't eat it."

"Seafood or eggs? Yeah, I know. I got them mixed up. Here you go, Princess, chicken salad."

"OK, so you heard about that too." I unwrapped the sandwich slowly, suddenly uncomfortable.

"Don't start overthinking it," Slade said. "Single blokes have got nothing much better than to gossip."

"Yeah, but I don't even know you, and you're making custom sandwiches for me based on my dietary preferences."

"And if one of the girls had done it, what would you say?"

"Thanks."

"So, what's the difference?"

"Well…"

"Well, what? It's different because Nerida doesn't want to fuck you? Don't count on that one, you should see her with a couple of drinks in her. Her and Stevie… Let's just say I learned a whole new bag of tricks that night. Most single guys here are gonna try and get in your pants, that's a simple fact. Thing is, what are you going to do about it?"

"I don't have to do anything about it, according to Kelly."

"That's right, you don't. But guys…" he reached into the cooler and pulled out some grapes, picking one off and digging his thumbnail into it and quickly pulling the skin off, before offering the green blob to me. "They're gonna keep trying to find that currency, that tipping point which turns a no to a yes."

"What's that?" I asked, looking at his hand.

"A peeled grape. They're always talking about them being the height of luxury in books and films."

"It looks like snot."

"Have a taste."

"Seriously, green blobby snot..."

"Just try it woman! Put it in your mouth and taste. It might be great, or it might be gross. You can always spit it out. Stop thinking so much, and try it." He rolled to his knees, grape still held outstretched, moving until his hand brushed my lips. I rolled my eyes and tried to take it from him but he shook his head. "Uh uh," he said, and pressed the gelatinous glob to my lips. I opened them and took it.

It just tasted like grape. Watery, sweet and a little weird, as instead of bursting with juice in my mouth, it just got rendered to goo with a few chews. I swallowed it and threw my hands in the air. "What was the big deal?"

His face immediately split into a broad grin. "You took the grape."

"So?"

"This is how it works here," he said, shifting over, his grey eyes burning into mine. "Until you high tail it off to the married quarters, locked up tight, every single bloke will be looking for that innocuous thing to get under your skin, to get closer, to find an in."

"But I don't have to say yes."

"If I had said I would have you eating out of my hand when we first got on the quad, you would have said I was dreaming. Yet, here we are."

"That proves nothing. Eating a grape isn't the same as having sex. At the risk of sounding terribly provincial, I want to see where things go with Shaun before I start eating other people's grapes."

"You will and you should, but it won't be just him. No woman here sticks to one guy. Shaun would probably think all his Christmases had come at once, for a while. Then he'd get paranoid, wondering if today's the day you're finally going to succumb, trying to keep up with who the most likely candidates are, and working out their plays before they even make them. We're all reconciled to the fact that it's gonna be one girl and multiple guys."

"Yeah," I said, "but this is just your play. You want me to focus on your view of things, make me give you a chance to show what you have on offer."

"I got no problems showing you what I have to offer anytime you like, princess," he said, getting to his feet and pulling his shirt off in a few quick movements. Seriously, blokes were like trained strippers here, always on the verge of getting naked. He dropped the garment to the ground, revealing another well-defined chest. I almost rolled my eyes. Didn't anyone have muffin tops here? He was broader and heavier in the shoulder than Shaun, with a smattering of dark hair that trailed down to disappear under his waistband. When he saw my eyes move his hand went to his fly, but I held my palm out to stop him. His hand froze, his eyes boring into mine.

He's right, in a way, I thought. There was a part of me, a selfish, greedy part that I didn't really like dealing with, that wanted to touch that different but beautiful flesh, despite the fact I still felt the ache inside me from Shaun. In some way, that was what prompted it. Being drowned in wave after wave of intense pleasure awakened me to the possibility of more. He was equally compelling physically, but he would be something new again. He would touch me, caress me, push me in ways Shaun hadn't. Ways that may match or transcend the pleasure of last night. Years ago, I'd watched the movie *Alien Resurrection*. It was confusing and weird because I hadn't seen much of the franchise before, but there was scene where Ripley descends into the Viper's Nest. She lies there amongst a thrashing, writhing nest of alien monsters, the dark skin pulsating and twitching. It was both totally repellent and somehow, sexy. In some ways, that's what this place felt like, a sea of beautiful male bodies to fall into oblivion with.

"You can touch me if you want," he said huskily.

"No, I can't," I said, putting my hand down. "Not yet."

He nodded, some of the tension going out of his body. He shifted his weight, his eyes meeting mine more naturally now. "You're right, you know," he said, his voice a low rasp. "I am making a play, just like anyone else, but I want to believe it's a little different. Guys here, they'll promise you anything you want, any position, any combination, any kink... there'll be someone to give it to you. You can go the route Nerida did and try to exhaust that, but someone will keep on coming up with something new. But me, I'll treat you like an adult, Julie, whether you want me to or not. I won't bullshit you, won't try and seduce you with pretty lies, try to keep you from seeing what's really going on behind the scenes. There is so much I want to tell you, but I can't yet. Just know, if you need the truth, I can give it to you."

"At what price?" I asked.

"I already told you, we're always looking for a way in. That's mine. So, now that you've been able to resist the mesmeric sight of my chest and we didn't end up as I hoped, rutting in the dirt during work hours, we better get back to it. You OK?"

"Yeah, but I'm going to feel really weird riding on the back of the quad with you."

"Don't worry about it, princess. I'll enjoy it for both of us."

WE ENDED up going back to the admin sector, and he showed me the basics of quad bike riding so I could take one solo. He was right, there were guys who appeared outside doors and hanging around in the car park, watching, watching, watching. Buddy just ran in circles and barked at me. Some tried to come over and offer advice, but I waved them away. Slade smiled as I got back on the quad and attempted to follow his instructions better. His approach was blunt and definitely unique, but for some reason, I liked the lack of bullshit. While I had no way of verifying this, I felt like I was on more solid ground with him. I was dripping with sweat by the time he called it a day, putting the bike back in the shed and ignoring Ethan and his crew's frank interest as I did so. Slade led me up to the bar in the mess hall, and I sculled the cold beer he put in front of me in two goes.

"Hey, tough day?" I turned to see Shaun standing there, looking a little worried.

"Hot, tiring, illuminating, glad you're here now." I swung my arms around his neck and dropped a kiss on his mouth. He gave Slade a nod and then turned his attention to me, initiating another kiss and letting it go as deep as it could in polite company. When I pulled away, I saw every guy in the immediate vicinity had his eyes on us. I shook my head and took Shaun's hand as we headed to the tables. Guys filled all the seats around us in dribs and drabs, and as soon as my plate was put before me, several shot out and tried to take it to go and fill it.

"If you ever want a chance with me, put the plate down now," I said in a low growl. The dish clattered on the table untouched. "Listen to me, and spread this to all your mates, as I will only say it once. Everyone needs to back right off. I'm not interested in anyone trying to push, persuade or seduce me into anything. If you want my attention, start talking to me like a human being, let me get to know you as work colleagues. I have no problems separating sex and love, but I don't like fucking people I don't like. Tonight I want to have a nice meal with Shaun, and I don't want anyone disrespecting him or me by trying to muscle in on that. Are we clear?" There was a chorus of mumbles and grunts that I figured was as good as I was going to get. I turned to Shaun, who was smiling, a little surprised. "Do you want to get something to eat?"

8

Everything was a lot more low key after that. Shaun and I ate and talked a bit about our day, though I glossed over Slade's conversation. I wasn't ready to talk about that yet, I think. Finally, we put our plates in to be washed and wandered outside, hand in hand. I turned to him and drew him in for a kiss, long and lingering. "So, my place or yours?" I said with a grin.

Oh, no, I thought when I saw his face. It was that all too familiar look of guy apprehension that came from the knowledge that they were going to have to disappoint me, and they were really hoping there wouldn't be a scene about it. I swallowed, I'd been so sure... He was happy to see me, held my hand during dinner, had returned my kisses. I took a step back, then another.

"Jules..."

"It's OK," I said, hearing a quaver in my voice and hating myself for it. I ground my teeth, determined to keep my cool, at least until he left. "I shouldn't have assumed."

"Jules, I've got to work. There's a bunch of houses..."

"You don't need to explain," I said. "Go, and I'll catch you some other time." He sighed, glanced down at his feet and then shook his head. He walked off towards the admin sector and disappeared into the darkness. "What are we going to do, Bud?" I asked, kneeling down and scratching his chest.

"Julie?" I looked up and saw Finn was coming over. "Everything alright?"

"Yeah," I said quickly, then realised I was heading back to my bungalow with just my dog and my clothes for company. I couldn't even head out for a drive, I had no idea where to go. "Actually, is there any way to get a TV or a magazine out here?"

He smiled, "Come this way."

"Now," Finn said, standing outside the front of a building I'd never been to before. "Just know you're always safe here." I looked at him and the building behind him, listening for the thumping sounds of music and was that...?

"Oh, yeah, fuck me harder..." I heard someone call in a muffled whimper.

I narrowed my eyes. "Just what is this place?"

"It's the social club. Don't worry," he said, and he opened the door and walked in. I stopped short of peering around the doorway, but was in every other way entering the room with serious trepidation. It looked like a converted shed with a bar along one side and a woman I'd never met serving beers, a couple of pool tables, a dartboard, small TVs on the walls showing various sports and races, and a huge flat screen TV showing hardcore porn with a semicircle of couches surrounding it. All full of men. I looked at the screen briefly and sure enough, there was one woman and whole lot of erect penises. *This is beyond a way to keep the peace*, I thought, *this is the norm here.*

As if by magic, all heads turned our way, almost at the same time. I felt the need to go straight back out that door, the combined gazes of twenty-odd guys and one chick more intimidating than I would have thought. "Don't worry," Finn said. "It's through here." He held out a hand and I took it, kinda wanting the moral support right now. He pulled me past all the punters over to another doorway on the far wall. Once we slipped inside, the bow chicka wow wow soundtrack dropped away, and instead of beer, I could smell musty books. "Sorry," he said. "It's the only way to get here. This is our library. The magazines tend to be a bit out of date, but beggars and all that. Anyway, pick something out, and I'll show you the borrowing procedure."

"Wow," I said, moving towards the stacks without even thinking. It was a tight space, but there were shelves upon shelves of books. I walked past westerns and military and around to my favourite, romance. I ran my fingers along the spines, smiling. There were a lot of old faves there that I could totally re-read, but I was looking for something new. The erotic romance shelves seemed to be overflowing with books, I noticed with a smirk. I picked up a few I hadn't read and put them in a pile without too much thought. It was only when I had a whole bunch I wanted to borrow that I realised I was going to check them out in front of my boss. I looked down at the books. They always had to make it real obvious what was inside the book, black covers full of pictures of rippling muscles and gasping women. *Why couldn't they have something nice and discreet?* I thought darkly. *I don't exactly want to advertise that I'm going back to my place to read mummy porn to my superior. Though we did just walk past a bunch of blokes watching orgies together so...*

I squared my shoulders and walked up to Finn, holding the books out, the top one had a cover with a naked woman writhing with pleasure sandwiched between two naked guys. Right now, I figured this could work as a training manual for this place, help me understand the dynamic here. "I'd like to grab these, please." Finn's eyes flicked down to take this in for a moment, but he only smiled politely.

"Over here is where you book them out." I followed him, weaving between the stacks until we arrived at a lending desk where Brandon, the guy I'd met at Nerida's, was sitting, feet up on the bench, reading a novel with a very similar cover to my choices.

"Hey," Brandon said with a wide smile, tabbing his page and putting it down. "Got some stuff to borrow out? 'Sheets of Fire'? Nice! There's a great scene in there where the alpha... Sorry, I don't want to spoil it for you. What else have we got? Some Felicity Blaze, she's great, good characterisation as well as smoking hot. Ms Walters is always good if you want something sweet. Bree Carter, *Highlander's Whore*... Just hang on, I reckon I have something you'll love." He disappeared through the shelves as I tried to make an intensive study of the patterns on the concrete floor. I was conscious of Finn standing beside me and couldn't be sure he wasn't chuckling quietly. Brandon arrived back with a book and put it next to my pile. It was called *The Vixen's Pleasure*, and had a beautiful red-haired woman sitting on a throne with a smug smile on her face, a cluster of hot looking men lounging indolently by her feet. "Reverse harem, so plenty of guys and not like the old love triangles, she keeps them all..." He took in my wide-eyed look and stopped mid-spiel. "Look, I'll sign it out to you, no pressure. So will two weeks be long enough?"

It was either going to be plenty of time, or not enough if I went full bonobo and decided I needed to get some vixen's pleasure myself. I could film it and reduce the company's porn bill. I rolled my eyes, only I could go to a smaller community and feel more like a provincial noob. "That'll be fine," I croaked out.

"Well, if you need more time, let me know," Brandon said with a wide grin. He had a longer, leaner, more graceful look than many of the guys here, but that smile... He was still one of the hot guys. Belatedly, I realised I was discussing my guilty pleasures with men I worked with. Hot men I worked with. I watched him scan each book and then bundle them into a brown paper bag, just like liquor or porn.

"Thanks," I said, dully.

"Not sure if you'd be into it, but we run a book club every Thursday. We sit and talk shit about the book of the week. This week is Vixen's. Shaun comes sometimes." His voice sounded hopeful, but I was busy trying to imagine a room full of muscly guys discussing the gender politics and geopolitical implications of erotic romance books. Though if that was where Shaun had learned his tricks... *Fuck*, I thought, wanting to smack myself in the forehead, maybe I just needed to walk around blindfolded so I could start treating the fellas here like normal guys.

"Sounds interesting," I said politely. "I'll let you know."

"While we're here," Finn said, perfectly calm, the smug bastard. "Can we organise a TV and set top box for Julie? She has nothing at the moment at her place."

"Zeke was supposed to have sorted that before she arrived," Brandon said with a frown, jumping on his computer and shooting a quick email. "Probably was hoping she'd be forced to come down to the social club and watch the crap they got playing there."

"The woman getting it in every hole?" I said. "No thanks, I'd rather go and stare at my walls."

"I keep trying to tell them. If they made things appealing to women, other than Daisy behind the bar, they might actually get some feminine attention, but y'know. Be good to have more chicks down here."

"Why do guys do that?" I asked, feeling bolder. I couldn't very well get any more embarrassed, could I? "Watch porn together? Like, I understand if it was gay porn and you wanted to bone the guy next to you, but an extraordinary amount of straight guys seem to like watching girls getting fucked as a group. Aren't they uncomfortable, all those hard dicks around them?" I looked from Brandon to Finn and back again, and was cheered by the fact they seemed to be looking embarrassed now.

"I got nothing," Brandon said with a shrug. "Never something I've been into."

"Company, I assume," Finn said. "Guys get lonely here."

"Well, thank you for the books, Brandon."

"Anytime, I'm here most nights," he said handing me my bag, his fingers lingering over mine. "If you ever want to talk books or need another recommendation..."

All of a sudden, the mood in the room changed. One minute he was this geeky book nerd, happy to help me find something to read, then the next those grey eyes grew hooded as they bore into mine, his fingers hot against my skin. Almost involuntarily, my gaze dropped to his lips, full and soft, and as if in response to my gaze, his tongue flicked out to lick them. For a second the walls, the library, Finn all dropped away, and I felt an almost full body flashback of the way Shaun's tongue felt inside me last night.

"Thanks," I forced myself to reply.

"Lemme know if you get into Vixen," Brandon said with a smirk, nostrils flaring slightly.

9

I left the library in a rush, not even taking in what porn was playing now on the big screen. I stumbled out into the cool night air to where Buddy lay, panting in the dirt, clasping my books to my chest.

"Look," Finn said, "if you've got nothing on tonight..."

"What? You want to take me to the office sex club next?" I snapped out. I wasn't sure why, Finn was unfailingly polite, though perhaps that's what bothered me. I was gasping and blushing and stammering like a little girl with a very wet, dirty secret between her thighs, and he was always Mr Cool.

"Nah, that only runs on a Thursday. If you want me to make introductions I could..." I shot him a murderous look, and he burst out laughing. "Sorry, I was just being facetious. No, I was going to say did you want to come over to my place and watch some TV? I should have shown you where I live anyway, in case you have any issues, but I have a pretty impressive DVD collection."

"What? Like what they're watching in there?" I quipped.

"There's some, if that's what you're into. No, I was thinking more..." *Netflix and chill?* my brain supplied helpfully. "...a good comedy."

Such was my unstable mental state that I was both relieved and disappointed by his response. I was starting to wonder if sexually induced psychosis was a thing, I just seemed to be walking around constantly, horribly embarrassed and horny as fuck. *It's because you aren't comfortable with what you want,* my brain commented. I looked down at *The Vixen's Pleasure* and thought *that's not what I want* and *I totally want to give that a go with as many guys I can find* at the same time. I sighed, I was straight up torn. I knew this, this was a popular trope in romantic fiction. Female lead is offered sex or a relationship with a guy she didn't like or thought was too good for her or acted like a wanker towards her or had a lifestyle incompatible with hers, yet her vagina throbbed only for him. Cue: Should I? Shouldn't I? Should I? Shouldn't I? ad nauseum until the leads finally fucked and went off into the sunset to live happily ever after. I looked into the bag at the Vixen. She didn't seem too conflicted, more like the cat that got the cream, and not of the dairy variety. I glanced up at Finn who was waiting patiently, thinking god knows what while I indulged in this little rumination. "Yeah, sure," I said.

There was more than a little deja vu as I walked up the hill in the dark with another strange, attractive man. I'm not ashamed to admit the darkness changed things a little for me. It was as if by dulling down the extreme visual stimulus, I became a whole lot more aware of what was around me. I could hear his breath mixing with the night air, feel the warmth radiating off his body as we walked side by side. The breeze gave me tantalising whiffs of spicy male scent. Fuck, this was just like when Shaun walked me home. Were we going to pash on the porch or progress a whole lot further, as I was going to his place? Kelly's advice about seeking permission before making it with the boss came to mind, as well as some tantalising yet uncomfortable mental images of what that would look like, or with Slade or both of them... Damn Brandon and his book recs, he was putting ideas in my head I didn't need right now. "Well," Finn said, "here we are."

It was similar to mine, though maybe a bit bigger. It had a better sized kitchen, a fair-sized lounge room with another flat screen and... one couch. It was a three-seater, but I still looked at it for long enough for Finn to notice. "Sorry, I don't have many people over... Well, can I get you a drink?"

After the day I'd had, the only response was *fuck* to the yes. Instead, I said much more politely, "Sure, what do you have?" I ended up with a rum and coke, and took a seat on one end of the couch. *Not awkward*, I thought, *not awkward at all.* "I haven't had all that much time to see how you are going. How have you found your first few days?"

Probably how the girl in the porn movie feels, wondering which dick is going to go where, I thought, *or Alice in Dickland, completely bemused by all the weirdos, yet strangely turned on. I don't know what I'm doing, what I should be doing, or who I should be doing. Like all the rules I've ever been told about romance and love and sex and guys are wrong, wrong, wrong, and I'll be fucked if I know what's supposed to replace them.* Instead I took a hefty mouthful of my drink, enjoying the sweet burn as it went down. "Oh, it's been OK," I said instead.

"The guys are treating you OK?"

Well, Shaun treated me greeeeat last night, I thought, *though I'm sure that's not what you wanted to hear. Seriously,* I fought the urge to shiver, *rocked my world. Slade is determined to tell me the truth, the whole truth and nothing but the truth, which is curiously appealing right about now. Probably all part of his evil plan. There was me, shutting down his advances, and him with that gorgeous fucking body, out of loyalty for a guy I'd spent one night with. I should have just fucked him in the dirt,* I thought. *Hmm...* my brain helpfully supplied a wide selection of mental images of what that'd be like. *He looked like he had a huge dick too. Wonder if it was curved, you know so it rubs...*

"Julie?"

"Hmm, yeah, they've been fine."

"I know many of the women who come from the outside to work here, they find the male attention a bit overwhelming at first. Just let me know if that gets too much."

Was it too much? Too much to get work done, that was for sure. I had no idea how people followed Kelly's clinically delivered work conditions: work then play. Maybe if you no longer had to worry about when you got laid, it became just like having a shower, sleeping or having a shit, just part of day to day life. I took another long swig of the drink and was surprised to see I had finished it.

"I'll be honest," I said. "I don't really know how to deal with it. For the past few years, I've been living in a semi-ghost town with the retired set, and my only chance of getting laid was when someone amenable came through. This place...it's an embarrassment of riches, except I'm the one who's always embarrassed."

"I know you don't want to hear this, but you needn't be. We don't have the same hang ups about sex and attraction here. You seemed to have a moment back there with Brandon. He won't be anything other than pleased and flattered, and perhaps optimistic something might happen between you. You're not being disloyal to anyone."

"So everyone here is genetically incapable of getting possessive or jealous?"

"Of course not, those are basic elements of our natures. But so is anger, envy, malice... These are all unacceptable in most workplaces, yes?"

"Yeah..."

"Well, we've just added a few more sins to our list of unprofessional behaviour. Just because we're a workplace that's open and accepting of sexual and romantic behaviours, doesn't mean you have to engage in any of them. If you don't want this, what's the issue?"

Yes, what is the issue, I thought. *They all sound like they'd give me a raise for creating better staff morale by fucking a bunch of them, but that isn't the barrier.* No, like most women, I'd been raised in the cage of what men wanted and expected from a sexual or romantic partner, and what these guys were proposing was a radical departure from that. I was a rat in a cage, and I was too scared to venture out, expecting to get electrocuted even though the door had been opened. *All day long I think about fucking...* my brain did the best imitation of Korn it could.

"No issue," I said, wanting to end the conversation. "Do you mind if I grab another drink?" I got up when he said it was OK, topping up his glass as well. I walked over to his shelf of DVDs while he turned the TV on. "Comedy?" I said with a grin. "Most of these are rom-coms!"

He shrugged lazily, "What do you want to watch?"

I picked one and it was the usual fare. Couple meet, are attracted to each other, but klutzy heroine and uncomprehending romantic lead struggle to get it together, and hijinks ensue. It felt good to laugh, which became a whole lot easier after the second, third and fourth drink. Then the heroine and the romantic lead started to have sex. "So what's the appeal of these films for you?" I asked, slinging my arm along the back of the couch and turning to face him. Finn took a bit to pry his eyes away from the actors getting naked.

"It's exotic to me, I guess, one man with one woman. It feels kind of... titillating in a way."

"What? One girl, one guy is kinky for you?"

He sighed and paused the film, turning as well. "Me and most of the men here were raised by a mother and several dads. That's ordinary, garden variety relationships to us." I snorted at this. "You were obviously raised very differently. Watching a rom-com with characters similar to what I grew up with would probably be equally as odd and alluring to you."

"But you're sitting in your house, watching films like an old maid. You're gorgeous, with those eyes. I can never tell if they are grey or blue." I drew in to take a closer look, and he looked back steadily. "And you've got this hair." I ran my fingers through the ends and sighed. "It feels like silk. Why does it feel like silk? Every guy I've ever been with, their hair feels like hair... Anyway, what was I talking about? Oh yeah, and you have this amazing bone structure..." I ran my hand down the flat of his cheekbone. "You're my boss, I shouldn't be touching you, should I?"

He reached up and held my hand in place, "You can touch me if you like."

"Mmph..." I groaned, "Nope, nope, nope. I remember, Kelly said to talk to her first, so I better not. I am so screwed if I lose this job."

"You're not going to lose your job. You talked to Kelly about me?"

"I didn't mean to. It was supposed to be a hypothetical, but she so knew I was hot for you."

"You're hot for me?"

"You, Shaun, Slade, pretty much everyone, even that huge guy with the scary sized dick. I feel like I need to carry around spare undies constantly, as I am always wet. Like I need a maxi pantyliner to save my clothes. Like, you wouldn't even have to use lube if you have a massive cock like everyone else here, wet."

"That bad, huh?"

"It is bad, even if it doesn't sound like it. I never knew what guys meant by blue balls before starting here. My clit aches, like all the time. Funny thing is, it means I go off in the sack, multiple times even, which I've never really been able to do. Before if I tried, it was like so much work, and the orgasm was super weak...it never seemed worth it, y'know?"

"That's difficult for me to imagine right now," Finn said.

"But while it sounds great, it's really distracting, especially on the back of the quad with all the vibrations..." I shuddered involuntarily. "I had to think of nuns and dead kittens the whole time to stop from coming on the fence inspection. Hey, maybe that's who I should go and see! Slade wanted to fuck me in the dirt in the forest. Do you think I'd get dirt and leaves and sticks in my bum if we did?"

"I'm sure he'd make that happen if you wanted it to, though I would suggest there would be safer ways to get you off if you wanted anal stimulation."

"That's not what I meant!" I said, slapping a hand on his chest. His other hand snaked up and took a hold of that one as well. "God, like I'd want that monster in my butt. I'd never shit again!"

"There are ways, but I agree, it would take some time to learn to do. Do you want me to get Slade?"

"What and bring him here? When you're here?"

"Yes, that's what I've been trying to tell you. You could have both of us, or any other combination, if that's what you want. Trust me when I say, everyone is waiting to see what it is you want."

"Wait, do you mean...?" I moved my head closer, as it was difficult to see him clearly. Then all of a sudden, I was too close, my mouth only centimetres away from his. Up close, I could hear the harsh sound of his breath coming fast, see his eyes flick from my lips to my eyes and back again, watch his Adam's apple bob as he swallowed, his tongue swiping briefly over his lips. I reached out and touched them with my fingers, wanting to see if his mouth was as soft and slick as it looked. His tongue shifted again, grazing my fingertips. "Do you...?"

He moved slightly, bringing my awareness lower down. I wasn't sure how I'd gotten here, but I was straddling him and could feel exactly what he wanted. "That makes you hard?" I whispered.

"Not him," he said, "you. Your smell, the softness of your body, these curves, the scent of your arousal like thick, sweet honey... I know he'd feel the same, and we would treasure the opportunity to show you just how much we want that."

"So..." My brain was muzzy with drink but somehow, I knew I was hanging on the precipice of something huge. I couldn't think or speak, so I acted. I moved forward and pressed my mouth to his. Sharp flashes of arousal twisted inside me as he groaned, his kiss initially careful and precise before his hands dove into my hair, and he pulled me closer. He tasted of sweet rum and tobacco, his fingers like iron when they slid down and yanked me against his hardness.

But he pulled away first, resting his forehead on mine and gasping for breath. "We can't..."

"Ring Kelly, she can approve a quick HR request in the middle of the night," I pleaded. "Then ring Slade..."

"You want us?" he asked, a wild note of hope in his voice.

"You're smoking hot and packing serious heat," I said, reaching down between us and giving him a bit of a squeeze. God almighty, were average length guys like the ones with small dicks here? "Why wouldn't I?"

Somehow, that was the wrong thing to say.

"We can't, not tonight," he said in a much firmer voice. He took in my inarticulate growl of frustration. "Trust me when I say I know exactly how you feel, but you're drunk. This isn't consent, this is lowered inhibitions."

"Are you fucking kidding me? In a place where everyone wants to fuck me, I can't get anyone to fuck me? This is some grade A bullshit right now!"

"Julie, Julie!" I tried to wriggle out of his grip and instead, we fell back onto the couch, his body lying heavily over mine. He pushed himself up on his arms, and said, "You talk to Kelly, and tell me and Slade you want this, nothing will stop us from closing the deal. I mean nothing. If we have to lock away all of the liquor on site and give everyone a three-day holiday, we will make it happen for you. But Julie, conscious consent is sexy, a woman looking me in the eye and telling me just what she wants me to do to her is sexy. Not this, not alcohol making the decisions for you."

I wriggled my hips under him, "Your body seems to be saying otherwise."

"Yeah, well, a stiff prick has no morals, but I do. Let's go to bed..."

"That's what I've been suggesting!"

"And sleep. You make the decision in the morning, in the cold light of day, and we're yours, baby."

He got to his feet, leaving me lying there, head spinning, feeling slightly nauseous and not the fuck sure what just happened. I grumbled all the way to bed and had to be stopped from stripping off entirely, Finn forcing me to wear my undies and shirt. As soon as my head hit the pillow, I was out.

10

I woke to a world of pain. "Unnh..." I groaned, holding my head. My brain was pulsing in counterpoint to my heartbeat, sending waves and waves of agony through my body. I opened my eyes a slit and gasped as harsh arrows of light seemed to pierce my brain pan. I screwed them closed, and that hurt as well. I rolled over and buried my head under a pillow, a pillow with a distinct masculine scent. *Oh, fuck*, I groaned, *I was in some guy's bed.*

"Morning." I peeked out from under the pillow to see my worst nightmare. My boss was standing at the edge of what I now realised was his bed, coffee in hand, dressed and neatly pressed, looking down at me. What had I done?

"Did we...?"

"Have sex? No, though not for want of trying on your part. I wanted to be gentlemanly, but you did not seem inclined to take no for an answer, right before you passed out."

"Oh, no!"

"You did however, ask me to ring Kelly in the middle of the night and clear us having sex."

"No...." I groaned into the pillow.

"Can I take from your reaction that you don't want Slade to come over and have a threesome with the two of us?"

"I didn't suggest that...did I?"

"Yeah, you did. He's waiting outside right now, just in case you were sincere."

"I can't come to work today," I said, pulling the pillow tighter over my head. "I'm sick."

"A hangover isn't a legitimate reason for a sick day," he said, yanking it off my head. I screamed some sort of harsh gurgle, jerking my head under the blanket as quickly as I could. I might not have come by it legitimately, but I had a grade A headache right now. "Your dog has been fed and has somewhere to be today. Be out the front of the bungalow in twenty minutes. I've left some clean clothes for you on the bed, as well as some spare knickers."

"What do I need them for?"

"You told me all about how distressed you were, being wet all the time. Like, you wouldn't even have to use lube if I have a massive cock like everyone else here, wet."

"Fuck, fuck, fuck..." I said, smacking my head against the bed, even though it caused brightly coloured stars to flare painfully behind my eyes.

"Twenty minutes, or I'll assume you've changed your mind, and you want to take Slade and me on. You won't have to get out of bed all day, I promise."

I thought about it for a moment. I know, I'm weak and depraved, but god almighty... I swung my body upright, feeling my belly swirl and then clench painfully. *I am not going to hurl, I am NOT going to hurl*, I told myself. Once I felt safe to move, I staggered into the bathroom.

Maybe having a threesome wouldn't be so bad, I thought as I walked outside. I resisted the urge to hiss like a vampire at the obscenely bright morning light, but only just. I saw Slade, Finn, and some other guy in army fatigues leaning up against what looked like an old Range Rover, all with the same smug male smile blokes got when they saw a lady in distress. I walked over to Slade and pressed my body against his, saying, "I will suck your dick if you gimme your sunglasses for the day." He laughed, pulled them off his face but held them out of reach, eyes flicking from my right to my left eye and back, like he wasn't sure if I was serious. Not a bad idea, I wasn't, probably. Then his grin grew wider, and he held up a poisonous green bottle of Gatorade.

"Then what will you give me for this?" he asked, swishing it around. It fizzed weirdly.

"What's that?" I asked, jamming the dark glasses on my face.

"Two extra strength aspirin and Gatorade. I got the cure for what ails ya, princess."

"Oh, you big, beautiful man..." I reached for it, but he yanked it away.

"Ah ah ah..."

"I'll give you my first-born child."

"Nope."

"A lock of my hair."

"Nope"

"A lock of my pubic hair?"

"Only if I'm picking it out of my teeth."

"Dude, gross. Alright, what do you want?" His grin went wide, slowly enough that I could easily guess every little thought he was having as his lips moved. Pretty sure I was naked in most of them. "Well?" I said, because I wanted the damn aspirin. Fuck knows where I was gonna get some of that out here. Maybe Doc Hobbes would help...

"You'll hang out with him after work today, yes?" Finn said, plucking the bottle out of Slade's hands to his surprise and handing it over to me, obviously sick of our stupid antics.

I looked Slade over, his hooded hazel eyes looking right back. I could think of worse ways to spend my time, particularly as it was likely to feature me asleep. "Yeah, alright."

"You going to join us, boss?" Slade asked, not looking away from me. His grin made it plain he'd heard all about last night.

"If I'm invited..."

Oh, shit, I thought, *what was I bloody thinking last night?* Army guy, who I'd yet to be introduced to, was also looking at me with that same naked interest. What had Finn said? My brain seemed to slosh around painfully in my skull, rather than provide accurate memories. 'Everyone is waiting to see what it is you want.' Yep, that was it.

But I didn't have to decide today! I popped the lid of the Gatorade bottle and swallowed the drink down, it tasting like both manna from heaven and fizzy, slightly salty bile. I forced myself to scull it, some of it running down the sides of my mouth and spilling down my neck. I jerked back when I felt a tongue running up my neck to catch it. Slade laughed when I spat the last mouthful out, not even caring that it went all over him. He just wiped his eyes and grabbed me around the waist, "C'mon beautiful, we're going to the gun range."

11

Army guy was Aaron, apparently. He introduced himself once we bundled into the car, Slade taking the back seat, moving to sit right by my side and pulling my hand into his. "Y'know, I'd find you a lot hotter if you were a bit distant and unapproachable, like from the other side of the backseat."

"Oh, don't you worry," he said. "You'll find me plenty hot enough tonight."

"Now I'm just scared," I mumbled, and the whole car started laughing. Fucking men. "Why are we going to a gun range, again?"

"We're going to see how well you shoot," Finn said, looking at me in the rear vision mirror.

I looked from one to the other, disbelief plain on my face. "Are you fucking serious?" I grated out. Extra strength the painkillers might be, but I still felt like warmed over shit.

"Sometimes we get wild animals that come into the compound. You're restricted in the places you can go until we gauge your gun proficiency," Finn said.

"And this has to happen the day I am stupendously hungover?" I said.

"I'm free, and Aaron's back from a trip to town. Seemed like the best time to get it done."

I mumbled something about Finn's parentage, which just set the rest of the car laughing again. Apparently, I was nowhere near as quiet as I thought I was, and hilarious to boot. "What about some breakfast, then?" I asked. "I could murder a greasy bacon and cheese..." Aaron leaned down and plucked a wrapped white object from the cooler between him and Finn and passed it back, eyes on the wheel.

"Is that...? Oh my god, it's still warm! Wait, what do I have to do in exchange?"

"Anything you want, honey," Aaron replied, his lips twitching as he watched my expression in the rear vision mirror. I wasn't comfortable with that, but dear god, pain relief and wellbeing were just a few bites away. I peeled the paper away to reveal a fluffy bread roll chock-a-block full of bacon and cheese. I took a bite, not giving a shit that bits sprayed everywhere. Today was gonna be messy, no matter what.

Slade groaned, shuffling back so as to get a better view of what I was doing. "Stop getting horny watching me eat," I said, spitting crumbs.

"Too late," he said, and reached down to adjust himself. My eyes widened when I saw an indication of what he was packing down there, but I kept eating.

I STUMBLED out of the car, feeling mildly better with food and medication in me. I was pretty sure they thought they could put something else in me to make me feel even more awesome, but I instead marched up to the door of the range. I turned the handle and stepped inside ... and wanted to walk right out again. Blam! Blam! Ratatatatatata! "Oh, fuck," I groaned, grabbing at my ears, my headache back with a vengeance. The place, unsurprisingly, was full of men shooting guns. "Here," Aaron said, and put some ear muffs on me. Now it sounded like a muffled gun fight was happening around me.

"So, what do I have to do?" I asked, probably too loud.

Aaron smiled, moving over to one of the walls and producing a key from his pocket to unlock the cabinet there. He pulled out several guns that looked way too big and scary for me to be on the other end of, and tossed them to Finn and Slade before grabbing his own. He held it so the stock tucked into one shoulder, the other hand holding the grip thingie at the front. "Wmm dmm omsmm," he said.

"What?" I said, pulling off one ear protector.

"We'll go to the range outside."

Yay, I thought, casting a dark eye at the dusty paddock that served as an outdoor range. Less noise but more sun, and I wasn't sure what was worse. I was sweating already, that funky mix of sour body odour and alcohol leaving the building. I was gonna be so sexy when Slade finally got me for alone time.

"So this here is a blah blah gun thingie," Aaron said seriously, showing me his fine weapon. "It's great for blah and manly things."

"Uh huh," I said.

"So to use it, you do blah, blah and blah and then slowly squeeze your finger on the blah..." Boom! A hail of bullets came firing out of the machine gun thingie and into the target some metres away.

"Right," I said, swaying slightly, "Don't squeeze the blah too hard. Boys always say that."

"What?" Aaron's eyes snapped to Finn. "You sure she's up for this?"

"I need her ready to go beyond the gate. No gun, no gate," Finn said.

"There's no rush..." Slade said.

"She's employed to be my offsider, so yeah, there is a rush," Finn snapped.

"This got anything to do with last night?" Slade asked. "Because stampeding into this..."

"This is too early," Aaron said to Finn. "Once we know, she'll be able to handle this no problems, or she won't. But right now..."

"That might not happen," Finn said. "She needs to be able to defend herself." All of the men fell silent after that.

Aaron shrugged, taking one of the guns and passing it to me. "Never point a gun at anyone you don't intend to shoot," he said, pushing the muzzle so it faced the targets. "Be aware of what is in front of and behind your target. Keep your finger off the trigger until you decide to take a shot, and leave the safety on until then."

I held it in what I thought was a mirror image of his pose. He sighed and came to stand at my rear, putting his arms around me to correct my hold and stance. I wasn't sure this was strictly necessary, it felt like maybe he was trying to cop a feel. I arched my hips back slightly, so my arse grazed his groin. His body turned to iron, and he became very still. Slowly, he pulled away. "Chamber a round, then take the safety off and give it a go. Just be careful, there'll be some recoil." Right, the safety. Where was the safety? Aaron sighed and flicked it for me, and then gestured for me to proceed.

I had no fucking idea what I was doing. The last time I'd shot a gun was some peewee air rifle my brother had been given by my uncle. We'd gone out with Dad and Pa and Uncle Bill, and learned how to shoot cans in the home paddock when I was ten. Well, I was committed now. I looked down the barrel, my hands starting to shake. *You should back out, back the fuck out*, my brain screamed hysterically. *You can hurt yourself or others. This is part of my job*, I retorted. I couldn't follow Finn without showing I could do this. I squeezed the trigger gently and...

Blam! I'm not totally sure what happened, but somehow I was lying in the hot dirt, staring at the sky, and Finn, Slade and Aaron were all standing over me. "Are you OK?" Finn asked, eyes wide.

"Princess, if you wanted to get out of the date, you just had to say," Slade said.

"I told you it was too early," Aaron said to Finn.

"Yeah, alright," Finn said with a curse. "Let's get Doc Hobbes to have a look at her."

WHICH WAS how I ended up lying on the cold metal bench in the doc's surgery, my head throbbing worse than before. "So, what happened?" she asked.

"Julie had a go with one of the rifles and wound up on her arse," Slade said.

"Weapons training? That'd be better done after the full moon, wouldn't it?" she said, flashing a torch across one eye, then the other.

"She needs protection," Finn ground out.

"So assign one of the young bucks. They would be more than happy to protect her."

"I'd be happy to volunteer," Slade said.

"Me too," said Aaron, meeting my eyes with a steady gaze when I looked at him in alarm.

"She's supposed to be my offsider."

The doctor glanced up at Finn without expression, then sniffed. "Well, who better to protect her? You can take her past the gate if you're by her side. Sooner the better, I think. She seems OK, someone's going to have to stay with her tonight, wake her up every couple of hours and look out for any sign of brain injury. Slurred speech, dizziness, vomiting... Anything out of the ordinary, give me a call on my mobile. So who's going to do it?" The room went silent as the guys eyed each other.

"My night tonight," Slade said with a shit-eating grin.

"Hey, if you want to spend it with her flat on her back, spewing, be my guest," Aaron said.

"Yep, but then I get to hold back her hair and clean her up and rub her fevered brow," Slade said. Aaron's brows pulled down into a frown.

"Slade, take one of the bikes or carts up to her place and collect her dog from Nerida's. Aaron and I will take her up in the car."

"Sure thing, boss."

I started to push myself upright on the table, but Finn swept me up in his arms, despite my protests. "Give Slade these," Doc said, handing Aaron a box of medication. "We have to wait until the aspirin has cleared her system, but she can have two of these after eight hours."

12

So there I was, lying in bed with Slade sitting in a chair at one end.

"You can lay down," I said, my voice raspy with exhaustion, "as long as you'll sleep. I am so not up for anything else."

"Wouldn't dream of it, princess," he said. "Which is why I'm all the way over here. Go to sleep, I've got to wake you in a couple of hours, but I've got a book to keep me company."

"Well, if you're sure…" I mumbled, burying my head into the cool, clean pillow. I dimly heard his chuckle as I drifted off. Sweet, sweet oblivion. As I start to doze, the pain faded away so quickly I let out a languorous sigh. The removal of pain is almost as good as sex after a while. I felt the soft sheets around me, the comforting weight of the blanket as I went deeper and deeper…

I lay on a bed covered in red silken sheets that slipped sinuously as I moved. I opened my eyes a crack, and saw that I'd been sleeping on a massive four poster bed with gauzy white curtains hanging down from the canopy.

"Hello." The mattress dipped as someone came and laid down beside me, pulling my body against theirs. I looked over my shoulder to see Slade, looking much cleaner but with the same reddish-brown scruff of a beard, his hair a short crop of a slightly lighter colour, gazing down at me. He reached over and caressed my face, and I saw his bare arm.

"Are you naked?" I asked, rolling over to face him. He ran delicate fingers up my arm, trailing over my neck and cupping my jaw, brushing a thumb over my lips.

"I can if you want me to be. Your wish is my command," he purred, running the flat of his hand down my neck and collar bone, my nipples pulling tight in anticipation of his callused caress, but he veered off down my ribs, rubbing up and down them, getting closer and closer to my butt. My clit began to throb lightly, sure that he was going to slip his fingers between my thighs and...

Instead he pulled me closer, so our bodies meshed, and his hand dropped down to my waist, lingering in the small hollow at the end of my spine. It sent curious shivers through my body. "So..." I gasped, "you'd do anything for me?"

"Within reason, love. Talk to me about what you want, and I'll see what I can do." His mouth was suddenly busy, lipping at the skin of my neck and shoulders, the prickle of his beard a tantalising tickle. "Tell me what you want," he said, skimming his palm up, up over my stomach and ribs, getting closer and closer...

"Uh..." I moaned, but his hand returned to my jaw, drawing me in for a kiss. I wanted dream Slade to caress and pluck, tug and suck and spear his fingers inside me. Freed from pain, my sex drive came rollicking back, twice as strong. I felt the slickness between my thighs as they moved restively, and I dug my hands in his hair, tangling my tongue with his, pushing my body against his, wanting and seeking more.

"What do you want?" he insisted as I fought to catch my breath. "I'm not doing it until you ask. Tell me, Jules."

"Tell you what?" I whined, writhing, trying to drag my nipples across his chest, anything for some blessed friction. He pulled back, pushing me down on the bed and clasping my wrists. He reared over me, shutting out the light, holding me within the broad shadow of his body. He kicked my ankles wide but didn't settle between them, even when my hips bucked underneath him.

"What. Do. You. Want," he said.

"Touch..." I whimpered.

"Touch what, Jules? Just say it, and I'll do it. Touch what?"

My eyes flicked open to find I was in my normal old bed, top pushed up around my neck, the sheets draped around my hips. Slade hung over me in the exact position I'd been dreaming about. "What's going on?" I said, blinking. My body throbbed, not struggling to make the transition from sleep to awake like my mind was.

Slade jerked back. "You were still asleep. Fuck, Jules, I'm so sorry. I was trying to wake you up, trying to do it gently, and then you started moaning and talking back to me..." He turned to leave, but I grabbed his arm. God, his body was like iron.

"It's OK," I said.

Yeah it is! my body said. *Let's tell him what we want and get things started. Now a little tweaking on the nipples, not too forceful. Both at the same time would be just grand...* I shook my head, trying to bring my attention back to the concerned looking Slade. "I was half awake and was kinda dreaming you were doing and saying the same things..."

"We alright? How's your head? Still hurting?" I nodded. "Let me get you your meds." He disappeared, returning a moment later with a glass and some pills. I pulled the sheet up to cover myself and then swallowed them down. "Lemme have a look at your eyes," he said, coming in close. I smelt the tobacco on his breath as he looked at one, then the other, and felt the heat coming from his body as he bent over me. He reached up and cupped my chin, turning it towards the light a little, bringing my mind back to the feel of his stubble scraping over my skin. "Apart from the pain, no light sensitivity or dizziness?" I shook my head carefully. "OK, well, go back to sleep, and I'll..." He went to pull away, but I didn't let go of his arm. His eyes went from my grip, then back to me. "Princess...?"

"I want..." His hazel eyes grew dark and hard as he watched my mouth move, like it was the most fascinating thing in the world.

"Mmm..."

"I..." He took some pity on me, tangling his hand in my hair, then dropping the other to run his palm across my collar bone. "I...."

"You gotta say it, Jules," he said. "Men, your mum, society has been teaching you all your life not to. But here, you gotta make sure the other person is clear on what you want. You might have noticed, most of the guys here are bigger and stronger than you. The thing that protects you is spelling out what you want." I made an inarticulate growl, my eyes dropping down. I couldn't keep staring into his, it felt suddenly too close, too intimate. "Your instructions are like a contract. They make it clear what people want..." his lips grazed over mine, "and what they don't want."

"Gah!" I flopped back down, instantly regretting it when the pain in my head flared in intensity. "You guys are always pushing me! Do this, accept this, be open to this! Maybe I just want to be swept off my feet. Did you ever think of that? Maybe I want you to push me down on the bed, turn me on with awesome foreplay, and then let me see what I want to do from there!"

"Well, OK, princess. I can definitely work with that." All of a sudden, my wrists were caught together and pulled above my head, forcing my back to arch and my tits to thrust out. He dropped his head to one, his tongue flickering out. I whimpered as he circled my nipple with the tip, the sight as much of a turn on as the sensation. He blew on it and smiled as the skin puckered. "If you consciously give away control..." he said, pulling back and ripping off his shirt, then pulling his belt free. He fed the tongue through the buckle. "Then you can get it back, anytime you want..." I looked at him wide-eyed as he caught my wrists in the loop, pulling it tight enough I couldn't pull free, then tying it off against the bedhead. "You don't like what I'm doing, you want me to get you free, you feel dizzy or sick, you say the word Buddy, right?"

"What is that?" I looked up at the belt. "A safe word?"

"Been reading some BDSM mummy porn, or are there some hidden depths there, princess?" he asked in a low rasp, moving down my body until his head drew level with my breasts. He looked up at me with a sly smile, then wrapped those lips around my nipple and sucked.

"Uh!" My body drew up taut as a bow, struggling to move under the intense onslaught of sensation, his mouth sending rolling waves of pleasure through my body. Just as I struggled to get my head around that, his other hand circled the other, plucking and stretching the tender tip, almost to that point where intense pleasure bordered on pain.

"I... I..." I gasped.

"No need now, princess," he said, letting my nipple pop loose. "You want to be swept away in something bigger than you? I'm your man. You don't have to say a word unless you change your mind. Now, where was I?"

I don't know how long he took, lavishing caresses on my breasts, but by the time he pulled free, the tips were throbbing right along with my clit. The air itself seemed to caress them almost painfully. He pulled away, toeing off his socks and then removing his pants. He smiled when he saw me watching, pausing and taking it a little slower with his underwear. I swallowed when I saw him bob free, thick and curved and tending to veer slightly to the left, just like I'd thought. I would have rolled my eyes that I was looking down yet another huge dick, but all I could think of was how it was going to feel going in. I'd had a boyfriend with a similar orientation, though not quite as blessed as Slade, and knew from experience that the tension between his body and mine as his dick was forced away from its natural bend for a while, would create the most amazing drag inside me. I had to clench my legs together to cope with the sharp feeling of need.

"Uh uh..." he said, pushing the blanket down and then removing the sleep shorts I'd put on. It was probably a bit shameless, not wearing undies under my pyjamas and sleeping in the same room as a guy I barely knew, but right now, I didn't care. He tossed them over his shoulder and spread my ankles wide, settling on his knees between them. "Well, look at that," he said almost reverently, reaching out and running a single finger along the top of my thigh.

God, so close… "You are so wet and pink…" His fingers slipped
between my folds for a brief moment, leaving me gasping in frustration, and he smiled when he saw the slick moisture on his fingertips.

"Please…" I whined.

"You'll get yours, when I'm ready." His fingers trailed through my
pubic hair, the featherlight touch both tantalising and nowhere near
enough. I slammed my head back on the pillow, not caring that it
hurt anymore, the ache in my clit almost seemed worse. I almost
screamed when his hands dropped down to my ankles, so far away
from where I needed them, curling around them and slowly wending
their way up my legs. Every scrap of my attention was on those two
points of contact, my breath coming in pants as he moved closer and
closer…

Which is probably why we didn't hear anyone at my bedroom
door. I nearly jumped when it snicked open, Finn's head appearing in
the gap. Whatever he was about to say froze on his lips, his eyes
instantly drawn to where Slade's fingers travelled, growing darker as
they finally, finally traced the length of my seam.

"I… I was checking to see how she's going," Finn said.

"Can't very well check from over there," Slade said. I wanted to be
embarrassed, to fight free of the belt and draw the sheet over myself,
and be the suitably blushing employee I thought I should be. But all I
could focus on was Slade's fingers slowly working deeper, spreading
me open and…. "How swept away do you want to be, princess? You
really want to shake up those small-town morals?"

"Not like this," Finn said in a hoarse whisper, shaking his head as
if breaking a spell.

"I dunno," Slade said. "She seems kinda amenable." I closed my
eyes and let out a long, hard groan as he pushed two fingers slowly,
inexorably inside me. That first stretch… I could feel his fingers push
outwards, creating an intense feeling of being full. A third finger
came quickly afterwards, shoving in and out with long slow
movements.

"Oh, fuck!" I cried, something tightening like a vise deep in my
pelvis. Right now, I didn't give a fuck who was in the room, I just

wanted something hard pounding between my legs, pushing my boundaries, giving me just that little bit more than I could cope with. Those light plucking touches at my breasts, and that hard suction. Caresses curling around my legs, flickering over my clit, dragging me closer and closer. "I'm gonna..." I gasped.

"Shh, princess..." was all I heard as I bit back a cry. Those fingers pulled away from me, leaving me stranded on that precipice, so desperate for just one flick more. Instead, Slade settled on the other side of the bed, his hand lightly caressing my breast but not enough, far from enough. I made inarticulate noises of protest, but Slade just bent over and forced his tongue inside my mouth, his kiss hard and brutal. "Look at him," he commanded, pointing to the doorway when I lay there panting. My eyes flicked over obediently. "He's holding himself back by a thread. He wants to drop to his knees and bury his head in your cunt..." I squirmed as his words almost, almost conjured that feeling for me. "Suck your clit, force his tongue inside you until you burst all over his face. Are you going to let him?" My eyes flicked from Slade's to Finn's. I could see it, smell it almost, Finn's desire. His fingers were almost making dents in the doorframe.

"Can I?" he rasped.

I wanted it. Fuck, I wanted it. I was so close to coming, and it would be glorious, I knew it. Ripples and spasms of wanton golden pleasure, taking me out of my body and... As if knowing he needed to up the ante, Slade's hand slid lower, spreading me wide before Finn's gaze, his fingers a dizzying shift of sensations, pushing inside me, pulling at my clit, circling it with his thumb, smearing my wetness around with his fingertips. It didn't seem to have rhyme or reason to it, but my arousal was slowly ratcheting up higher.

"Answer him, princess, or I stop. You don't have to say yes, but answer him."

"Ah..."

Slade watched the indecision flicker over my face and then shook his head. "Fuck! Can he watch? I'll make you come so hard, princess..."

I nodded. Both of them moved in unison, Slade going down on

his knees between my legs, Finn to Slade's chair. I no longer cared what my boss did as a broad tongue flicked over my clit for a few passes then lips closed around me. *This is like a hate fuck*, I thought as Slade speared his fingers inside me. The three jammed in so quickly, it kinda hurt for a second, and then a pleasant burn started up. "Oh, fuck!" I cried as he drew me harder into his mouth and curled his fingers upward.

When I came, it was like the rest of the world no longer existed. I wasn't a body inside a room with two other bodies, one of them sucking my clit. I was this disembodied cloud of pure unadulterated pleasure. I almost started crying, it was so intense, like the ache of getting your heart broken but so, so much sweeter. I was dimly aware I was screaming, that my shoulders were hurting, that Slade was going to give me a beard rash of epic proportions, but I just didn't care. I was so high, I wasn't sure if I could come down.

When I did, Slade was moving over me, dick in hand. He released the belt from the bedhead, making certain the skin there wasn't hurt. *Oh, yeah*, I thought. I was soft and languid, and swollen with pleasure. I was pretty sure I could go again without too many strokes of that beast. He knelt between my thighs, shifting until he could drag his dick over my over sensitive flesh.

"So wet," he groaned as he forced his dick to rub against my whole cunt, from clit to the mouth. The bulbous head caught as he moved, my wet flesh trying to draw him inside me where he belonged, but he just kept rubbing himself against me.

"Fuck me," I said, happy enough to tell him what I wanted.

"No."

"Stop playing Slade. I'm aching for you."

"Good," he said, eyes snapping away from watching my body part for him. "I want you to ache, high and deep inside you. You're having a lovely time, getting lots of attention, no one really pushing your boundaries. If you didn't want this, I would not care, but I have considerable evidence to prove otherwise," he said, jabbing the head of his dick into me for a moment, making me scrabble to try and force him deeper. "Feel that ache and think of this over the next few days.

When you're ready to deal with your own shit, I'll fuck you as hard and as long as you want."

He closed his eyes, bending over me and focussing now on the slip of our flesh against each other, refusing to push his dick into me, just using it as a means to rub against my clit. He got me there again no problem, but as planned, when I came it felt somehow less as I ached, empty inside. He shot his load across my stomach with a painful groan not long afterwards, pausing to catch his breath. He looked almost sad as his eyes opened, and before he pulled away, he laid a slow kiss on my lips.

"You can watch her," Slade said, getting out of the bed and grabbing his clothes after untying me.

I DREW the sheet up with a shaking hand, unable to look at Finn as my arousal was trailing away. *Well*, I thought, *there's no secrets now.* I buried my head down into my pillow and stared at the wall, not sure what to do.

"I spoke to Kelly today." *Oh fuck*, I thought, screwing my eyes up tight. "She said if you're interested in pursuing something, you need to come and see her. She has no issue, but she wants to hear it from you. She's worried we're all putting pressure on you."

"Come here," I said, patting the bed. There was a long pause, and then I heard a rustle as he moved. I think he toed off his boots, and then I felt him lie next to me, making sure there was as big a gap as possible. "I like you, Finn," I said, not looking him in the eye. I couldn't get this out if I did. "I don't know you very well, but you're hot and kind, and you seem to have the respect of your team. If you weren't my supervisor, you'd totally be worth spending time with."

"But…"

"But you're my boss, and I'm seeing just how woefully unprepared I am for this position. I can't ride a quad, shoot a gun, or make up a dog's feed bowl without looking at a recipe. You know I'm willing to try, today has to be testament to that…"

"Yeah, you were not in a good place."

"But I think I'm going to fail the performance review when it comes up. I don't know how I can't, I can't do anything useful. Unless you switch me to a cook or kitchen hand position, I'm no use to you."

"Ah, Julie," he said, pulling my chin up. "I wish I could tell you... It's not going to be an issue, I sincerely think that."

"Why?" I looked down pointedly. "Because I make your dick hard? That's no way to secure a job. What happens if you lose interest?"

"I..." he frowned, rolling his eyes in frustration. "Look, the most important performance review you had to pass was Doc's eye test."

"What? Her 'little project'?"

"It's not. I guess you could say that this place acts more like a family. People who are a genetic match for the family, get to stay, even if they are completely useless, which you aren't. People who aren't would get to the end of the month, and a reason would be found to let them go."

"My eyes... What the fuck? That makes no sense. I'm paid to stay here because of my genetic makeup? For what...to have sex with your family? Am I some kind of whore? Or is this... Is this some kind of breeding program? Is that what the queens are?"

Finn paused for too long, his face too carefully smooth. "No, of course not."

"I have one of those implant things in my arm. None of you bastards are taking it out, not for any money. I'm not anyone's brood mare."

"That's not what I mean! Look, it's 12 more days to the full moon. It will become apparent by then, trust me. I'll sign anything you like to say that no one will force you to have a child."

"What the fuck is going to happen on the full moon, Finn? Finn?"

"Jules, you can wait here until it happens, do what and who you like. No one will force you, coerce you or ask you to do a thing until then. Once it's over, we'll know better what your role will be, just know you will have one."

"Well, that's clear as fucking mud. You're asking me to take a lot of faith."

His eyes went hard. "From what you told me, you were broke and homeless and worried about your dog. I've offered you food, board, a wage and free medical to wait here until the full moon, with a promise in writing that no harm will come to you. If you want to walk out that door and drive away, I'll pay out your wages myself and make sure you have a full tank of petrol. Are you likely to get a better offer than that anywhere near here?"

I swallowed my anger down. My heart was racing, and my head was starting to ache again. Finally, I said, "Can I talk to people? Ask questions? Go to the married quarters?"

"Sure, but don't push them. You treat them with respect, and I'll never have an issue with what you do. But you'll report to me, once a day. Are we clear?"

"Fine."

"Go to sleep, Julie," Finn said with a sigh.

13

H e was in the kitchen when I woke up, drinking coffee and wearing a t-shirt with the sleeves torn out and a pair of old jeans. I took this in and frowned. "Day off," he said with a grunt. "I've got..." The door opened and closed, and Brandon walked in. He inspected my ratty pyjamas slowly, a smile spreading over his face, like they were high end lingerie. "He's going to take you for the day."

"Mmm," Brandon said, stepping closer, his grey eyes almost glowing in the morning light. "What's that I smell?" His nostrils flared. "Eau de Slade?" He glanced at Finn, then back at me. "Nice, but you better get dressed." His eyes dropped to the sheer fabric of my top, "Wear something light. Today we get hot and sweaty."

My eyes flicked from Finn to Brandon. What did that mean? Here, it could mean anything from digging ditches or having sex or digging ditches and having sex. The two of them just watched me without a response, like some kind of predators up on a hill. *What?* I thought, *What fucking now?* But there was no point in asking them. No one really told me anything, unless it was about what I was doing that day or trying to get me into bed. I stomped over to the bathroom and had a quick shower, putting on an old pair of jeans and a light white top with some embroidery around the neckline, figuring that would have to do.

"Wherever we go today, I'm gonna ask each and every person, you know that, right?" I said to Finn when I came back out.

He sighed, "Would be shocked if you didn't. Look, I've got a date with the DVR, it's been a hard week." He looked at Brandon. "Have her come by mine on your way home."

"Will do, Boss."

"That OK with you, Julie?" Finn asked.

"Fine."

BUDDY JUMPED up when I went outside, gambolling around my feet. "We're in the truck," Brandon said, moving to open my door for me, standing so close I had to brush past him to get inside. My dog jumped in over me and sat right in the middle of the bench seat. "Here," he said, leaning across me and plucking a travel mug from the centre console, "Black, no sugar."

"Just the way I like it," I said, looking at it with a frown, then taking a sip. It was the perfect temperature.

"So, how do you feel about casual public nudity?" Brandon asked as he got inside the cab.

My eyebrows shot up, "Is this some kind of date?"

He cracked up laughing at this, his teeth white against his bronzed skin, "Ah, Jesus, I'm sorry. I was trying to channel Cable Hilton from *Billionaire's Bedroom*. Y'know, go all smouldery and a bit suggestive. I could see your mind ticking away... Sorry, I never thought that line would work. I assumed you'd know I was taking the piss and punch me in the arm or something. Nah, we're doing the morning deliveries. Today is the majority of the camp's rec day, so it's mostly a beer run, though we will be heading to the married quarters and the farm. Finn figured that would give you access to plenty of people to ask your questions."

All of a sudden, I felt like a bit of a brat. My life had experienced an upturn coming here. I'd checked my pay slip and even for the few days I was here, I was paid very, very well, and here was my boss giving me the opportunity to talk to people about that which he couldn't. Weird sex stuff aside, everyone here was pretty good to me, and now I felt strangely disloyal for wanting to know more. *But I need to*, I thought with a frown. There was something seriously weird about this place, apart from the romantic stuff, and I needed to know what it was to be able to relax and work out where I fit.

"Delivering beer? How does that involve nudity?" I was about to find out.

"Here, you take this one," Brandon said, handing me a slab of beer. "Just head inside and dump it on the kitchen counter."

This sounded simple enough. I walked up the stairs, opening the fly mesh sliding door, and there before me was a sea of half-naked men. Draped over three couches and a bean bag, was one muscle rippling body after another. Tattooed or clean, dark or light or in between, there had to be six or seven guys there. It looked like the after party of a gay porn set. One slept face down on the couch, revealing a very nice arse in a pair of tight cotton boxers, another was sitting on the floor, legs akimbo, head and arms resting against the seat. Others lay passed out on the floor or snuggled into beanbags. Every single one of them was bare chested and wore only a pair of sleep shorts or undies. My mouth went dry from hanging open for so long, and I stood there frozen, still holding the slab of beer.

"What's the hold up?" Brandon asked, coming behind me. I heard him set down his load with a thud on the porch. "Ahh, now I get it." He cast his eyes over the sleeping bodies with a slight smile. "I'm trying to imagine what this would feel like. How would I react if that was a sea of half-naked hot girls?" His smile widened. "You must want to dive on in and see if you could make it to the other side."

"I-I..." I stammered, but I didn't get another word out. Brandon rapped on the metal door frame, loud enough to wake the dead, and wake they did. Eyes flicked open as one, blinking for a moment. I heard groans and curses, and then their vision cleared.

"What do we have here?" said a guy with the greenest eyes I'd ever seen, and blond hair that fell in waves to his shoulders. He got to his feet, towering over me of course, and came closer, the rest of his mates following behind en masse. I took a step towards the doorway but blondie said, "Uh uh," and slid it shut behind me. "You're the new girl."

"Uh, yes, Julie. Here's your beer."

"Macca," the guy said, and took the slab, passing it to the darker haired man with a beard behind him. He placed the beer on the counter and returned to play his part in the human shield of man flesh that boxed me in. "Come in, take a seat." The men moved as one, creating an avenue of bodies that led to one of the couches they had been sleeping on. "I apologise for the mess, we went on a bit of a bender last night."

"A bender where you all ended up down to your jocks? What kinda bender is that?" I said, looking them up and down. I meant that to be a sceptical thing, but damn! I wasn't sure I gave a shit what had gotten them to this state. A guy with longish sandy hair steered me towards the seat with a hand on my tailbone, plopping me down with Macca and his dark-haired offsider sitting down on either side of me. I swallowed as I felt those long, hard thigh muscles against mine, the rest of the guys now reclining by my feet or standing in a line across the sliding door.

"We've been meaning to approach you," dark haired guy said. "I'm Blake."

"Nice to meet you. You have?"

"Yeah," sandy haired guy said, "I'm Rhett. You're gonna need a pack if you are going to stay here. Shaun, Slade, you won't see much of them until you've made your decision..."

"What?" I interrupted his spiel. "What's happening with Slade and Shaun?"

"Until you've decided who your pack is, the guys you've slept with will hang back, see if your other partners are ones they can live with. They may start banding together, showing an obvious preference for the blokes they reckon should be in the pack. Some of them will form blocs, start making their moves as a group to try and influence your decision. Then the fighting starts."

"I'm sorry, what fighting? Kelly said everyone was cool and groovy about this stuff."

Macca chuckled at this. "Well, it certainly doesn't take place during business hours, does it? But a bunch of red-blooded blokes all wanting the same thing? C'mon love, you know that's not going to happen."

"You take us on, all the work is done," a guy with long, dark hair at the back said, "We all get along, you don't have to go through the drama of choosing. We'll all move to one of the bigger places on the other side, and then you can relax and have every need catered to by seven guys who want you."

I was going to start laughing at that. Seven guys I'd met five minutes ago ready to settle down and fuck me stupid for ever and ever? It sounded completely ridiculous on paper, but the thing about sitting with a whole bunch of dudes in their undies, I could tell at least physically they were into the idea quite easily.

Brandon walked in with the last load and said, "You coming?" Then he took in all the men seated around me. "I'll make the next delivery and then come back, OK?"

"You could join us," Jake said. "She smells like she's into you and as long as you're not a dick, we could make room. You gotta better chance with us than on your own."

This made Brandon stiffen. "I know exactly what she smells like. I'm not interested in this little power play you got going on. I'll find my own way, the same as my dads did. It's the woman's choice, it always has and always will be. You guys, you're trying to take that from her. Julie, are you OK here?"

"I ..." should have gotten up and walked out. They were very good looking guys, but they could be kitten killing, axe murderers for all I knew. Macca chuckled when Brandon walked out, and they all seemed to shuffle closer. I was enclosed in a very manly cocoon.

"You choose us, and you'll see just what we can do," Macca said. "Seven guys? You'll never be left unsatisfied. You can keep coming and coming, there'll always be someone to take you there." His hand landed on my thigh, feeling warm even through the thick denim.

"We're bringing in good money," Blake said, placing his hand on the other leg. "All of us are either at the mine or in the barracks. Lot of hazard pay."

"You'll never have to lift a finger," Rhett said as the guy at my feet slipped off one shoe and began pushing hard with his thumbs into the sole of my feet. I fought to hold back a groan, but one of the others noticed and started massaging the other foot. Blake jerked his head at one of the guys standing by the door, and I watched him stalk around to the back of my couch, his hands slipping under the neckline of my blouse when he arrived, fingers digging into my shoulders.

For a few selfish moments, I let myself go with it. I could feel the hands on my feet forcing the muscles to become soft and supple, those on my thighs creeping higher and higher. For a moment, I knew I could meet a need I'd never really acknowledged before, the need for more. My last real relationship was with Trevor Noakes, a guy I'd been to school with. He'd been a few years ahead of me and then left to help his dad run the local car yard. He was a nice looking guy, nothing on these blokes, but he had a full head of dark hair and a twinkle in his eye that made it look like he was always having a good time. We had an active sex life, he gave a shit about my pleasure, but... We'd be lying there, both having come hard, revelling in the afterglow, and a sneaky little voice at the back of my mind asked for more. My cunt would be wet and swollen, my clit still throbbing, and if I had more touches, more licks, more dicks pushing into me, I could keep this pleasure train going and going... I never said anything, frightened at what he might say and feeling like the most selfish bitch in town. Plenty of my girlfriends bemoaned their self-centred boyfriend's lack of technique in the sack. I was one of the lucky ones but... This was that opportunity, I realised as I let my eyes close. I would never get to the end with these guys, never want for more. I'd have a string of fingers and lips and dicks to keep wringing the ecstasy from me, until I just couldn't anymore. Another set of hands took up their place on my shoulders, the fingers digging now into my collar bone and moving lower...

"Tell you what," I gasped out. "You tell me what happens on the full moon, and I'm happy to give the lot of you a test drive." My eyes flicked open, and I smiled when I felt the hands still all over my body. Those many eyes that had been burning into me with smouldering gazes now looked wide eyed and worried.

"Babe," Macca said, not moving his hand from the top of my thigh as he came closer, "we want you to have whatever you need..."

"Then give me answers."

He stopped and placed his forehead on my shoulder, "We do that and we're gone, exiled, never to come back. We don't have family out in the country to go to. Beyond the Sanctuary, there's nothing for us."

I snorted at this and pushed their hands off me, only semi-regretfully. "You guys are young, good-looking, fit. You could easily get a job stripping at the very least, but seriously, if you're working in the mines there's plenty of work in that industry going all over the country."

Blake shook his head sadly, "It's always going to be the Sanctuary for us. We were all born and raised here, and this is where we'll live all of our lives."

"But if you went to town, you'd have no problems finding women, believe me. The way you guys look, you'd have women throwing themselves at you. Better looking, richer."

"We don't want other women," Macca said, moving so his lips rested against my neck.

"We want you," Blake said, mirroring Macca's actions.

"And I want answers," I said as I got to my feet. I picked up my shoes and then stepped free of the insta-harem. "I have no idea what happens on the full moon. Does it happen to me? Do you guys all go bug nuts and rampage around the countryside? Is there an epic surprise party, and you're all just really committed to making sure I don't know about it? Seriously, this place has me tripping balls as it is, seven hot guys begging to fulfil my every whim, but I need to know what's going on. I've never even had a threesome before, and I'm prepared to go in that room and do whatever you like, for answers. That's what I need, answers."

"Fuck," Blake cursed, adjusting himself from what was apparently an uncomfortable angle. He looked meaningfully at Macca who just shook his head.

"Where would we go? There's no Mackenzie's left in the county, not that remember this side of the family," Macca said. He looked around at the other guys, and they all appeared similarly despondent.

"There's also no promise of anything beyond this one fuck," Rhett said, taking my place between Blake and Macca. "We'd lose our jobs, all of our savings, our homes, our families. We'd lose everything for one taste of pussy. I'm sure it's just dandy and you are a spitfire in the sack, but that's not enough to turn my back on all I've ever known. Honey, I get you want to know what's going on, but you're looking at this all the wrong way. You could spend the next two weeks on the company's dime, exploring every sexual position and scenario you've ever thought might make your pussy twitch, and no one will be concerned."

"And the thing that makes us nuts is on some level, you want this," Macca said. "Your nipples are just about burrowing through your shirt, and I reckon your cunt would be wet enough to drown me if I could get my head between your naked thighs."

I rolled my eyes, "Seriously? That's your rationale for fucking you and your mates and going unquestionably to meet my unknown fate? That I am horny? I'm always horny, have been since I got here, which is weird." I thought about it for a moment, I wasn't usually this turned on, even back at high school and full of hormones. "That's nothing special. Ever since I came here, I feel like I'm a cat in heat."

Apparently, that was the wrong thing to say. Every guy in the room froze, then Macca came over and dropped to his knees, burying his nose into my stomach. "What the fuck are you doing?" I cried but he held me close in an iron grip, taking several long sniffs, lower and lower. "Fuck off!" I said, and shoved him away. He got to his feet and turned to the others, shaking his head. "What the fuck is wrong with you? You're not a dog! You want to sniff my butt next?"

"What's going on?" Brandon said, arriving at the front door.

"This dickhead sniffed me!"

Brandon looked at Macca with a disbelieving expression, "You can't have gone that long... If she was, we would all know, so keep your nose to yourself. So, Julie, you get anywhere with these guys? No? You wanna come with me?" I nodded. "Catch ya next Saturday, fellas," he said, waiting for me to walk out and then letting the sliding door slam shut behind us.

"You OK?" Brandon asked as I got back into the car. Bud had gone with apparently, keen to keep finding new smells to sniff. That said a lot about Brandon's character, that my dog was prepared to leave me and go with him.

"I...don't know."

"Look, don't worry too much, if you can. I know it stresses you out, not knowing, but if my word's worth anything, I can tell you it will be OK. What's coming? I've never seen it hurt or harm anyone, emotionally, physically or spiritually, if that helps."

"It's not a big orgy, is it?"

He laughed at that. "No, not unless you want it to be. If that's what worrying you, I can say it's not in any way sexual."

"Strangely, that's both a relief and a disappointment."

"Jules, you gotta let that patriarchal bullshit holding you down go, love."

"Really, that's your response? Feminist theory?"

"Think about it," he said. "You have two different types of people in a heterosexual relationship. One of them is big and strong and muscly, and capable of one orgasm before needing half an hour or so before he can go again. The other is often soft and curvy and sweet."

"Yeah, I get the idea."

"And can, but not always, have orgasm, after orgasm, after orgasm, if that's what she wants. Why would the big muscly one use all of his power, verbal, political, social, whatever, to demonise the women who want to exploit that delightful biological quirk to its fullest? She's a slut, a whore, she has a mental illness, she shouldn't be able to keep custody of her kids, or get a job unless it's on her back. It's fear, love, that the all consuming hole that provokes so much pleasure in him is not wholly satisfied by him. He is not enough."

"You've been reading some Freud at the library, haven't you?"

"But seriously, I don't know how you can't see it. Men have used their control over women for so long, you girls keep perpetuating it without any interference from them. Wives don't want to lose their husbands, so they toe the line. They raise their daughters to toe the line so they'll have a chance of marrying, to have their own daughters and perpetuate the cycle. It's mothers who perform female circumcision on their daughters, not fathers."

"Really, you don't think that's a bit of a jump from my reluctance to fuck those seven guys back there?"

"Fuck them, don't fuck them, doesn't worry me. Have sex with no one here, if you like. That's the point, *if you like*. The attention you are getting right now is largely because you're ambivalent. You're into it sometimes, and not others. Guys don't know whether to approach you or not, whether you want it or not. Because there's so few women here, they'll keep asking, just in case you say yes."

"I have said yes, twice."

"And everyone knows that, which of course, means hope springs eternal. If you seriously don't want what anyone's got to offer, say no a bunch of times and people will stop asking, I promise. But if the only thing holding you back there was inherited sexual repression... well, you should imagine that you are on some kind of exotic tropical island, where the culture is very different to your own, where it's expected that you will operate using a new set of sexual mores."

"Are you hoping to talk yourself into my bed? Is that it? Did Slade say he talked me around, and you thought to try the same?" I said, looking at him through narrowed eyes.

He laughed. "Nope. Can't say I'd be sad for the chance but..." This earned me a long look, and when his eyes went back to the road, he reached down and adjusted his dick to what was apparently a more comfortable angle. "There's a lot of guys rushing to get into your pants. Me, I'd like us to be friends. Your hot, hot, very willing friend, if you decide to choose me. But if you don't, still a good friend." I laughed at that. "As your friend, I'm just saying, don't let a bunch of dead, old guys stop you from having fun. You have power here, a lot of it, don't be afraid to use it."

"With great power comes great responsibility."

"Spiderman?"

"The French Revolution, I think."

"Well, whatever. Just treat the people you are with respectfully, and you should be fine."

14

We sank into silence until we reached the next house. The guys were awake there thankfully, but similarly underdressed. It had been warm last night, but I was comfortable in my jeans and top, so I wasn't sure why they were stripped down that far. They looked very interested when I dumped their beer and food on the counter, but I stopped them cold with a question about the full moon. Brandon just smiled and shook his head as each guy backed right off after that.

"Now, we're heading to the married quarters, so there'll be bigger boxes. I'm going to take you somewhere special first though, OK?"

"Where?" I said frowning.

"You'll find out in a second. It'll be fine. Just trust me."

We drove through the admin sector, past a lot of sheds and buildings I was still yet to visit, and then back up the hill. The houses were a lot bigger on this side I realised, with sprawling gardens filled with children's play equipment. Brandon skipped all of them, heading down the third row and pulling up outside one three quarters the way along the street. He smiled as he got out of the cab. "C'mon."

We picked up the boxes and Brandon got the gate for me, walking up a pretty white stone driveway to a house with a huge porch running around each side of it.

"Hey, honey!" I heard a feminine voice call out. The door opened and a beautiful woman of slim build with long dark hair arrived at the door. *Am I meeting his girlfriend?* I thought. That's something I'd never really asked about, if blokes had multiple girlfriends as well. She was pretty enough to be so, which sent a stab of jealousy through me. Where did that come from? "Did you bring our stuff first again? The neighbourhood is going to kill me if you keep doing this. Especially Phyllis, you know how she is about precedence. Oh, who's this?" Her eyes flicked to me, and then the broadest smile split her face. "Is she...? Have you...?"

"Mum, this is Julie. She's the new girl, Finn's offsider. Julie, this is my mum, Janice."

"Nice to meet you," I said.

"Come in! Come in! So you're from the outside world, huh? Your head must be spinning right about now." She turned to Brandon, "John and Bill are at the pub, but Adam and Duke are in the den looking over the books. Go and grab them." He walked down the hallway obediently. "So how are you coping, honey? I'm a Sanctuary girl myself, but my best friend, Carissa, I still remember when she first came here, poor thing. Her head was spinning for weeks."

"Spinning would be a polite word for it. The way people live here is just so different," I said cautiously. I didn't want to just blurt out that I thought it was weird that she had four husbands and looked only a little older than me.

"The harem thing? I know from Carissa that the way we do things here is quite unconventional. Maybe I should introduce you, might help you adjust?"

"Ah, yeah. And then there's that full moon thing."

"Still not telling you what's going to happen until afterwards? I've talked to Kelly about this for years. I don't think it's the right way to go about it, but I'm not the matriarch here."

"You can't fill me in at all?"

"Not without losing everything. Kelly runs Sanctuary well, and is a fair and reasonable boss, but that is absolutely no go for her. I'm sorry, it'll be OK though. Once you find out, it'll probably be a let down, I think." She saw my face and reached over and rubbed my arm, "I know, honey, it's not fair. Look, some people are coming around for a BBQ this afternoon. Carissa will be there, you want to come and meet her? She'd have to have a lot of advice about how to cope in the next few weeks."

"Yeah, sure."

"So, how's my son treating you?"

I was giving Brandon a glowing recommendation when two men came into the kitchen. One of the guys was tall and had that big, bulky, muscled look bodybuilders have, with a short crop of greying black hair. The other looked like he could be Brandon's dad. He had a similar lean build, covered in compact muscle and waving dark hair that fell to his shoulders. Both of them took me in and burst into smiles. "So, this is Julie," big guy said, taking my hand. "I'm Brandon's dad, Duke."

"And I'm his other dad, Adam. Johnny and Bill will be pissed they missed you. Did you have any plans on tonight? We're having a BBQ."

"Janice just invited me. Yes, that would be lovely."

"So, how long have you known our son?" Duke asked.

"Duke, don't give the girl the third degree," Adam said.

"You're going to make the girl nervous," Janice said.

"Mum, Dad and Dad, I know you'd like to grill Julie, but we have more deliveries to make. Phyllis will have rung the front office and made a complaint right about..." he looked at his phone as it began to ring, "now. I'll bring her by tonight and you can talk to her, respectfully, without asking a million invasive questions."

"Son, we just want to get to know the new lady in your life," Duke said.

"Well, she won't be in my life if you guys have your way, so cool it. Think back to grandma and the grandpas..." Duke and Adam winced at that. "Exactly, so chill. Anything you want us to bring?"

"Just Julie," Janice said with a warm smile. "We'll see you later."

· · ·

"SORRY FOR THE PARENTAL OVERKILL. Every time I'm seen with a girl, they lose their shit. Duke gets all 'who are you that wants to see my son's junk' and Janice and Adam act like cheerleaders, overexcited by everything. John's much more low key, he'll just offer you a beer, and Bill's usually too stressed out with running the mine to worry about what I'm doing."

"So, that's who you grew up with. What happened when you wanted permission to do something? Did you have to ask every single one of them?"

"Nah, just Mum. Though if I knew she'd say no, I'd ask Adam or Bill. If they said no, I'd just keep asking, hoping to get a better answer."

"That sounds...so confusing."

"Not really. If Bill was my only dad, I wouldn't have had much of a male role model growing up. I love him, don't get me wrong. He makes tremendous sacrifices to keep the family going, but having multiple dads meant there was always someone to care for us kids. Duke made sure we got our homework done and brushed our teeth, John patched up scraped knees and told us stories every night before bed, Adam got us drunk the first time. Said he wanted us to do it under supervision, but Mum freaked out."

"Us? You have siblings?"

"Yeah, a twin sister, Brady. I know, Brandon and Brady is naff as hell, but Mum liked it. You'll meet her tonight, she'll bring her husbands and the kids, especially now you're coming."

"I'm starting to feel a bit intimidated."

"Don't be. People want to have a gawk at anyone new, it's too small a community not to, but they won't get too crazy. Just say hello. Here we are, Queen Phyllis's."

He pulled the truck up outside a very large house with a perfectly manicured lawn and fence around the perimeter. An older woman came barrelling out as soon as we arrived, striding over in a cloud of orange chiffon. "Where have you been, Brandon Meares! I was told you would be here by ten o'clock at the very latest. You know you are supposed to come to my house first. I have a formal dinner tonight and it's now 11:30. I don't know how I'll get it ready in time."

"Delivery times are estimates only," Brandon said, getting out of the cab.

"That is not what head office said. They definitely said 10 o'clock. I even got the officious little snip, Karen, to send me an email in writing confirming this."

"Better take that up with Karen," he said, rolling the back door up and jumping in to start sorting out the goods.

"And what's this?" she snapped, turning those scary green eyes on me. "I don't know you. Are you...? You're that single girl who wants to break up happy marriages! How dare you bring someone like that here? And with some flea bitten mutt in tow. There are mothers and children!"

"What the fuck?" I said. "You crazy... Oh! Hi, Al."

A stream of men came out the front door and made their way down to the truck. Al, the married guy I'd met at the mess, was one of them. "Hey, Julie. You giving Brandon a hand today?"

"Yep, I think this is yours," I said, passing him a box of produce.

Her eyes went from Al to me, and then narrowed. "You know this woman? This is what I keep telling Kelly. We need to create separate settlements! There's no reason for settled packs and the single to mix at all..."

"Which means you wouldn't see the kids at all," one of the men said to her. "Love, go inside and have a drink and calm down. The girl is delivering groceries, not hawking her wares on a street corner."

"I might have to cancel tonight," Phyllis said, her voice starting to waver. "I'm feeling one of my spells coming on."

"Buck, walk her back to her room. Don't let her take anything," Al said to one of the other guys. "Dom, Earl, get the patio ready. Make sure you're careful at the corners. You know how she freaks if there's any dirt there. Jock, Henry, put the groceries away and we'll start on the dinner. Thanks Brandon, appreciate you making us second on the list."

"No problems, Al. See you next weekend."

The goods disappeared into the hands of the many men, as fast as Brandon could hand them out. Earl took Phyllis by the arm and marched her back up into the house, and she whimpered the whole way.

"Something to keep in mind if you go with a big pack," Brandon said once we got inside the truck, "everyone's sure the constant histrionics are Phyllis's attempts to maintain control of her blokes. There's three more out at the mine, so she's got eight in total. Eight sounds awesome at the beginning, when it's all red hot passion, but once kids start coming... Her chances of getting to all of them and meeting their needs is not good. Instead she runs around being a ball busting bitch to keep everyone beholden to her, rather than there for love."

"There must be more to it than that," I said, looking out the window. "Al seemed like a reasonable bloke, he's not going to be emotionally blackmailed into staying."

"Maybe she gives head like a vacuum cleaner," Brandon said, laughing when I started to make gagging noises. "Yeah, just like that."

"Ew! Ew! Ew!"

15

The rest of the deliveries went without a drama. There was one young family with a new baby that was super cute. Mum was breastfeeding bubs as we came inside, the three dads rushing around, trying to take the boxes from us, fussing over the mother, and managing to trip over each other in the process. When the child started crying, a dad dropped the box he was carrying, thankfully not the one with the eggs in it. Mum just reassured him calmly, getting the baby back on the nipple and redirected him to the job at hand. She thanked us for the delivery and asked idly how I was going. I mumbled something appropriate, transfixed by her placid beauty, completely absorbed in feeding her child.

"OK, we've got to head back and pick up the next load from the warehouse, then we're heading out to the farm."

"So there's a whole farm connected to the Sanctuary? I had no idea this was a whole self-sustaining community when I came for the job. I figured everything got shipped in."

"Some of it," Brandon said. "You're about to see where the supplies are kept."

· · ·

WE PULLED into a shed I'd never been to before. It was filled with floor to ceiling industrial shelving that contained household goods of every description. "How does this all get here?"

"Someone does a run with one of the long haul trucks," he said. "I do it sometimes. You could come if you wanted, return to civilisation for a day. Alright, maybe get out and stretch your legs as stacking the truck is going to take a bit." He yanked his shirt off and tucked it into the back of his jeans.

"And you need to do this shirtless?" I asked, my eyes running across his bare chest. He wasn't as puffed up as some of the other guys, but he was all muscle and sinew.

"It's hot, shitty work, but it's all made a whole lot better when you look at me like that." He grinned and then loped off into the shed.

"C'mon Bud, let's get some food," I said. He sprang to his feet and ran in the direction of the mess hall. I was just starting to put something on my plate when the sirens began to wail. My head jerked up, and I saw everyone drop what they were doing and run for the entrance. Bud started to circle and howl, obviously distressed by the noise. I followed the group outside at a slower pace.

Bam! I turned to see the gate to the mine rattle on its frame as something massive slammed against it. "Get the guns! Get the guns!" people yelled, running to the various buildings. Bam! Bam! Bam! What the fuck was that? Brandon had said I would be safe, that no harm would come to me on the full moon, then why were people flying around in a mad panic, looking for guns? It was like World War III was about to break out. I walked slowly towards the barrier, avoiding the flurry of people around me, peering past the mesh into the darkness beyond it, trying to work out what was battering its way through the gate. Bam! I heard a scrabbling noise, then a god awful screech, like something sharp dragging itself against metal. Bam! Bam! I should've been worried, tearing off and screaming from here, because I could see the pins on the frame were starting to bend. Bam! Bam! Bam! Then I heard it, a sound that had my blood running cold. An unearthly howl, like a wolf's, yet totally unlike. It was as if it came from a throat coated with broken glass, forced through vocal cords made of barbed wire. Too late I realised that moving closer to something that was making that sound was not wise, that everyone was racing to find weapons for a reason. Smash! The gate flew wide and something that looked like it had crawled from the gates of hell stepped out.

Buddy dropped down into an aggressive stance, growling ferociously at the beast that had broken down the gate. It was big and black and somehow, indistinct, as if made from smoke as well as flesh. It had four paws that moved slowly, almost gracefully towards me, bright red eyes that glowed within its smoky form and a long snout, like a wolf's, that was currently scenting the air, scenting me. "Oh fuck!" I finally gasped, my brain now realising how much danger I was in.

"Julie! Julie!" I heard people call dimly, but I couldn't heed them.

"Buddy!" I cried as he slunk closer to the beast. He dropped down into a crouch, his legs coiling. "Buddy, no!"

I threw myself at my dog, but he leapt at the same time, jaws open wide. The black thing's eyes flicked to my pup for just a moment, and that was all it took for it to pluck him from its flesh and throw him wide. "Buddy!" I sobbed, seeing him lying there, motionless. I ran over to his side, no longer caring about the hell beast, but it did not return my sentiment. I was slammed to the ground, getting a mouthful of dirt for my trouble, gasping for breath but unable to get any air, as I had been completely winded. *Can't breathe! Can't breathe!* I thought hysterically, fighting to fill my lungs, but I was no match for the huge weight on my spine. The horrific growl was now deafening in my ears, so much so that the sound of guns being fired was almost a muted counterpoint. I felt my shirt rip as I managed to wriggle free enough to lie on my back, and was greeted by the monstrous face of the beast. The red eyes bore into mine, it's stinking breath washing over me. I tried to shimmy away from it, tears flowing freely, but it placed both of its paws on each of my arms. I screamed when its claws buried themselves into my skin, using air I didn't have. My vision was starting to fail as I gasped, my lungs fighting to fill as the beast's head drew closer and closer. "No!" I whimpered, "no!" I lost consciousness just as those terrible jaws descended.

16

I woke with a start in a room I'd never seen before. I was lying on
a metal gurney, attached to a whole lot of machines that went
ping. I looked at the IV in my arm, the curtain surrounding my
bed and realised, I was in a hospital. I plucked the shapeless green
gown away from my body and saw long rows of stitches. It was weird,
the moment I looked at them was when I felt the deep aches and
superficial itches on each wound site. *What the hell...* I thought, and
then it came back. The smoke beast had hurt me. I glanced at my
wrists and sure enough, there were thick bandages around them from
where the animal had clawed me. *Oh, god*, I thought, tears beginning
to rise. *What had happened to Buddy?* "Buddy..." I cried softly, my
vision overwhelmed with a flood. I'd had him since he was a pup, all
fluffy and falling all over the place. I remembered having to puppy
proof the fence four times before I could stop him from trying to
come to work with me. Then it was a kaleidoscope of images, of
Buddy asleep with his head on my lap, of him running away with a
stinking rabbit corpse, not letting me take it, of having to wash him
afterwards and him woo wooing as I did so. Buddy curled up in a ball,
sitting on the passenger seat of my car, looking excitedly down the

road as we travelled, searching for a new home. "God, Bud," I sobbed, "I'm sorry..."

Yelp! My head whipped up and my heart felt like it was going to jump out of my chest as I heard the clatter of doggy steps on the concrete floor. *Woo woo!* The green curtain was pulled aside as my dog barrelled in, whining and crying so much I started crying too. He tried to leap up on my bed but it took two goes before he landed on me, whimpering and licking and snuggling in as close as he could. "Bud," I said, holding his wiggling body to me. "Buddy boy!"

"I wondered what all the noise was about. You're feeling better, I hope?" Doc Hobbes had joined us, pulling the green curtain back to reveal Finn and Kelly as well. She picked up the chart at the end of the bed and then consulted the various machines around me. "We'll leave the IV in for the moment, but I think we can remove these now," she said, reaching inside my gown to pull sticky sensors from my skin. "Now, would you like a drink?"

"Yeah. Buddy, sit down! Yes, but first, I want some answers. Just what the hell is going on? What was that thing that attacked me? Is that what you are keeping at this place? Is this what the full moon is about?"

"No, no, Julie, please lie down and let Doctor Hobbes finish her observations..." Kelly said.

"If you think I'm going to stick around for the next few weeks to find out what happens on the mysterious full moon..."

"You won't have to. We've talked and we'll let you know as soon as the Doctor finishes. She needs to sign off that getting news like this won't impede your progress."

"She should be fine," Doc said. "I've had a look at her stitches, she still has a day or two before they are ready to come out, but they're all healing well, no sign of infection." She turned to me. "You'll need to take some antibiotics. Always with food, and don't miss any. The infection you're fighting can be virulent, we've already had to give you some intravenously since you were brought in. I'll talk to you about how to care for your wounds after you've spoken to these two."

"Ok," I said, looking at Kelly and Finn. "Talk."

Instead, Finn started to pull his shirt off. "Are you serious? Is the answer sexual or a strip show?" I snapped.

"He can leave his clothes on if you prefer, but they will be shredded in the change. In the hope of reducing our clothing bill, we usually strip down before we do this."

"Do what?" I asked, my eyes flicking wildly between the two of them.

"Can he take his uniform off and show you? He won't touch you, not for a moment, I promise," Kelly said.

"Fine." I wouldn't have thought it possible, but I watched Finn get naked without a twinge of arousal. They were scaring the shit out of me. The only things I could think of that they might need to show me nude were porn related or monster of the week kind of stuff. Apparently, option number 2 was the correct one. I watched open mouthed as he hunched over, his body moving in a series of lightning fast stretching, snapping, shifting motions until a huge white version of what had struck me down at the gate stood where Finn was. Buddy was up on his feet, then down at the foot of the bed, sniffing wildly. All I could do was stare.

"This is what the Sanctuary is for," Kelly said. "This is what we keep safe. This is what we all are, what we believe you are."

I DIDN'T WASTE any time. I yanked the IV from my arm, which stung a lot more than when they show people doing that on TV, and jumped free of the bed. "Julie!" I heard Kelly call as I ran, pushing aside the curtain and flying down the ward, past empty beds and other cordoned off areas. I saw the big shed door exit and started to really put on speed, Buddy sprinting beside me. I emerged out into the light, eyes blinking, looking wildly around to see where to run to next. Instead I saw my car, idling, just outside the hospital with Brandon sitting in the driver's seat. "Julie!" he called and opened the passenger seat door.

He's one of them! my brain insisted. Yep, he was, and he was in control of my only way out of this crazy place. I jumped into the seat, letting Buddy into the back, and slammed it shut before locking it. "Julie, I know you're panicking. The car is full of petrol, and I have some money for you." He handed me a wad of cash in an envelope. "That's 1000 bucks. It'll get you to the next town and keep you going until you can get a new job, if that's what you want to do. If you want me to drive, I'll stay. If you want to go on your own, I'll get out and you can take the wheel. What do you want to do?" I looked back at the hospital and saw Kelly and Finn, still in white beast form, emerge in the doorway.

"Just drive!" I snapped.

For a while, all I could hear was the hum of the engine, the rasp of my lungs as I tried to catch my breath and Buddy's panting. We peeled out of the Sanctuary complex and headed out onto the highway, back the way I'd originally come. I watched the trees and scrub flick by, until my heart rate slowed down to normal. Brandon turned to look at me, as if sensing the immediate crisis was over, and smiled tentatively.

"You're one of the them too, aren't you?" I said flatly.

"Yep, everyone you've met is in some degree a wolf."

"So that's what that is, a werewolf?"

"Not what we called it in the old country, but it will do for now."

"And the thing that attacked me?"

"Yep."

"Your parents, Shaun, Slade..."

"Yep, all of them. Some, like Nerida, are genetic hybrids. It can be hard to do, most humans are instinctively repelled by us, but when we live in human communities and raise our kids there, that repulsion seems to lessen. There have been instances of humans having children with us. You are the result of that."

"I'm going to turn into that...thing."

"That's why we wanted to wait for the full moon. You either would or wouldn't, and then we'd know where you fit in the community, what your strengths and weaknesses are."

"So what, if I didn't turn, I'd be given my marching orders?"

"No, but like Nerida, you wouldn't do any of the frontline jobs. The stronger wolves keep the weaker members safe at the Sanctuary."

"Obviously not, or I wouldn't have these lovely scars to show for it," I said, thrusting my wrists at him.

"If you turn, you'll lose those scars. But that wolf, it wasn't one of ours. It attacked you because of your value to us. An unattached female is worth more than her weight in gold. He would have taken you through the gate, to his community. I can't tell you how you'd be treated there, but based on the reports from the others, not well."

"So, I'm a scrap of meat to be fought over."

"No one thinks of you like that. If we did, you'd be caged and raped repeatedly, like in some of the fucked up communities. But part of the urgency for us guys in finding you mates comes from a protective urge. Mated wolves emit the same kind of repellent vibe to other wolves as we do to humans. It certainly can be overcome, some sick individuals relish pushing past it and assaulting women, but they are few and far between."

"So if I'd decided I wanted a relationship with Shaun or Slade, that's it, everyone else would find me a turn off?"

"For as long as the affection and commitment lasts. That's part of Phyllis's paranoia, that at some point one of her pack will start becoming attractive to others. If that happens, she'll know that the love has died."

"I don't want this," I said, almost in a whisper. I'd thought my words had been drowned out by the sound of the engine, but Brandon's hand snaked over and took one of mine, giving it a squeeze.

"I know," he said, and on we drove.

WE PULLED over at the first petrol station we saw and got some food and drinks and some clothes for me. My stomach was just about turning itself inside out from hunger. Then I remembered Doc's words, I was supposed to take antibiotics to keep my wounds from getting infected. I looked over the rows of stitches raking down my body in the toilet mirror, and they all appeared healthy and pink. If Brandon knew about the medication, he would turn the car around, no matter what I said. I yanked on the clothes and stuffed the hospital gown in the bin. Feeling better now with a belly full of food and drink, we drove away and kept on driving, further and further from the Sanctuary.

The next major town was five hours away, but there were a few smaller places that had a pub, a petrol station and a shop a little closer. We stopped at one, Gordonvale, three hours later. "Feel like a beer?" Brandon asked, pointing to the pub. I nodded, glad for anything that might make me feel a bit calmer about today. We stepped inside, Buddy at my heels. I worried that they might not let him in, but saw other people's cattle dogs lazing under tables or under their owner's feet.

"What'll it be, love?" the barmaid said on automatic, looking up at us and then flinching slightly before recovering her professional smile.

"Two beers thanks," Brandon said.

She poured the beers and expertly started chatting to us, obviously pushing herself to be polite. "So, you out here seeing the sights?" I thought back to the endless plains of scrub and wondered what she was talking about.

"No, we've come from the mine down the road," I said.

She frowned at this, "The mine? There's no such place, not for 200k of here."

"Yeah, there is," I insisted. "It's about five hours away, northwest."

She shrugged. "I've lived here my whole life, never been a mine nearby. Must be a new place. Been bloody quiet about it, haven't heard anything about hiring."

I nodded, wanting to end this weird arse conversation. We took a seat away from the other punters in one of the corners. "So, what the hell was that?"

Brandon sat on one of the stools and took a long sip of his drink. "The Sanctuary operates in a weird space."

"Of course, it does."

"The way I had it explained to me, is it's like a membrane. Only those things that have permission can see it or go in or out of it, anyone with some wolf genes. Everyone else just sees dirt and trees."

"So my place of work plays Jedi mind tricks?"

He grinned, "From what I heard it's witch mind tricks. Cost a lot of money back in the day."

"So that's how they knew I was one of you, when I found the Sanctuary."

"Ah, no, that was confirmed when you saw the ad."

"Seriously, magic wanted ads?"

Brandon got up and walked over to one of the other tables and picked up an old newspaper there and passed it to me. "Take a look."

I opened the classifieds and there it was, over and over, the same offsider job advertised in every space. "So why didn't they tell me what was going on?"

"Because everyone runs, just like you did. Kelly thought it would be better to wait until we know if people can turn, so there's less time spent chasing after people and making sure they're OK. If it turns out you can't change, and don't want to stay at Sanctuary, no harm no foul. If you do, well they deal with that when it happens, rather than freaking people out about something that might not happen. I meant what I said, the full moon was never going to hurt you."

"We should get a room for the night," I said. I just wanted to climb under the covers and shut out the world right now.

"Ok, one or two."

"One should be fine."

THE BEER HAD HIT me pretty hard, I realised as I got to my feet. I was feeling kinda drunk already, but I guess getting bitten by monster beasts took it out of a girl. The room was dark and smelled musty, but I dropped down on the bed as soon as we got in the door. "Are you OK, Jules?" he asked, but I only heard his words dimly.

"Hot," I said. "Turn the aircon on, will ya?"

A hand was placed on my forehead, and I knew Brandon had something to say about that but I missed it, dropping almost immediately into sleep.

17

"She's burning up! She should have taken her damn medicine. I told Kelly to leave the explanations until she was out of the woods."

"What are we going to do, Doc?"

"Get her back to the hospital. What else can we do? You all need to be prepared to lose her. I'll put her on the strongest antibiotics I've got, but I don't know if they'll help much against the lycan strain. If I was in a major hospital with more resources at hand.... Get her in the van. I'll hook her up and do my best."

I SLOWLY CAME BACK to consciousness, and wished I hadn't. "Unh!" I mumbled, it came on me so fast. I whimpered ineffectually as it felt like someone was smashing into my skull with fists of iron, my heartbeat sounding like a bass drum being pounded at 100 decibels, and I burned. As my awareness of my body grew, so did the feeling. I was so, so hot. *I'm burning!* I thought, fear clogging my throat. I needed to get up, to run, but I was made of lead. I cried as all I could do was shift restively. Nothing helped, nothing provided any respite. If anything, moving exacerbated it, sending slashes of pain through my

body as I did. But I couldn't stop. My skin felt like it was surely beginning to crisp and blacken. "Uh...uh..uh.." I felt the hysteria rise, I
couldn't escape this, I couldn't get up, leave, kill whoever was doing
this to me because this was me. My body had betrayed me, turning
on me, threatening to crush my awareness like a bug. My back curved
into a harsh bow, the muscles trembling with the effort and unable to
stop.

"Fuck! She's regaining consciousness. Up the tranqs, 20ml!"

"Is that wise? What if this is the change? She's been here for days,
the full moon is coming..."

"She'll be dead before then if we don't get her sedated! She's
knocked the fucking line out. You two, hold her down, I don't care if
you bruise her, just keep her steady. I need to get this back in, and I
don't want to rip a hole in her vein."

"Arrrgh!" I shrieked as bars of iron were wrapped around me. I
needed, had to move, to somehow get away from what was going on.
My throat felt like it was scraped with glass, but I screamed and
screamed. It was the only way, either that or let the pain take me
whole. Something cold and hard was shoved in my arm, I tried to
yank it from the harsh grip but instead, was forced to fight for breath
as I was squeezed inexorably. I panted madly and moaned, then felt
the spread of a cold heaviness inside me. I whimpered, not yet willing
to believe that there was a way out of this hell, that I might not have
to endure this agony.

"She'll be out in 3...2..."

SOMEHOW, I was standing on a plain of grass. It spread out towards
the horizon until it shifted into some bluish coloured hills. I heard a
slight hiss and looked down to see the grass ripple as a light breeze
swept through it. *Where the fuck am I?* I heard something move
behind me and spun around to see another of those smoke wolf
beasts standing before me. "Fuck, fuck, fuck," I said, jerking back
from it and ending up on my knees. I scrabbled away but it merely
stood there, watching me with curious glowing green eyes. When it

became apparent it wasn't going to chew me up right now, I stopped where I was and took a closer look.

It seemed to have the body of a normal wolf, just much, much bigger. Its fur was indistinct, though. In places, I could see the strands of grey ticked fur clearly, and in others, it looked as if the fur was made of smoke, wisping away and dissipating into the air. It didn't have the usual greenish yellow eyes of a wolf, instead it regarded me with eyes that seemed little more than glowing lights. Noticing that I was no longer retreating, the wolf settled down onto the ground, eyes on me.

"What the fuck are you?" I whispered.

I didn't see the wolf's mouth move but I distinctly heard someone say, *You.*

"WHAT'S HAPPENING! She's fitting again!"

"Febrile convulsions. She should have taken those fucking drugs! The antibiotics aren't working, we need some of the little used ones they save for resistant strains, but god knows if they'll sell them to us, or we can get them in time. There's every chance she'll go septic."

"We need to keep her alive until the full moon. It will take care of it."

"Forgive my concern, but you don't know that. I can't plan her care assuming she'll turn."

"She'll turn. I feel it."

"Are you sure what you are 'feeling' is real? Or is it just wishful thinking? How the hell did the dark one get past the guards anyway? She should have had a guard on her at all times."

"We haven't had a serious incursion for years. That's what convinces me that she'll turn. They know, we know. Just keep her alive, nature will take care of the rest."

18

"Hello," I said to the creature. This was a dream, I'd worked out. Every time I fell into REM sleep, I came back here and the wolf was waiting.

Hello, it replied, sort of. I never caught its lips moving or anything like speech from the wolf, but it replied nonetheless. Its voice sounded kind of hollow and echoey.

"So, I've never tried to have a conversation with an animal before. Well, I've never expected a response. That usually means you're crazy. Maybe I am, maybe that's why I never wake up... Anyway, what are you?"

Tirian, it replied.

"And what's a Tirian when it's at home? Or is that your name?"

It tilted its head to look at me and then said again, *You*.

"OK, I get it, you reckon you're this hitherto unknown part of me. You're not human, you don't look like an actual wolf so..."

I am Tirian.

"Oh great, circular logic. Look what is a Tirian? Any Tirian?"

It chuckled, the fucking smoke monster chuckled. *Tirian is... smoke wolf beast?* Its green eyes scanned mine, as if pulling my mental image of it directly from my brain. *Not accurate.*

"I get that, that was my placeholder description until I got an accurate one. You obviously know and are supposed to be part of me, so how about you explain?"

Yes, I will show you. The 'Tirian' got to its feet and looked over its shoulder meaningfully.

"You want me to follow you?"

No, ride.

"SHE'S LOOKING BETTER."

"God almighty... She's not better, she's sedated as much as I dare, just short of killing her. She screams whenever she regains consciousness, the entire time. This is why I went into veterinary science, this is bloody cruel. She's not improving. She's not going to improve. We need to discuss amputation. Her hands, and one of her feet."

"That's not going to happen. The full moon is only days away."

"I'm not sure if she'll make it. Can't anyone force the change on her? If I have to bury this girl because of this... consider it my last act of employment. This is not what I signed up for."

"I understand. We can't force the change. The one that could... he's not on our side of the gate. He would take her with him once she was healed, and we'd never see her again."

"I get the importance of females to your kind, but seriously, at this point you don't think this would be a better option than what's happening now? She's dying, and we're letting her."

"A lifetime of rape and forced child bearing? If we're wrong and the change doesn't happen, then we can look at more desperate options. You have your instructions, Doc, follow them."

I WAS RIDING a wolf across a fantastic landscape. It was a blur as we moved, but I saw more things shift as we travelled than was normal. It was like we were bounding from one realm to the next, and each time the wolf's paws hit the ground there was something different: icy tundra, an old growth forest, a field of sunflowers, a rocky mountainside. Then finally, we stopped. We stood on the crest of a hill, looking down at the valley where a village had been built. It was a small cluster of houses, smoke curling from the chimneys, chickens pecking the soil around them. "*Watch*," the Tirian said. As if on fast forward, I saw a rapid flicker of movement, people coming out and going inside the houses, hunters bringing home meat, farmers bringing home crops, children playing, women hanging out the washing. Then it drew dark, and I wasn't sure if it was because it was night time, or because of what happened next. Great armoured men swept into town, crushing everything in their path. Thankfully I only saw glimpses, but children's throats were slit, women were raped and men slain, fighting hopelessly with spades and hoes. Afterwards, there was a smoking ruin and a tiny group of tattered people, standing lost in the wreckage. Slowly, I saw the town get rebuilt. Houses grew from shelters, crops were planted, cows and chickens returned, children were born and families grew. Then the sky became dark.

"Oh, no!" I murmured, hand going to my mouth. Another group of men, different armour and with different colouring, came through and did the same. The view of the village sped up until I saw the cycles, rebuild, rape and pillage, rebuild and rape and pillage. Until one day, the raiders who came looked different. Taller, they didn't wear armour but the skins of wolves, the skulls perched on their heads like helmets. They slashed at the inhabitants with curious spears made from a crystalline material that had been knapped to a series of razor sharp points. They killed the children and the men, and left them lined up in a gruesome tally of their days work, but they left the sobbing women alive for a different purpose.

I wish this part went faster, the constant grinding rape. I saw flickers of it only, yet it was too much. Mouths stretched in screams as man after man took his fill. I saw blood and semen running down the legs of the women when they staggered to their feet, only to be knocked down again. The women grew big with child, huddling in rudimentary structures against the cold, the men now slower moving, less interested in brutality as they had achieved their goals. They then left en masse, weapons shouldered, disappearing like smoke into the forest beyond, leaving their victims to survive the winter alone. Their limbs became thinner and thinner as their bellies grew, many just resting listlessly for hours inside a primitive lean to, staring glassily into space. One woman struggled to her feet, staggering over to the fire to put more kindling on it, the fire fighting to survive in the whipping wind. The extra wood only smothered the remaining flames, and it died away to a wisp of smoke. She looked at it, completely aghast, unable for the moment to believe this bad luck. She dropped to her knees, her face a mask of despair, the pain so raw there I wanted to shut my eyes and pull away. The Tirian, forgotten, pushed me with its muzzle to pay attention. I didn't want to watch her die, her pain reminded me of...

Her hands clasped together as she emitted a heartfelt prayer, tears sliding down her cheeks. I didn't know what she was saying but I watched her lips move rapidly, like she was pouring out her soul to her god. I expected that to be the beginning of the end, for her to slowly starve or freeze to death. But instead, a woman appeared before her, tall and wearing a gown of faded grey green, with long reddish brown hair. She dropped to her knees, her dress unsullied by the ashy sludge and surrounded the woman's hands with hers. The pregnant woman's eyes went wide, she babbled something, then moved her hand to her mouth as if to stop more from coming out. It didn't work, soon she was gesturing to the village, to the other women and then to her belly. The red-haired woman bent down, touched her stomach for a moment and then shook her head. The pregnant woman's gestures grew wider, more desperate, her fingers stabbing in the direction of the other women, but the redhead shook her head again. Defeated, the pregnant woman's head dropped down and slowly she collapsed in on herself. The red-haired woman looked the village and the victims over critically, and then tapped her finger to her lip. The only sound I'd heard since we came here, a wolf howl, sounded in the distance. This seemed to give the redhead an idea, and she swept her arms out in a great gesture, turning to make sure she included all of the women in it. Every single one of them shifted into a smoke wolf beast, sorry, a Tirian, though their bellies remained swollen. The Tirians shifted restlessly, taking in the changes for what felt like a second, and then the far off wolf howl called again. Now a pearly white Tirian, the praying woman's head jerked up, then she yipped at her pack mates, and they left the ruins in a flowing mass.

What came after was dizzying. Flash after flash of human children being born from their Tirian mothers, the women returning to human form, now sleek and well fed, to care for their children. New villages were built and children grew. When raiders came, the women instantly shifted into Tirian form and tore the flesh from their bones, teeth cutting through armour like butter. Now the raiders were lined up in a neat line, as the women spoke to their bloody faced children. As they grew, it became apparent there were more male children than female, and that it was the women who ran the village. The original praying woman acted as leader, right up until she became grey and wizened, a horde now of young men and women at her feet. When she died, her badge of office, a crystal necklace that looked much like the spear head of the wolf raiders, was passed to the next woman. Time sped up, showing woman after woman after woman taking the necklace and the position, bands of men standing with one woman, children milling at their feet. This started to flick by so fast, my view almost zooming out as I saw many villages with the same cycle of women stepping up and leading their people. Then, I saw the gate.

Made from rough-hewn stone, looking much like the smaller standing stones in Europe, a woman and several of her men sniffed around it in Tirian form, jerking back when a blue light flared between the rocks. The white Tirian, the female, touched the blue with her nose and... I blinked and saw that I had returned to the original plain where I first met the Tirian. Though now when I looked over my shoulder, I could see in the distance the set of standing stones they had gone through. "So that's how they got into my world," I said, "through a gate?" The Tirian nodded. "And that's how I came to be. Someone from here, like that, was one of my ancestors."

. . .

"She needs to be brought out of the coma in three days."

"It'll take longer than that to reduce her dosage safely..."

"You don't get it, Doc. Whatever health emergency you're predicting will be resolved once she shifts."

"You... Fine, if this is what you want, I'll leave you the instructions. I am done with this. This, this was handled badly, all of it. The policy of keeping people, particularly the girls, in ignorance has to change. Better that you have them bolt out into the world beyond, than this. I've kept my peace in the past, as there's been no real casualties but--"

"Your concern is noted. Go back to the surgery after you've written the instructions. We both thank you for all your hard work."

"Don't be tempted to drop the tranqs too early. She can die from seizures before the full moon, easily."

"We will follow your instructions to the letter."

"Doc, I'll stay with her, right to the end. Slade or Brandon can switch with me when I need to sleep. We'll do what we can, around the clock, I promise."

"If that's what you've decided, I'll leave the instructions in the hospital office. Good luck."

"I think--"

"Just wait... OK, she's gone into the office. Go on."

"I think I should give her some of my blood. It could help the transition, and keep her going until the full moon."

"And it will bond her to you, almost guaranteeing you as the leader of her pack. Apart from the riot that will incite with the men, I'm not sure tying you to the girl without her permission is wise. She's had blessed few choices since she's come here, and I am loathe to take more from her unless we have to."

"We'll monitor her, but I want latitude if it comes to it."

I was on the back of my Tirian, and we were moving like the wind. I whooped as I felt the rush of the breeze on my face, my wolf beast covering ground like a racehorse on steroids. I gripped my thighs tight around her ribcage, but it didn't slow her down. Finally, she stopped in a stand of trees. I slid off, my toes burying themselves into the spongy, mossy turf. She jerked her muzzle, drawing my attention to what lay beyond. I dropped down into a crouch, peering past the tree trunks. There was a beautiful waterfall, the water clear as glass, pooling in a sandy hollow. Perhaps my wolf wanted to swim? I went to get to my feet and walk towards it, but my beast kept me down with a paw to my shoulder blades. She indicated I should sit and watch. I settled down against the cool soil and waited.

He moved so quietly, I hadn't realised he was there until he appeared from between the trees. It was the black Tirian, the one that hurt me, I'm sure. His eyes gleamed red, and he was huge, his fur a furious plume of smoke. He made his way down the slope and to the water with precise steps, dropping a bundle on the bank and lowering his muzzle to drink. His head jerked up, I watched the drips fall from his muzzle, and he scented the air, taking in long whuffing breaths. I froze, not that that would prevent him from smelling me if the wind went the wrong way, but I couldn't stop it. I remembered those knife long claws and those razor teeth... I looked up at my Tirian and started to shift, wanting to get on her back and run and run... She looked down at me and shook her head. We were in luck, he seemed to almost shrug it off. Instead he walked into the pool, submerging his body, and when he popped his head up to take a breath, he was a man.

I studied the broad, well-muscled shoulders and long, wet black hair. He looked much like the guys at the Sanctuary, the same tight, hard bodies, but his had seen more action. White scars raked down his torso, partially covered by spiky black tattoos. He scrubbed at his skin, then scraped his hair back from his face, walking towards the bank, water running down in rivulets across his washboard stomach. I didn't care how fucking cute he was, he nearly bloody killed me. Once he'd finished, he stepped free of the pond, reaching down into the bundle for a cloth to dry himself and some clothes to put on. I was forced to watch his toilet by the heavy paw of my Tirian, though I didn't know why. Not until he reached down and retrieved a familiar looking white skull. I watched him with my heart in my throat and my heartbeat loud in my ears as he placed it on his head, tweaking it until it sat just so, before he looked up and met my eyes.

19

My eyes flipped open wide, and I sucked air into my lungs as if I was dying. The pain was back again, a sudden surprise, as while dreaming, I was freed from all of that. I couldn't seem to get enough breath in, it was like my lungs were made of lead, my chest unable to expand.

"Jules! Jules! You're OK, you're OK." I saw Finn's face swim into my field of vision. "Just take slow breaths for me, in and out. Get her a drink of water!" he snapped at someone beside the bed. Brandon arrived back, holding out a glass of water with a trembling hand. "Little sips, Jules," Finn said. I tried, but my throat felt as if it would close around it, drowning me. I coughed and most of it splattered on Finn, and I noted the blood that came out along with it.

"C'mon princess, you got this. You've been swallowing like a pro for ages," Slade said, trying for a smile, but it came out shaky. "C'mon, my girl. Keep breathing, or we've got to put you back on the machine. You don't want that."

"Let's unhook her," Finn said.

"I'll carry her out onto the grass. The moon's about to rise. Maybe if she's under it..." Brandon said, but I smelled the stink of fear on him. They all stank of it, like the sour scent of unwashed bodies.

"Fuck it, let's try. What else can we do? If she shifts with this stuff in her..." Finn said.

Slade moved to my arm and placed a hand above the bend. "This is going to pinch, princess, but you're a tough girl, aren't you?"

I watched them fuss over me like a corpse, because that's what I was close to being, I realised. I smelled of death, stinking, sickly, sweet rotting death. If I could have raised my head, I would've seen the wound sites had gone rotten. The bandages at my wrists were pristine, but I knew they hid a sight much more awful. I couldn't move, I couldn't speak, I couldn't even breathe as Slade's hand closed too easily around my arm like an iron band. Something peeled away from my skin, feeling like it was pulling the flesh with it. I squeezed out a whimper, and all eyes whipped to meet mine. "I know, love," Slade said, and I heard the tears in his voice. "I don't want to, princess, but I have to. I'll try to be quick."

Maybe he was, it was hard for me to say. My entire world was pain, and it was all I could pay attention to. Something was pulled from me, feeling like it grated and tore as it came off. I cried out, but no sound came from my desiccated voice box. I was frozen in a curve of agony, unable to do anything other than blink as the waves of it crashed over me. I was moved, I felt the sensation dimly but it couldn't take my attention away from the pain. They held me around the shoulders and under my legs, because that's where the muscles shrieked in protest. I felt like I was going to throw up as the swirl of motion sent my head spinning, but there was nothing to come up. Instead, my abdomen clenched and spasmed weakly, sending further spikes of pain. I was laid down on the ground finally, the guys coming to sit beside me. I wanted to scream at them, force them back and not hurt me further, but all I managed was a slight spastic moving of my limbs.

"Give her the blood," Slade said. "I'll fight every cunt here if I have to. She's not going to make it. She's been wasted away by that fucking prick's venom. Give it to her, now."

"You're going to do what?" I shifted my eyes slowly to see Shaun had arrived, his hair made golden by the floodlight behind him. "You take her choice."

"She's not strong enough to make a choice right now! The doc warned us, she might not be strong enough to turn. The blood, it'll at least give her a chance."

"Fuck," Shaun said, kneeling down beside me. "Jules... What they want to do, it'll give you some strength, but you'll be bonded to them, for at least a while." His eyes searched mine, looking for some answer, some clue. "She can't give consent, she can't tell us what she wants."

"Surely not to die would be high on her list," Brandon snapped.

"She'll come back strong and wanting to fight. This will put a target on your back if you do this," Shaun said.

Finn answered by bringing his wrist to his mouth, teeth sharper than a human's snapping out and making a tear there. "Open her mouth, Slade, and keep it open."

I saw my Tirian over Finn's shoulder, watching what she did. "Help me," I said, but didn't move my lips. She shook her head.

I cannot. You have to be strong enough to come to me. If you can, I can fix the rest.

"I can't!"

Then you will die. I kept you from the pain, stopped it from tearing your mind to pieces, let the chemicals they pumped into you have a chance to do what they intended, but you must take the final step.

"I can't."

You must.

"How? How do I do this? I can't even breathe!"

Swallow, my Tirian commanded.

MY BODY MADE the swallowing motion without even thinking as the salty metallic liquid filled my mouth. I dimly heard them all twittering on about it, but I focussed within. Moving my muscles, opening and closing my throat in a series of agonising movements, getting the liquid down before it went the other way, into my lungs.

Then, I became fire. It was different to before as it was not painful in the proper sense, I just felt a terrible heat spread through me but as I did, my chest opened and I could breathe more freely. My muscles relaxed and lay flat against the earth, loosening a tension I hadn't even been aware of. I swallowed, reaching up now to take the strong, hard wrist in my hands and pull it against my lips. I fought back the urge to moan as the trickle of crimson made its way down my oesophagus, spreading blessed relief through my body.

"It's happening," Finn gasped, "I can feel her fangs."

"C'mon, princess. You shift and no one will ever take you down again," Slade said, rubbing a hand over my forehead. I thrust both of them back, amazed when I saw them fly through the air to land far away from me. I tried getting to my feet, no, that wasn't right. I needed to be on all fours, anchored to the earth with my great paws, ready to fight off or chase down these men, depending on what I wanted from them. Brandon and Shaun remained close, only drawing away when I let out a godawful growl. I was getting hotter and hotter still, until it felt like all that was me was molten and liquid. I shut my eyes, stretching back, feeling things inside me pop and crack and rearrange. Then the dust settled, and all was well.

I smelled like earth, smoke and the wind now, all that a healthy animal should. I shifted restively, and my muscles obeyed without complaint. No, instead I felt a great coil of power in my gut that was itching to get out. My Tirian had disappeared, because I was her now. I could run for miles, cover massive areas in a few strides. And run was what I wanted to do. I looked around at the beings next to me, drew in the hot woody scent of their desire on each of them.

"You want to run, princess?" the big one with the fur on his face asked, baring his teeth at me. "You want to chase us down?" I threw back my head and howled my contempt at his words. I could smash his head against the ground with one swipe, and claw out his entrails if he tried to run. "Looks like we're going to have a mating run," the man thing said.

I growled in disgust, hackles rising at his blatant lack of respect. I was his better, his only appropriate response was to roll before me and bare his throat for my pleasure. Just as I was about to coil my legs and leap after him, the other man things stepped in my path. "Every bloke that's able to will be down here in moments, heeding the call. She's going to get drawn back to you, Finn, for the blood," the light furred one said. "Are we staying together? She's already picked us once, all except for Brandon."

"We should let her choose," the dark furred one growled.

"She has chosen. When she was human, she chose all of us, and she has to live with whatever decision the wolf makes when she wakes up. This way, she will be happier living with the end result."

The man things had obviously decided to submit to my superior strength. I took one stalking step towards them, then the next, growling my intention to gut the lot of them. I still had the taste of the reddish one's blood in my mouth, and it was so sweet. I looked forward to gouts of it splashing my muzzle as I tore into him. "Time to go," the reddish one said, his eyes already gone to green. I screamed my warning at him, not to make the same mistake as the other, not to take his other form, but in the next moment, the three of them were no longer man things. White and two greys, they howled their derision at me and then took off into the night.

I followed them on wing-like feet, seeing their forms disappear into the darkness, putting on extra speed to close the gap between us. Instead, a river of other Tirians came from every direction, running towards me, eyes bright in the darkness, heads down and taking one insolent stalking step after another. The stench of lust was so thick, it was almost sickening. I snorted to free myself from it, to retain my former fury, but another hunger woke. *This is the mating dance*, a voice said inside my head, and I knew then what that meant. They thought themselves contenders, thought they deserved the right to plunge themselves into me. I felt a lowdown ache that told me just how ready my body was for that, but refused to give in to it. I shook my head and growled as one, and then more, dared to draw closer. I opened my great jaws and rushed the impudent bastards.

It was heaven, the feeling of skin and flesh ripping under my teeth and claws, the spurts of blood in my mouth dissipating like smoke from my fur when it splashed me. The cacophony of yelps and growls was the purest music to my ears, making my heart sing, making me redouble my efforts. Bones cracked and guts dropped in steaming piles as I fought my way through, looking, looking for the strongest among them, the one who earned the right to be by my side. I found my way out the other side of the crowd without having found him. I laughed my wolf laugh, my muzzle dripping with blood in the cool night air, looking over the now greatly reduced group who had presumed and then turned tail and ran. I could feel him, out there in the dark, the one I wanted, the one I needed. Wolves followed hard on my heels but they did not have my reach, my speed. I howled in mockery before effortlessly tearing away from them.

Once I broke into the forest, I was hit by a wall of sensory information. Smells, like dead leaves, rotting animals, trees mouldering into the soil. Bright harsh pine resin, and the crunch of needles under my feet. The haunting calls of night birds, the flutter of wings, the snap of branches under animals' feet. And there, off a ways and to the left, my prey. I dropped down low, I had a fair distance to cover until I found them, but the need to stalk was strong. He was it, the thing I needed, the thing that made my insides burn again, though much more pleasantly. I knew what it would feel like when I covered him, my body hot against his, the wedge of his dick working itself inside me. I would howl and convulse, and it would go on and on and on... *You'll need more than one for that*, the voice said. I laughed, there was plenty to go around.

I wove through the trees like a shadow, the grey of my fur mottled and perfect for blending in on a silvery night. I looked like moon glanced foliage or bark on a tree, impossible to see. I shifted so that the breeze washed past me, bringing me the tantalising sent of the one I wanted, and washing mine away to taunt those who dared to follow. I crept through the forest on silent feet until I found him. I crouched down on the crest of a riverbank, watching him drink from the river, his white body stark against the darkness. There were reddish marks marring his fur, but he seemed unconcerned by them. His head pulled up from the water, smelling the wind and listening to the far-off howls. I opened my mouth in a wolfish smile and then began my slow descent. My steps were concealed by the sounds of him lapping, I dropped down into the undergrowth each time his green eyes flicked around, but he continued to drink. I coiled my legs under me as he stood in the small stream, panting hard to catch his breath, then I struck.

I leapt the distance between us, crashing into his side, forcing him on his belly in a growling scrabbling mess. I attacked fast, avoiding his razor sharp teeth and claws, and then snapped my fangs around his neck. It was as if I'd pushed a button. He lay half in, half out of the water, limp under my grip, and I remembered the taste of his blood. I wanted it, to close my jaws and rip out his throat, to take that blood into me, but I had other hungers that needed satisfying first. *Not in this form*, the voice said, *you'll need to shift back for this.* My eyes flicked around me as I held the male pinned, looking for signs of threats. It was hard to discern, my nose clogged with the delicious scent of blood and receptive male. I pulled back from his neck, planting a paw on his chest and then with a twist, I was in my other form again.

Instantly the world seemed quieter, duller. I looked around, trying to recapture the sensory carpet I had been able to discern while Tirian, but it was lost until I turned again. I could call it, that form, I realised now, at a moment's notice. We were the same coin and with a flip, you could get one side or the other.

"Jules." I looked down and saw my hand was planted on the smooth chest of Finn. He licked his lips as my eyes raked his body, taking in that he was hard and thick for me. That's what I needed, I felt a sharp hard twist of pleasure inside me as I felt how swollen and wet I was. My cunt dripped with need for him. He would slide in with ease, spreading me wide, just beyond that pinch of pain that settled into a hard, desperate bliss as he began to move. He watched me wide eyed as I placed one hand next to the other and started to lower myself down.

"Jules, no!" he said, and I snarled in response. How dare he stop me? He was there for my satisfaction, I had a need, and he was well-equipped to meet it. All he needed to do was sit there and enjoy the ride. "I need to get you ready. You've been lying in that bed for weeks, the water, and I'm...bigger. Let me make it good for you, Jules. You're going to want it hard and often tonight, and for a while after that, probably. I don't want you hurting any more, Jules. Please."

He will make it more pleasurable for you, the voice in my head said. Why did I need him to do that? I knew exactly what would please me, he just needed to get on board. My cunt would be a vice, squeezing the pleasure from him as I took mine. Why did he not submit to this?

"Jules," he murmured, shifting beneath me, my hands slipping to his shoulders as his lips grazed my body, glancing touches that made my skin come alive. When his mouth surrounded my nipple, I yipped as the demanding yet soft caress sent a wave of warmth through my body.

"Is this what you mean to do?" I gasped as he moved to lave the same attention on the other nipple.

"Mmm hmm..." he said, his teeth grazing my skin.

"Then let us get out of the water. I will permit this."

"There's a campsite about five minutes away. I didn't have a chance to do much, but there is a bed roll there. Better than fucking in the dirt."

"Take me there."

20

I followed hard on his heels, holding myself back from what felt natural, striding off in front of him and leading the way. I heard his pants come as he ran down the dirt track, but I had barely raised a sweat by the time we reached the campsite. A warm fire crackled within a pit, and there beside it was the promised bed roll. "Lie down," I said, ready now to satisfy this urge.

"Not quite yet," he said. He held up a hand when I started to growl, and then fell to his knees, a pleasing posture. He looked up at me and then moved into my body, burying his head into the hollow of my hipbone before turning and placing hard, wet kisses on the skin, moving down and down until...

"Uh!" I cried in surprise. My legs were closed, and yet his tongue managed to worm its way into the top of my slit, the wriggle flicking hard against my most tender spot. My thighs spread automatically, and I grabbed his head, forcing it in deeper. He groaned as he shifted his angle, licking up and down my seam. I yelped, it was not enough and too much all at the same time.

"God, I can't take this slow. Your scent is driving me mad," he said, and then buried his face in me in earnest. I was alerting all around me to our presence, but I no longer cared. I could take on a hundred, a thousand of them, such was my desire. Inside, my cunt clenched as his tongue worked its way lower, to that achingly empty place that was dying to be filled. "Lie down, I can get to more of you," he said, panting.

I laid down on the soft bedroll, and he was between my legs, pushing them wide in the next moment, a furious feeding thing. His tongue wiggled inside me, helping to abate the ache a little, but I needed something harder, faster. The pressure of his mouth and chin against my slit made me shift, jamming my body down harder, wanting, needing more. "You're close," he said, pulling back and then closing his lips around my clit.

I saw stars, my vision went white and then dissipated into a series of flashes as my pelvis tightened and ached in response to his sucking motions. It was coming, something huge. My whole pelvis began to shake, I couldn't relax, couldn't let this just happen. "Now Jules," he murmured against my flesh and then jammed three hard fingers inside me.

"Uh... oh fuck!" I screamed. My body snapped tight around the intruders, then spasmed in wave after wave of overwhelming pleasure. I felt cramps in my tailbone and up my spine, but that seemed to only make it more intense. I had barely finished when the fingers were pulled from me, and he shifted.

"You'll want to be on top," he said, rolling me over so I straddled him. He produced a small tube of clear liquid, and I watched open mouthed as he worked it onto his dick. "You can control how fast or how deep you want to go."

Yeah, I could. I looked at him with slitted eyes, he was able to provoke great pleasure, but he seemed to be assuming that gave him more authority than it did. Nonetheless, there was a spot in me that needed to be stroked, and his fingers had been unable to reach, no matter how brutal. I nodded and moved over his cock, and then worked it up inside me. "Oh yeah..." I hissed. This was the real thing, what I really needed. The lips and fingers were nice, but only a prelude to this. An incredible sense of rightness settled over me, pleasure flickering up and down my spine as I felt the stretch. It was hard work, he wasn't lying, he was big. A little bigger than I needed, but I couldn't find the desire to stop. Instead, there was a terrible excitement, like this was some kind of cliff and I was just about to jump off of it.

"Ah!" I hissed as I felt a wrench of pain. I did not want pain, pain was the world I had spent all too long living in. His hand snaked up and his thumb began to circle my clit, which turned the pain into something else altogether. I worked myself up and down, up and down, letting my body grow used to the intrusion, finding myself going lower and lower.

"God, Jules, I've wanted this for so long," he hissed. I smiled, of course he had. Then, I began to move in earnest.

It was like running as a Tirian, the drawn out, loping movements, but this wrung quite a different feeling. Each downward jerk of my hips forced his cock hard against my aching spot, his dick dragging against it, almost painfully, but making me feel most tremendously full. I felt an incredible swelling deep inside, as if each stroke forced more and more blood into my tender flesh, until I was bloated with pleasure. It sat oddly for a moment, how soft and swollen I felt, how hard he felt pushing into it.

"Jules..." he tried to grab my hips and slow me, afraid he wouldn't be able to keep up, but I shook my head. He was there for my pleasure, I would take what I wanted from him, and if he failed me, I would not choose him to help me with it again. My eyes bore into his, and he seemed to realise this, his hands clawing at the bedroll, a vein popping out on his forehead as he strove to hold back. I smiled lazily, slowing my strokes somewhat, just revelling in the feeling of him in me. "Jules...please!"

"You don't need to draw it out, princess." My head whipped around, and I saw Slade appear, hard and naked from the darkness. "We're all here for you." He dropped down to his knees behind me, and his big hands covered my breasts, his calluses rasping over my nipples as his lips trailed down my neck. "Let him come, and then move on to one of us. We'll keep coming until you can't." His hand was a light pressure on my hip, yet somehow my pace picked up. I felt

Finn buck beneath me, forcing himself up higher, probably too high, but I couldn't seem to stop. "How about a bit of this?" Slade said as one hand slipped south and then flicked at my clit.

I no longer knew who was fucking who, everyone was moving, and the beautiful ache inside me was becoming bigger and bigger, expanding until there was nothing left but this horrible hunger. I needed more. Another hand plucked at my nipple and someone's mouth fastened itself to mine, their tongue parting my lips, and I welcomed them into my throat. "So close..." someone gasped, and I knew what they meant. The fingers on my clit closed around my nub hard, almost pinching, then pulling the tender spot away from my body.

"Oh fuck..." I cried, and then it happened. A long, languorous trickle of pleasure radiated out from my cunt, which then erupted like an earthquake of ecstasy, the aftershocks felt all up my spine and down my legs. I pulled the cum from his body, my cunt like plucking fingers surrounding his hardness, forcing the tremulous spurts to burst within me. "Ah!"

"Come on, princess, let us take care of you while Finn has a rest." I was plucked from my position and deposited into the arms of another man. I looked up to see Brandon. His eyes were wide, flicking down my body to the wet spill between my legs and then held my gaze.

"We haven't...yet," he said, "I thought I'd have some time to work up to it with you, but..."

"I want you," I said, smelling his rich smoky smell. His breath seemed to catch in his chest. "I want you to be here. I want you in me."

"Well, how about you come here and see what that mouth can do, while Brandon shows you what his does." I turned to Slade who knelt before me, insolent expression plastered on his face. His smile grew wider as my gaze narrowed.

"I could gut you where you sit," I snarled.

"Yeah? But you'll have a lot more fun if you don't. You want fucking, not fighting. You got that already, if the stink of blood on you means anything. I'll give you what you want, you know that, princess. Any hole, any way, I'm your guy. As long as you can tell me how you want it. I'll give you everything I have, but right now, I'm just asking for a little bit back. You've had a lot of meat in your mouth tonight, just take mine. Though, without the teeth if you can."

I pulled myself from Brandon's arms and stalked over to the smart mouthed man on all fours, and then grabbed his head and yanked him to me for a kiss. It was hard, and our lips stung as his tongue tangled with mine. I yanked myself away as the ache began to start again. I shoved Slade down onto the ground and then ran my nose down his body, smelling the sweat and the blood and the desire there. He had a gash across his hip, not too deep, and I trailed my tongue over it, tasting the residue. "That's...uh...not the meat I was thinking," Slade said.

"Shut up or I'll fuck the other one."

"Never really got off on pain before, but unnh..." he said as I dug my useless blunt teeth into him "But maybe moon madness is good for something. Now how about this?"

He shoved my head lower, but I stopped, easily holding off his straining muscles. He began to arch his hips up, trying to get the tip of his erection to graze my lips, but I pushed him back down with a finger. "Oh, god, princess! I would just about do anything right now if you'd... ahhh!" I slid his length into my mouth, swirling my tongue across his sensitive skin as he went deeper. "Oh fuck!" he yelped as I tilted my throat, and he went in further. I swallowed, the hard muscles closing around him. He tried to jerk free, "Too much, I'll..."

"Don't let him come too soon," Brandon said, trailing long fingers up the backs of my thighs. I pulled back from my ministrations, leaving Slade gasping, and looked over my shoulder. Brandon just smiled, intently watching his fingers slide over my flesh, gentle enough to make me want it harder, almost tickling. His hands flattened over my buttocks, running his thumbs down the edges of my cunt without actually touching anything that begged to be stroked. Finally, he met my gaze. "If you go slowly, he can come in your mouth right at the moment you come with me inside you." My eyes swivelled back to Slade, and I looked down at his twitching dick.

"Don't come before I tell you to," I said.

"Well, don't fucking deep throat me. Do it all you like after this night, just not now."

"I'll do as I please," I said and then ran my tongue up his length. Brandon's hands began to move again. His fingers rewrote my flesh in a crisscross of pleasurable strokes, gentle and not too demanding in themselves, but the lack of contact with my throbbing core only made me pay more attention to what he was doing. Over time, a fingertip ran up the inside of my thigh, moving higher and higher, only to veer off and land on my butt, which had me cursing. My clit throbbed, even though he wouldn't touch the bloody thing. It was amping up my pleasure, even as I fought the urge to snap orders at him. I bent my head and applied myself to my other task.

Wanting to savour his flesh now, I ran my tongue up and down Slade's length, swirling and sweeping, much like Brandon's strokes. He bucked his hips, trying to force it back into my mouth, but I pulled away, not resuming until he was flat against the ground. "I'm starting to wish I took the other end...oh!" I wrapped my lips around the head of his dick and sucked, hard. "Oh...oh...oh..." he began to pant. A sharp pinch on my butt cheek had me pulling away with a snarl.

"Don't let him come too soon. All you have to do is keep him worked up until I've finished working you up."

"Get on with it then!" I said.

"Why?" Brandon said with a smile. "This gets you hotter, will make you come harder. When I touch your clit..." My hips jerked as one of his fingers lightly grazed it. "...You feel it much more intensely. Do that to him, make him desperate, make him beg for it. You're the queen, bring him to his knees."

His words felt right, so I turned back to Slade and saw his eyes go wide as I dropped my head down to his groin. Brandon began his light trailing caresses again, this time up my inner thigh. He started at my knees and then drew long circles from there to my lower thigh, then again slightly higher, and again. My cunt clenched in anticipation of those fingers splitting me open and touching me where I wanted to be touched, but he stopped mid upward stroke and said, "Touch him." Growling at being ordered around, I moved because I wanted those fingers in me, now. I stuck out my tongue and heard Slade hiss as I trailed the point of it up the throbbing vein that ran the length of his dick. His sound of pained pleasure was music to my ears. I traced the skin under the head, flicked it over the opening, collecting the weeping salty fluid there.

"Princess, please..." Slade gasped, and I smiled.

"That's right," Brandon said, and I was rewarded by his hand trailing along my seam. I laid my head against Slade's hip and groaned. My skin had come alive, the hardness of his fingers against my slipperiness caught my whole attention. My legs widened instinctively, wanting to open myself to him, catch them in the mouth of my cunt and have them...

"You stop, I stop," Brandon said.

"It occurs to me that I don't necessarily need you at all," I said, getting up on my knees and turning to him. I shifted until my body was over Slade's, and then spread my legs and moved until my cunt was above his hard dick. His hands wrapped around my hips, and he held me as I worked the head against me, slowly shifting so he began to move inside. I closed my eyes, half in pleasure, half to mock my disobedient servant. "Oh, yes..." I gasped and rolled my head. I'd intended it to be more play, but the angle, the position was shoving against that place that always seemed to ache deep in me. "Mmm..." I arched my back, which only increased my pleasure. I snapped my hips and Slade's fingers dug even deeper. I felt the tremors in his broad forearms. Dimly, I heard Brandon shuffle, but I focused on the task at hand, much more pleasurable, and then I gasped, eyes open wide. Brandon had moved between my legs and buried his head into my cunt. He looked up at me, frozen in motion, and then his lips closed around my clit.

"You're gonna have to stay still for this, princess," Slade grated, lowering my hips and then pushing himself up into me. My eyes rolled closed as the two of them got to work. The contrast of the silky soft caresses of Brandon's tongue and his suckling mouth, and Slade's rigid thrusts sent me limp, and I fought to keep myself upright. I felt at sea, tossed around by forces larger than me, my pleasure pulled from me rather than as a result of my own actions. This rankled me a little, but the dual sensations... I chose to surrender for this moment, they worked to maximise my pleasure. I could knock them back into line afterwards. Brandon's lips became more demanding, sucking hard on my most sensitive spot, almost pulling the flesh from my bone and wringing intense sensations this side of pain and pleasure. The muscles in me grew tight and tense.

"Get her there," Slade snapped. "Can't...much longer." Brandon's mouth grew hungry, and Slade shifted his angle slightly and... *Oh, fuck!* That aching spot deep inside swelled in response, plumping out under the hard thrusting attention. I felt the prickle of orgasm, little pinpricks of pleasure all starting to fire at once, and then... Slade rolled into me as my body twitched and pulsed, cutting through my response until he finally slammed in as far as he could go, jerking and spasming against me.

I slid off Slade, legs trembling, and then got on my hands and knees. "More."

"On it," Brandon said. No more teasing touches, he rubbed his cock against my entrance and then slammed into me. Fuck yes! My body, still sensitised by orgasm, was ready to pick right up where we were. His pace was punishing. Instead of the slow build to orgasm, I'd almost stayed where I was, in the delicious state of pleasure just before you come, his hard thrusts keeping me there and pushing me higher. I spread my legs slightly, letting him shove in deeper so he bottomed out, making me feel completely full. His thumb swept along my folds as he fucked me, and I didn't know why until his hand snaked down my spine, to my butt. His finger was slippery as it swiped across my arse, gentle at first, and then insistent. I groaned as he pushed his thumb in, and then it all came undone.

I didn't know what he was doing, what I was doing, as the pleasure threatened to overwhelm me. It felt almost like an out of body experience, pure joyous exhilaration. The world, everything, was alright, a sweet, sharp place of endless ecstasy. I dimly felt myself coming and coming, like each orgasm provoked the next. I was helpless, swept along by the waves, completely abandoning myself to it. It took me a long time to come back to myself, but when I did, I found I was laid down in a cocoon of bodies, panting.

"You OK, princess?" Slade croaked. I couldn't piece together the meaning of the words, let alone a response. It was the sensation that I noticed most, the feeling of all of this hard flesh around me. My eyelids felt like lead, and the ache in my body had finally been sated, so I let myself go loose and fell asleep.

21

I woke up the next morning somewhere quite different. I was in a bed, a very big bed, inside a plain white room, the sun streaming in through a large window with a view of the forest. I was also not alone. I looked up to see three bodies curled around mine. As I shifted, I felt a twinge of pain, not sharp, more like a strained muscle or something. I glanced at my hands and then under the sheet, noticing I no longer had the stitches or wounds, not even scars to mark where they were. I was also clean, which seemed strange after last night's hijinks. Uh! I felt a spasm of pleasure down low, reminding me just how much fun I had with that. I rolled my eyes, I had surely had enough sex to last me for years to come. I felt the slickness between my thighs as I shifted, trying to climb free to my feet. Apparently not.

I headed into the kitchen after going to the bathroom, and looked around. The place smelled of dust and a slight dankness, as if it had been locked up for some time. There was a box sitting on the counter with a jug and some coffee, thank god. I looked out the window after putting on the kettle, and that's when I saw them. I moved to the door, unable to believe what I saw.

Rows of men sat or stood on the grass outside the house, watching. A ripple went through the crowd as I emerged outside, spines straightening, men getting to their feet. I felt the tension in the air multiply exponentially. My head snapped to the right when I saw one of them had camped out on the porch, his face a mask of blood. He winced when he got up, only managing an awkward hopping limp. His body was torn, that's the only word for it, I saw furrows over much of it, even over his scalp. Most of his hair was a matted bloody mass, but a few blond strands fluttered free, almost in mockery of his state. My hand jerked to my mouth. "Shaun?" He nodded slowly, each movement costing him.

"I need to shift."

"You're asking me permission? Of course, do that. Oh my god!" I watched his transformation, painfully slow. At times, it looked like his body was fighting against it, wanting to stay human. Finally, he collapsed and turned into a grey Tirian, whining mournfully, then came to lay himself at my feet. I looked back at the crowd, saw some of the men were unfamiliar, older, and thought back to what Brandon had said about the bonds between packs breaking down when affection ends. Is that where they had come from? Their wives' beds?

"What do you want?" I snapped. They just watched me with flat staring eyes, knowing what I did, that they wanted what the guys inside had. I looked them over for a moment and felt a pang of fear. Shaun had obviously stood guard last night and held them off, but how was it possible? He was only one, and they were many. "I don't want you! Any of you!" *Liar*, the voice in my head said. Helpfully, my brain supplied me a blow by blow memory of my fight with the horde of them. Part of my exultation was in the carnage I had wrought, seeing the scratches and gouges on their flesh as a celebration of this, and wondered what a more sensual experience with the group of them might be like. I grimaced, I'd just fucked two guys I'd not slept with before and had my first threesome, foursome, whatever. Taking on thirty odd blokes, irrespective of the fact I was now a shapeshifting wolf monster, was a bit beyond the pale for me. *What had happened to the ones I'd slashed and gutted?* I thought in belated alarm. My eyes searched for signs of old wounds that would let me know, but I couldn't see any. "If I choose anyone else for my bed, I'll let you know. But you stay here, you automatically get nothing. Now, get off of my property!" My voice held the echoey growl of my Tirian form, and the effect was instantaneous. As one, the men turned, some on two feet, some shifting to four. Shaun came over and rubbed his great head against my shoulder, and I dug my fingers into his fur. I was amazed that despite its strange smoky appearance, it still felt like raw silk. When I looked back into the house, I saw Finn in the kitchen, watching me with a small smile on his face.

I was still frowning as I went back into the kitchen to grab a coffee, Finn putting one in my hands and then surrounding me, his chest against my back, his arms on either side of me grabbing the bench top. I should have felt crowded, overwhelmed, but as his scent settled around me, the feel of his skin against mine, something inside me loosened and relaxed. "I just told a bunch of guys off, naked," I said, belatedly realising that clothes are usually a requirement for social interactions.

"Yeah, you did," he said, burying his head in my neck and trailing light kisses there.

"Shaun got fucked up last night. Seriously, he looks like he's been ten rounds with a meat grinder."

Finn pulled back a little, sweeping my hair back into place and took the hand without the mug in it. "He stood guard. Usually we would post more guys, but we didn't have more, and everyone was a bit...distracted. He did that voluntarily, with honour. He was worried because of the way the two of you had left things that coming to your bed last night would be a presumption. He was trying to prove his worth to you, Jules." I looked over at the huge animal who was curled up on the bare dining room floor.

"And if he hadn't?" I asked.

"No man here is as strong as you are now, not even several men together would be enough to overpower you. But a large group of guys," my brain flashed to the memory of Macca and his pre-made pack, "that can be harder to fight off. Now we know you can shift, we'll start training you. Aaron has a program worked out for you. Once the honeymoon is over, you'll start training every day."

"The honeymoon? Are we married? Is this arrangement permanent?"

"No, they call it that because everyone is..." He pushed his hands between my thighs and speared his fingers upwards, making me groan. "...very receptive."

Which was how I ended up bent over the kitchen bench as he went to work. He didn't draw out the foreplay like Brandon did. Instead, his almost rough caresses provoked a different kind of pleasure. I seemed to slip between the hard thickness of his fingers, a dizzying flurry of sensations rippling through my body as he moved more urgently, from sliding two fingers in a V along the sides of my clit, to shoving them inside me and spreading me wide for him. "Fuck me..." I growled, feeling myself drip in anticipation.

"But I--"

"Do it!" In the cold, hard light of day, my pushy Tirian behaviour seemed really weird, especially as I remembered how overbearing I had been last night. I couldn't seem to help it, it just slipped out, like getting snappy when sleep deprived. I heard a rustling and then all of a sudden, he was pushing in. "Oh, fuck..." I gasped, going up on tip toes, almost as much to move away from him, as to make it easier for him to get inside me.

"There," he panted once he was in deep, waiting, for me to move? For my body to adjust? I didn't know. His hand snuck around, then started to circle my clit, and I shifted, grinding down on him.

"Hard...fast..." I said, the cold stone of the bench top pinching at my nipples as they caught on the surface.

"But..."

"Not going to last long," I said, feeling a deep pressure build. Like many women, orgasm could be easy as falling off a log, or a far-off planet I was never going to visit, but was a process made a whole lot easier by my transformation. I could feel it now, a low down burn that I could reach for at any time. I could have multiple, hard quick ones, or put it off and put it off for one big payoff that would bring me to my knees. That knowledge, that surety, was enough to make me relax into his strokes. I hadn't realised how much anxiety about being able to get there had been ticking away in the back of my mind. I stretched out, my spine a flat line, and spread my legs further. "Harder," I growled.

I was so going to regret this later. He was too deep, too fast, but right now the stretching sensation that should have hurt just sent indescribable waves of pleasure through my body. His fingers dug into my hip, forcing me hard against him, and I closed my eyes. Something soft brushed against my lips, and my eyes snapped open to see Shaun in human form and healed, perched on top of kitchen bench with a question in his eyes. I drew him closer, my tongue burying itself in his mouth when our lips touched. His hands dropped to my breasts, circling and tugging at my nipples.

"Oh fuck!" Finn said, slamming himself hard inside me. I could feel every pulse of his cum. I moved automatically onto the bench top, crawling up beside Shaun, but he slipped off. I frowned, but he spread my legs wide and moved in, mouth open.

"Join me," I said before he made his first swipe. He paused, and then waited for me to reposition myself before climbing on top. His head ducked down to give my clit a few quick licks, so I wrapped my hand around the root of his cock and sucked the crown between my lips. His muffled moan sent a shiver of vibrations into my clit, which felt delicious. I responded by arching my neck and letting him push deeper down my throat. My hand crept up and trailed along the inside of his thigh before cupping his balls. They were high and tight, he wasn't going to last long, so I let my tongue wriggle along his length as he slid in and out. Right now, I was in a holding pattern, his mouth was a lovely sucking pressure, working me higher and higher, but I needed something more. As if thinking it made it so, long hard fingers pushed into me making me groan around Shaun's cock. His hips jerked at the sensation, forcing himself down a little further than I was used to.

"What a sight to wake up to. Turn her over, Shaun so we can all play."

I nearly cried out as the lips on my clit detached, but in a blur of motion, I was repositioned into the same position, except now I was the 9 rather than the 6. The hands in the room seemed to have multiplied. Fingers pushed in, circled my breasts, plucked at my nipples, ran over my butt.

"Pass me the lube," one of them said, and then a now familiar well greased pressure began to push against my arse. I nearly choked when it popped inside, my mouth going wide, and Shaun pushing his cock in deeper. The same feeling, of being carried along, swept away by the pleasure, wrung from my body. It was too much, a cacophony of sensation from so many sites, they were beginning to blend together into one overwhelming wave. The fingers in my cunt curled up sharply just as Shaun began to thrust, fast and erratic down my throat. I groaned as the orgasm finally broke, pulling me everywhere at once. Strangely, the sensation of Shaun's cum spasmodically spurting just added to it.

When reality reasserted itself, I found there were four naked guys around me, two looking drained and tired, the other two with lazy smiles. "How are you feeling?" Brandon asked, running a hand through my hair as Shaun wriggled free and climbed down off the bench top.

"Good. No, that's a manifestly inadequate word. I was dying, wasn't I?" He nodded. "I don't know how to put it into words, it's kind of overwhelmed, drained, hot, satisfied. Actually, that's probably the best word for it, satisfied." He, all of them, smiled at that. Apparently, that was the goal this morning. I jumped down next to Slade and Brandon and looked down. "But you aren't."

"Don't worry too much about that," Slade said, pulling me closer into a hug that Brandon quickly joined. "We are masters of rubbing a quick one out if needed. The early birds get the worm, so to speak."

"So you don't want me to..." I said, circling Slade's dick with one hand and Brandon's with the other. They both shivered in response.

"But if you're done..." Brandon said breathily.

"Yeah, but you're not. I get I was all 'do this, then that' last night, but I'm not about to turn into a dick just because I can grow fur at will," I said. "Let's go into the bedroom where small children are less likely to see what we're up to."

"No kids near the honeymoon house," Slade said, slinging an arm around my shoulders as we walked. "You guys coming?"

"I'm going to make some breakfast. I imagine everyone will be starving," Finn said.

My stomach growled in a Pavlovian response.

"Be right back," I said. "What about you, Shaun?" He seemed to be the least comfortable with the group. His eyes flicking to the other men, as if worried about their reaction.

"I'd love to, but I don't have another one in me for a bit, sorry," he said.

I SAW JUST how big the bed was when we re-entered the bedroom, it looked like several king size mattresses stitched together. Shaun reclined on one side, watching my hands run up and down the men's bodies.

"I think this is the first time I've really seen you," I said, suddenly feeling a little shy in front of Brandon. He was the guy recommending romance novels and talking about feminism to me a few days ago. He felt like something else altogether now. I shoved him back so he landed on the bed, looking a bit wide-eyed as Slade flopped down next to him. "Now, what was it you were doing to me last night?" I said, running my fingers gently up and down his inner thighs. He arched slightly under my ministrations, trying to direct my hands to where he wanted them, but I didn't play along. Instead I turned to Slade. Smirking at Brandon, I grabbed Slade's dick and licked it slowly like a lollipop.

"Oh, fuck..." one of them groaned, I wasn't sure who. I wrapped my fingers firmly around the base and licked from there to head, swirled my tongue and then back down again in few slithering movements. "Uh..!" it must have been Slade. His hips started to move, thrusting up desperately as I sucked his knob, trying to force it deeper into my mouth. "C'mon, honey, you want breakfast, and you've still got to do Brandon," Slade said.

"If you're going to complain," I said, releasing my hold. I smiled at Slade's hiss of frustration, and then shifted over to Brandon. He looked down the length of his body, arms propped up on his elbows as he watched me draw closer. This was the first time I'd seen him up close and personal; I hadn't been in the right frame of mind yesterday. He was long, longer than most of the guys, but not as thick and rigid, veins standing out proudly. I placed a careful kiss on his hipbone, prominent against his olive skin, slowly, slowly trailing my lips down, only to pull away at the last minute.

"For the love of all that's holy, I'll never tease you again if you... unh!"

"Mmmm..." I purred as I took him in my mouth, almost smiling around his length as his hips bucked at the vibrations.

"Gods, Jules..." he gasped as I stopped stuffing about, taking him deep and sucking hard. I jerked my head up and down his dick, feeling the involuntary twitches and shifts of his muscles as I pushed him higher. "Not gonna... Gonna come if...."

I rolled away from him as his gasps grew strained, chuckling at Brandon's howls of frustration, then turned to Slade. He watched me with slitted eyes, but his dick was still straining hard. "You little bitch," he said rolling to his knees. He grabbed my hair at the base and pulled me closer, trying to shove his cock past my lips, but I refused to open. He let go finally in frustration, he was beginning to learn. As a reward, I slowly swallowed his dick down and then began to move. Perhaps learning a lesson from Brandon, Slade stayed quiet, only the steady rasp of his breath giving his growing arousal away. He started to get my rhythm, trying to join in and thrust his dick inside my mouth, but I merely slowed my movements and drew back until I sucked on only the tip. "Jules, please!"

I pulled back and listened with a smirk for Slade's cursing to slow down. When he was quiet, I gestured to both of them to come closer. Their brows creased and they looked furtively at each other as they shuffled a little closer, then a bit closer again until finally, their twitching dicks almost touched. I grabbed each of them and took the almost out of the equation, ignoring their spluttered complaints and shutting them up with a long lick along the gap between them. My tongue was sandwiched between their erections, forced flat to caress the both of them. When I got to the heads, I pulled back and began to lick a figure eight that wound around each man's knob. I looked up to see if their protests were really in earnest, then opened and wide and did my best to take as much of them as I could inside.

"Unh!" their grunts were synchronised, both seeming lost in the sensations. It was uncomfortable and ungainly, I was sure my teeth were scraping them up something fierce, but neither seemed to care. I felt the slight shifts of their hips, the muscles of their buttocks taut as they struggled to stay stationary. I wrapped my hands firmly around the base of each guy, jacking them off as I sucked.

"Fuck Jules...."

"Gonna come," Brandon said. "Please...."

"Mmmm..." I hummed, and increased my pace.

"Oh fuck!" Brandon said and jerked forward, unable to stop his hips from snapping spasmodically in time with the gouts of cum shooting from him. Then he gasped and pulled away, too sensitive.

"So close..." Slade said, hands reaching for my hair. He kept his fingers light, just slowly, aimlessly caressing, all of his attention on his hard cock. "Jules!" he finally cried and shoved himself deep into my mouth, fingers like iron as cum shot down my throat.

"So," Finn said, appearing at the door as we all lay there gasping, "who wants breakfast?"

22

Kelly arrived halfway through the meal. Thankfully, I'd taken the time to pull on a robe, though the guys were still more or less in a state of undress. Finn's loose cotton shorts being the most formal dress, and then down to Shaun with a towel slung around his hips. She stopped at the door, hand raised almost tentatively to knock, looking through the glass into the dining room, her brows shifting, as if she couldn't believe her eyes. "You look well," she said finally, having come inside.

"A lot better than I did, right?" I said.

"Thankfully, yes. I knew you were one of us, that you'd be fine when you changed... Doc Hobbes will be very pleased to see you up and about. She'll be by soon to give you a check-up."

"Sit down," I said, indicating a spare seat. The tone of command in my voice was probably not an appropriate one, particularly as she was the leader of the community. No one said anything, but everyone noticed it. I could tell as the guys eyes flicked sideways and back to their plates, hands curling around cutlery. "Would you like some breakfast? Finn's made quite the spread."

"No," she said, not making eye contact, though she made the

effort to smile, "I had breakfast earlier. You must have a lot of questions."

"Not right now," I said, going back to cutting up my bacon. "I'm Tirian, and so are all of you. You live this side of the gateway because your ancestors came over a long time ago, and now you protect the gate from the dark wolves, like the one that bit me."

"How did...?" Kelly's eyes snapped up to Finn's. "Did you...?"

"No, they didn't have a chance to tell me much," I said. "I had visions while the doctor kept me sedated. I saw a lot of what I was, of our history."

"That's remarkable. I've never heard of anyone doing that before."

"Maybe it was a side effect of the black wolf's venom. Where's my dog?"

"Buddy is with Doc, she's been looking after him while you've been ill. I'll have someone bring him up once we see you've stabilised. This place is called the honeymoon suite, any new females who have come into their power take up residence here until she makes a decision about her pack. It gives her the privacy and space to indulge her desires, work out what will be best for her."

"My pack?" I said, looking around at the guys. "I don't have to make a decision, I'm not relinquishing any of them. As long as they want to, they stay here."

Shaun's face transformed, his smile so bright and intense I almost had to blink. I'd never seen anyone look so happy at something I'd said before. I caught his eyes, looking into the intense blues, momentarily stunned by his reaction.

"Now, Jules..." Finn said.

My head whipped around to face him. I'd had no more than a few seconds to enjoy it, and someone was talking to me in that 'be reasonable' tone. "Jules, we all want to be here..." he said, and one by one, every guy made it very clear that he spoke for them, "but a pack takes more than just desire. We'll be together for many, many years. Children may well come. You are making decisions about the future fathers of your children."

"Don't talk to me like that," I said in a low growl. "Don't 'manage' me, don't give me the 'see reason' talk..."

"The feelings after the first change are very, very intense," Kelly said. "I think your wolf is quite dominant, she's rubbing off on you, which is a good thing. We need more strong women in the community, but Jules, he's right..."

"Maybe he is, maybe he isn't. That's not what I'm disputing. I don't like being talked down to."

Kelly sighed and then rubbed her hand over her face, suddenly looking very, very tired. "Whatever decision you make, we will respect. As long as all of the members of the pack are willing, I won't stand in your way. But if you want my advice, and you probably don't, it is talk to the other women here. I'll send some of the others, Brandon's mum would be a good one, Carissa is another. They are also very strong, are high up in the hierarchy. If you are willing, they will tell you their stories about their packs, how they came to their current arrangement. You don't have to take anything they say on, but the perspectives of those who have gone before you can be useful, sometimes."

I felt restive, like I wanted to get up and pace, back and forward, watching this woman, this interloper who had come into my house. I wanted my dog and my stuff and my car with me, right now. I didn't want to listen, it was all very clear to me. This was good, the shining look of hope on Shaun's face was confirmation of that. I was where I needed to be, with who I needed to be with, I knew that with absolute certainty.

Which alerted me to the fact something might be wrong. I never felt this sure about anything. Decisions I made always were accompanied with a bit of healthy anxiety. Was this right? Would I be OK with the consequences? It was tempting, as I looked down that table at the smorgasbord of man flesh, equally on offer as the food, to just assume this was some kind of sexual nirvana I'd been moving towards all my life, but the old me shouldered her way forward for a moment and expressed concern. I didn't even know what a pack bond was, so how could I be ready to make one? I didn't really know these guys, not as people. I felt almost a tussle inside myself, hot possessive thoughts that eyed the gap between Kelly's hand and Finn's on the table with great interest, along with a cooler, more sensible voice of reason that recognised it was none of my business at this point who else Finn spent time with. I forced myself to nod, finding it difficult to get my neck to bend and I gritted out, "Set it up. Sounds like a good idea."

"I hope it is, truly," Kelly said. "You won't have many women come by here for a while. Tempers will be short as you adjust, but if you need any of us, please reach out. I'll go soon, but there's one more thing I must address with you. The other men, usually with a woman born on the reservation, they have a window of time to petition you for room in your pack. Just talking..." she said, watching as everyone began to stiffen and shift in their seats. "You are not in any way obligated to take any of them up on their offer, but it just helps settle the tensions with the single men if they feel they at least have a chance."

Slade, who sat next to me, dug his fingers so hard into the table he left grooves in the wood, and Shaun's eyes were wide with pain. When I looked at Brandon, he forced a smile and said, "You should do it. You have to know, if there's anyone out there you'd be more compatible with."

Finn nodded, "We'll be here, until you don't want us to be. You can't jeopardise anything with us by listening. We can even be present when they petition, if you like. Whatever you need, Jules, we're here."

"OK," I said, my words sounded weird and hollow inside my head, "set it up."

"Let's leave it for a few days, let tempers cool a bit, and then we'll do some short sessions."

"Fine" I said, "and what about work for me? For the guys?"

"Everyone involved is on indefinite leave until things are settled. Tensions are high. We've had to quell more scuffles than I can count since you shifted. I'll be in touch."

23

"This is a bad idea," I said as we pulled up at the meeting hall. My body was at war over the prospect of being introduced to other guys and deciding if I should add any more of them to my pack. My stomach churned, leaving me feeling slightly nauseous, and I felt the tension start to dig in at my temples. I rubbed my head, trying to ease the pain, which made the apparently scratchy lace of my bra rasp against my nipples, hardening them to points, making them throb with both the sensation now and the memory of what the boys were doing this morning.

"What's a bad idea?" Finn asked, sitting next to me. He placed his arm around my shoulders when he saw my expression and drew me closer. I fought back the urge to groan, drowning in the cloud of musky male scent, the smell of his desire, of the more earthy smell of our coming together this morning, not quite eradicated in the shower afterwards. My cunt ached from all the attention it'd been getting, yet I felt hollow inside, wanting more.

"Going to meet the guys," Slade said as he turned off the car and moved to face us. "Lemme guess, princess, you're nervous and horny."

"How do you…?" I said.

"I can smell the fear. It's a strong scent, kinda repellent, but a turn on at the same time. And horny?" He smiled and reached over, cupping my breast, his smile widening as I arched into his hand, whimpering slightly as his fingers closed over my nipple. "You're in heat, baby. Right now, it's your default state."

I shifted in my seat, placing my hands on the centre console and moving forward, forcing Slade back, so my lips grazed his. I wore only the lightest of cotton clothing, a pair of shorts I'd usually use as pyjamas and a short singlet. I couldn't bear to have anything heavier on my overly sensitised skin, but I knew it left the other half of my body only barely covered on Finn's end. His hand went to my thigh as if on automatic. "Let's blow this off, then I'll blow you. We can fuck and fuck..." I said.

"That's a given, no matter what happens today, baby," Slade said, pushing my shirt up and the cups of my bra down. I yelped when the calluses on his hands rasped against my bare skin. "Though I will hold you to that offer of a head job." I barely heard what he said, his clever plucking fingers had my full attention, right up until Finn's hands slipped under my shorts and into my dripping cunt. "Get her really worked up," Slade said over my shoulder.

"I know, this isn't my first rodeo," Finn said, though his voice cracked on the words. When I reached for Slade's cock, he pushed my hands back, holding them so they stayed on the console, then leaning forward to shove his tongue into my mouth. Sometimes they were like this, refusing to let me please them, worrying about coming before we got to fuck. My Tirian-self accepted this as her due, though I began to feel like I was devolving into a self-centred bitch, only caring about my own pleasure. That was a hard concept to keep in my mind as Finn's fingers shoved into me, driving the curl of arousal inside me tighter and tighter, and Slade bent his head to suckle on my sensitive nipples...until they both pulled away.

"What the fuck?" I said, frustration pushing the haze of lust partially to one side.

"That stopped the anxiety for a moment, got you out of your head," Slade said. Finn wrapped his arms around my waist and pulled me back onto his lap, so I perched on the solid lump of his erection. His hands cupped my arse, then reached back to spread my thighs wide.

"What do you feel when I show him your dripping cunt?" Finn murmured in my ear.

"Like I want him to bury his dick or his face in it."

"Then when someone walks in that door that makes you feel the same way, you know you've got a possible contender."

WE WALKED into the meeting hall, them smirking and me grumbling. I was painfully aware of the liquid slip of my overheated folds as we did so, which was apparently the point. They opened a door with a bunch of keys and ushered me into a small room that contained several chairs and a bed.

"What's that for?" I asked, but I already knew. "Test drives?"

"If you feel the pull that hard, then yes," Finn said, taking a seat on it, Slade sitting next to him. I looked at the two of them and my mouth went dry. It shouldn't, we'd fucked in every position possible in the last few days, but all I could think about was them on the bed, naked, me between them and... There was a sharp knock on the internal door in front of me.

"Take a seat, princess, you're going to be here for a while," Slade said. I paused, looking from him to the door. Who's behind it? Have I already met them? How will I know if I want them to be part of the pack? I felt like my ability to discriminate had fallen to the wayside. I never really chose any of the guys, just fell into a sexual relationship with them. Is there anything more to it? They seem to be hoping so, though I have no way of knowing as we rarely talk. There's always someone hard, and I'm always ready.

Slade chuckled when I picked the large wingback chair, covered in a plush blue velvet, then groaned when I hooked a leg over one of the arms. I instantly felt the stretch as I did so, my clit felt like it was popping up and taking notice. I would never in a million years have sat like this before the change, especially in front of strangers, but I wriggled in the seat, the tension in my groin starting to throb in a pleasurable way. "You're going to drive them insane," he said, almost gloating, "smelling like that."

"And us too," Finn growled. "Maybe we can cut the session short today. Say she's tired or something."

"Not gonna work. They know how bitches turn out in their first season. She could screw every man in that waiting room, and she'd still be ready for more."

"Stop putting ideas in my head," I snapped. The person on the other side knocked again. "Enter!" I said.

A well-built guy with wavy brown hair opened the door, freezing in the doorway, eyes dropping down to my crotch. He licked his lips, trying to look up to meet mine, but failing. Slowly, as if pushed down by an inexorable hand, he dropped to his knees before me. "I want to be considered for a place in your pack. Please." His eyes finally flicked upwards, the irises sporting a bright green sheen. "Please consider me."

I looked over my shoulder at Finn, who had appeared at my back, his hands resting on my shoulders. I moved on my chair, trying to push them lower onto the aching tips of my nipples, but his fingers dug into my skin, forcing me to stay where I was. The guy crawled towards me, something the Tirian inside me liked very much. I watched him moving very slowly through slitted eyes. "He's petitioning you," Finn prompted, trying to force me to think through the haze of lust. "What do you feel?"

I jerked my legs down, snapping my thighs shut, the man groaning in response. I looked over my shoulder and said, "The same as I always do, like I want him to shove his dick or his fingers in me or eat me."

"Yess..." the petitioner hissed, drawing a little closer.

"Stop where you are," I said, and the ring in my voice had him freezing on the spot. I got up from the chair, and the man at my feet had his eyes trained on my crotch as I turn to face Finn. "This is the thing, before I came here, I would never make a decision about a relationship based on lust. That's only useful for a one night stand. How am I supposed to decide who to tie myself to right now? I just want to get off. I want someone to touch, me, stroke me, lick me, fuck me. I don't give a shit who does it, it could be him, you or all of you, one for each hole…"

"Consider my interest piqued, love," Slade said with a grin. "I didn't think you were keen on that, but it would take some preparation…"

"Shut up, Slade," Finn and I said.

"But none of that would mean anything, it's just physical. I can't do this, Finn, I can't. Tell them I can't."

"OK, OK," he said, holding up his hands. "I understand what you're saying. It's just a tradition, but I'm sure there's a way around it. People tend to bond during the honeymoon period. I know it feels like it's all sex, sex, sex, but often it starts to turn into something more tender. Complaints were made that guys who weren't initially picked never got a chance to make a connection, so a formal petitioning was created, to try and alleviate some of those tensions. I'll have a talk with Kelly and see if there's another way."

"Please…" the guy at my feet said.

"No," I say, "not you. You are meat."

The guys all went very still, so still I looked around to see what the hell was wrong. The eyes of the man on the floor lost their green tinge and he got to his feet, eyes on the floor. "Sorry about that," he said, in a much more measured tone. "Name's John."

"Hi, John," I said, waving awkwardly. "I'm sorry, I don't know what I just said but…"

He shook his head and gave me a strained smile, "It's OK. I'll send in the next guy. See you around."

There was another knock at the door, but Slade crossed the room, putting a hand on it to keep it closed. "I don't think it's as hard as you are assuming it is," he said. "Maybe it is, for your human brain. You would normally date a guy, get to know him and then make a call whether to take a chance on a relationship, but your Tirian brain…" He poked his finger at my head. "I think it knows exactly what it wants, you've just got to get out of its way."

At his words, I was transported to the night I shifted, the horde of males surrounding me in a mob, thinking they could take me down, force themselves upon me. A wide smile spread across my face, I could feel the cool air against my teeth. I moved Slade to one side, then opened the door. Slade and Finn looked on approvingly, right up until I slipped through it and into what appeared to be a big waiting room beyond.

It was just like the first day of my "honeymoon", with sixty or seventy men sitting or standing around, waiting for their chance. The aircon felt cold against my bare skin, pulling my nipples tight, as I took a step forward, every eye trained on me, no one moving a muscle.

"Jesus fuck, Jules!" Slade snapped, grabbing my arm and trying to pull me back through the doorway. I planted my feet, I wasn't going anywhere, which probably wasn't a bad thing right now. Everyone's gaze fell to where Slade's hand gripped me, and the closest guys began to move forward.

"Everyone stop where you are," I said in an echoey growl. It felt like my voice filled the room, reaching every corner. I noted the twitches of muscles, the quiver in limbs as they all obeyed, willingly or not.

"What the fuck are you doing?" Finn hissed. "You're much stronger now, but there's more than enough of them here to take you down. We use the receiving room for a reason!"

I shook my head. "I'm not sitting here, waiting for everyone to drop to my feet. You reckon I'm going to 'just know' if there's anyone else I'm compatible with? Well, I'm about to go and find out." I turned to the group, "Don't touch me, approach me or do anything regarding me without my permission within this room. Actually, make that anywhere. I'm going to walk around, see if I get anything from any of you. If I do, you can come back to the house and we'll take it from there. If I don't, that doesn't mean the end of this, I'm willing to look at other possible contenders another time, when my head is clearer. But if I say no, that means no until I say otherwise. Don't hit on me again. If I decide later I'm interested, I'll chase you. Are we clear?" A round of nods and mumbled or grumbled yeses went around the room. I nodded then moved further in.

Coming closer, I could start to see the trees from the forest, or in this case, the individual guys from the crowd, and it was both an awe-inspiring and slightly intimidating sight. Some were in work clothes, some in casual wear and a whole lot wore only the minimum amount required for polite company. Bare calves and well-muscled chests abounded, framed by bulging biceps. I swallowed a lump in my throat as I drew closer, hit by a wave of heady, smoky, male scent.

Now I wasn't arguing with Slade, I could see his point. I would never have walked into such a large group of guys before, let alone ones that looked like this. Men seemed to take all the air in the room, fill it with loud voices and big gestures, so that I felt compelled to keep quiet or draw that raucous attention on me. I'd had plenty experience of that in the diner. Apparently approaching a table full of truckers, just doing my job and taking their order, was cause for blunt conversations about my attractiveness, about what they wanted to do to me and how willing they predicted I'd be. You always seemed trapped in a catch-22. If I tossed my order book over my shoulder and spread myself out on the table for their delectation, I was a slut deserving of no respect, but if I asked for the basic courtesy you gave any human being, I was a joke. I wasn't a joke anymore. I felt the hungry gazes on my skin, the internal thrum inside my body, and realised I was something that was completely alien: a powerful woman.

"You're all so good looking," I said to Finn and Slade as they trailed behind me. "This is some kind of peacock thing, isn't it?"

"That's Doc Hobbes's theory, though you're hardly a drab peahen," Finn said.

"Perhaps the peacocks feel the same way, enraptured by the shades of brown in their mate's plumage," I said. I stopped for a moment, scenting the air. There was something...something familiar there. I wove between bodies, letting my fingers trail across chests as I went, them standing as still as trees, until I came to a stop in front of a group of guys in olive drab. They weren't toting weapons but the close-cut hair and their alert yet relaxed stances suggested military. *Where have they come from?* I thought as my nostrils flared, then I saw him, the guy who'd tried to teach me to shoot. I flicked a hand and the group parted for me so I could stalk right up to him, tall with broad shoulders, arms crossed over his chest, hips thrown forward as he looked down at me. The arms dropped to hang loosely by his sides as I drew closer, and he shifted ever so slightly into my space, a small smile on his face.

"Good to see you, Aaron. I was hoping you'd be applying," Slade said. "We missed you on the hunt."

His eyes, a strangely amber shade of hazel, didn't move from mine for a second. "We got caught up subduing the unfriendlies trying to come through. There was a surge of them, feeling her call, I guess. I know I was." His eyes dropped to my lips, lingering as a murmur from the group made it clear the others had done the same. "Nothing other than Sanctuary security would have kept me away," he said, answering Slade, but talking to me. Finally, his gaze flicked up again. "We've been down to a skeleton crew since then, mostly married guys looking after the gate. The rest of us have been camped out here for days, waiting for a look at her."

"Looks like you're taking your fill now," I said.

His smile widened, his teeth a sharp white against the deep bronze of his skin, his stance shifting as he edged as close as he could before the boys started to growl. "I'm not even close to having my fill." He leaned down slightly, breathing in deep. "And by the smell of you, neither have you." He straightened up, falling back into his previous stance, "What do you reckon, sweetheart? You wanna see if it's good between us?"

Did I? He was big, almost Pete the Mountain big, and I admit a lifetime of chick flicks made something inside me quiver every time a bloke gave me a cocky smile. But did that mean I wanted to sleep with him? Possibly have a relationship with him? Obviously, Slade approved of the match, but would Shaun? Brandon? How did I negotiate this?

"Stop overthinking," Finn said, whispering into my ear. I leant against him, arching my back slightly so as to fit the hard length of him against my arse. Aaron's smile dropped at that, his eyes raking over me hungrily. "Touch him," Finn said, "you'll soon work out if there's something there."

I looked at Aaron with a cocked eyebrow, asking permission, and he just nodded, dropping his hands down to pull up the hem of his tight t-shirt. I watched every inch of the big brown body that appeared, mouth hanging open. It took a little nudge from Slade for me to reach out and place my hand against his skin. I felt a zing, shooting from my nipples to my clit in a split second, forcing a gasp out from between my lips. My hand slipped lower as a result, his abs clenching into a hard wall. "I'm sorry," I said, "that took me by surprise."

He placed his hand over mine and gently pushed it down lower, to his waistband. "My control's rock solid. You can touch me wherever you like," he said, his voice a low rasp, "and I won't move unless you tell me to."

My lips fell open slightly, my breath coming in faster as I considered what he said. "So, nothing I do will make you react?"

"Oh, there's a whole lot of reacting going on," he said, jerking his eyes downward, "but if you're asking am I going to start anything, then no, not until you say so."

I found myself grinning, unable to stop. His eyes burned into mine as I ran my finger down the fine trail of brown hair that ran from his navel to his waistband, watching his pupils flare, his breathing sped up as I toyed with the button. "What are you going to do with him?" Slade said, in a low growl, running his lips over my ear.

"I don't know," I said. "Right now, I'm just enjoying...touching without consequences, without expectations. That's OK, isn't it? If I walk away, don't choose you, that's no big deal?"

"Not a big deal?" He looked away briefly before glancing at me. He swallowed, then smiled. "Not sure if that's the word I would use, but sweetheart, I can see the dilemma you're in. Too many offerings, who do you choose? But, if you walk away leaving me harder than I've ever been, aching for you, well, I won't be in the minority, will I?"

I glanced about and saw guy after guy watching what I was doing. I went to snatch my hand away but a warm one covered mine and pulled it back against bare skin. When I looked back, he paused, as if asking permission, then pushed it further down his pants. My fingers closed around his hard length automatically, his smile spreading when I realised what he had down there.

I know some women think dicks are pretty ugly. I get it, especially if you're getting bombarded by unsolicited pics of them on social media, but me, I guess due to positive associations I've had with the handling of them, I considered myself a bit of a connoisseur of a nicely formed cock. One of the boyfriends I'd had in my early twenties had quite the package, and actually knew how to use it. Aaron's breath was coming hard now, his eyes rolling as his head fell back, my palm cupping and then rotating around the bulbous crown of his dick. It turned out the two of them were similar in proportions, and if he knew what he was doing, there would be that same almost punching sensation as he worked that big head up inside me. "He's in," I said, pulling my hand free. "I'll give you a go, and we'll see how things work between you and me, and between the guys." Aaron shuddered, coming to and then shifted himself into a more comfortable position, a huge smile on his face.

"I hope you have no reason to regret it." He nodded to his mates, who looked either pissed or envious. "Let the CO know I'm taking personal leave," he said as he fell in behind Slade and Finn.

"Got it, mate," one said, patting his shoulder. "Hope to see you married up and living the good life."

"Was there anyone else?" Finn asked, looking over the crowd. "Or did you just want to see how things go with Aaron?"

"One at a time," I said, moving closer to Aaron. His arms went around my waist, and I found that I fitted into his side as if I'd always been there. "Less likely to get overwhelmed that way."

"Home it is, then," Slade said. "Now, that rather intriguing suggestion you made before..."

24

Slade and Finn walked out, going around to grab the car. Apparently because I was with another man, it was safe to leave me alone. I stood by the big double doors of the meeting hall, Aaron at my side, watching the men begin to file out. Oddly, I felt a pang as they left. It wasn't that I wanted any in particular, I already had one I was reasonably sure I liked. I mentally smacked myself upside the head. I was getting selfish, because as they went, they took with them the potential thrill of finding someone else. Until he strolled through the door.

"It's over already?" he asked as he wove his way through the guys, a shit eating grin on his face. I didn't answer straight away, my eyes caught on the expanse of exposed male flesh in front of me. He wore a pair of well-worn navy work pants that hung low on his hips, looking like they could be pulled off with ease, and I found my fingers twitched to do just that. His chest was bare, less bulky than Aaron's well developed one, but there was a curious cat-like elegance to his lean build. He strolled over, green eyes boring into mine, shoving back the ragged fall of blond hair that tumbled over his shoulders. "So who are you, baby? The lucky lady in question?"

"She's not taking petitions, that's who," Aaron snapped, but my hand went out, hanging in the air for a moment in offer before the guy smirked and took it, giving it a firm shake.

"I'm Jules."

"Jack," he said, still holding my hand, letting his calloused palm rasp against mine before looking over his shoulder. "This is Hawk."

Oh, god, I thought. My heart jumped into a gallop from a standing start as Jack's friend walked up to the step. I watched his eyes widen slightly, but his steps never faltered, until he stopped to one side of Jack. The guy who I'd been watching doing the fencing, the one with the long brown hair, that was Hawk. "You two know each other?" Jack said, eyes flicking between me and his mate.

"No," Hawk replied, his voice a deep rumble.

"Jules, the car's pulling up. We better go," Aaron said, placing a gentle hand on the small of my back.

"Oh, right," I said, starting a little at the sensation of the unfamiliar hand on my skin. The singlet was brief enough that I could feel the heat of him. It said a lot about me that the sexual mores of this place were more disorientating than the fact I could turn into a wolf made partially of smoke. My Tirian shifted inside me, watching Jack and Hawk with a curious eye. Jack hadn't dropped the smirk the whole time, something she wanted to see if she could remove, or if that mouth was just as clever when it was full of me. And with Hawk, I felt a shiver, a need to shift, run, something I hadn't felt since the first night.

"So, this is your final choice?" Jack asked, eyeing Aaron, which drew an answering growl from him. "You're finished, squared away, ready to move into the married quarters?"

"No, I don't think so. This is still pretty new to me." Aaron's hand slid up the back of my shirt, rubbing circles on the bare skin between my shoulder blades. My eyes fell partially closed for a moment as I felt a rush of heat from that sure, slow caress. "Right now, I guess I'm just enjoying myself, seeing where things take me." Jack grinned at the breathy tone of my voice, watching the little gasp that came as Aaron's hand snuck around my waist and skimmed up along my ribcage. Jack's nostrils flared and he looked away, letting out a low groan, then laughing as he readjusted his dick in his pants.

"Well, alright then. We have to come by, check the bridal suite fence, especially as we have an unfriendly locked up on the premises thanks to the grunts. Kelly doesn't want to take any chances with you, love." I nodded, trying to keep my cool as Aaron's lips began to trail along my neck. I shifted under his touch, the light smattering of touches somehow making me more aware of what he was doing than something harder. "Maybe we'll see you around?" Aaron's teeth closed over a chunk of my skin, holding me still, triggering some sort of deep down instinct I didn't understand, pushing me into a state of submission before releasing me. I shook my head, all of a sudden feeling like I was drowning. There was too much, too much pretty, too much touch, too many hot guys bamboozling me with all this bare flesh. I took a little step away from Aaron, forcing his hand to drop, and Jack's grin grew sharper.

"Yeah, maybe," I said in a more even voice.

"Well, you have a...stimulating afternoon, love, if you can, and if you can't, we'll be by tomorrow."

Aaron leapt forward, ready to grab the guy, but I stopped his hand, watching Jack walk away with a wink and a swagger and Hawk looking back at us for much longer, with eyes I couldn't quite read. I schooled my face into a more pleasant expression, facing Aaron with a smile, and said, "Let's go."

"WHAT HAPPENED?" Slade asked when we got in the car, turning around to look at us from the front seat. Finn's eyes took us in via the rear vision mirror, but he kept his mouth shut. That was never going to happen with Slade. "So? You look pissed, and you smell horny," he said, looking from Aaron to me.

I propped my ankle up on the centre console, knowing that he would get a good view of my pussy up the leg of my shorts as I did so and sure enough, his eyes dropped down. "Default state, remember."

"Oh no, something's got you extra creamy, princess. I'd say it was soldier boy here, he sure looks stimulated, but that face. What'd you do? Tell him his dick isn't as big as mine?"

"It was Jack," Aaron said. "Hawk was with him, but he's never been a problem." I didn't look at him, but I could hear the clench of his teeth as he said the words.

"Jack? Really, princess? Fucking outsider girls, they always fall for the bad boy schtick..."

"Enough!" Finn said, his tone pure iron. "Right now, we're bringing Aaron back to the house for a trial, so he is the focus. As for any preferences Jules might or might not have, that's for her to explore, as is her right."

THAT KILLED ALL CONVERSATION. Finn drove us back to the compound, Slade jumping out when we got to the gate and punching in the combination. He looked calm enough when he climbed into the car, but he did not meet my eyes. We pulled up outside the house, Slade was out of the car the moment it stopped, ambling inside without a word. Finn paused with his hand on the door and looked at me through the mirror. "Take a moment, Jules, if you want. Bringing someone into the house, it has some meaning to it. Nothing for you to worry about, nothing that's permanent, but it's important to us. Take a minute, and see if this is something you really want to do."

25

The silence grew inside the car, a living breathing thing that was all of a sudden competing with us for the available oxygen. *Say something*, I told myself, *Something, anything, say something!* But I didn't want to. I was hit with a wave of resentment that made me think of being back home. *Pursue who you want, Jules, but not him. Listen to guys plea for me to have sex with them to keep the peace, even when you don't want to. Stay in this house, behind this fence, don't go through this gate...* It was tempting to view this place as some kind of hippy commune, but 'love' certainly wasn't free of expectations, here or anywhere.

I looked over at Aaron, who sat there with an immovable stillness that almost made him seem inhuman. You would have thought being one of the few females in a tribe full of hot straight guys would be just heaven, but it only was if you didn't give a shit about their feelings. This had to have been a big deal, getting picked, even if we didn't work out, and then I turned around and showed interest in someone else. I flopped back against the seat and sighed. His feelings weren't my responsibility, I reminded myself, but I couldn't let go of the idea that I was being a bitch. Then I felt his hand cover mine. I looked up, meeting his steady gaze. He didn't flinch away, but I could see in those golden depths, that he was holding himself somewhere safe, protecting himself from the threat I posed, of rejection.

"I'm sorry," I said, not knowing why I was apologising, but feeling like I needed to.

His breath came out as a hiss, then he nodded, "It's OK, I'll get one of the guys to drop me back."

Did I want that? I felt a rush of relief and a pang of loss. I shook my head, as if that would somehow clear it. *What the hell did I want?*

You do not have to do anything, today or tomorrow, my Tirian said inside my head. *You can return this man to his place, call on him another day.* I could, but I didn't want to. I looked over at him as I moved in my seat. There had been something quite nice going on there for a bit. *So, have him*, she said. *What stops you?* Yes, what did stop me? My Tirian sighed, *You are used to being the prey, not the predator. You are used to a man pursuing you, persuading you to make your choice. With the men inside, I took control, I took them. This is the first man you have chosen yourself, and it makes you feel uncomfortable because it is different to what you are accustomed to.*

Was that it? Evidently having had enough, my Tirian shifted within me, taking over as my mind whirled, unclicking my seat belt and moving so I straddled his lap, something that was considerably harder to do than I thought. The SUV was roomy, but he was a big guy. "Is this OK?" I asked, half of him, half of me.

"It's a distinct improvement on before. Silence isn't a turn on for me," he replied, settling his hands lightly on my hips.

This man may be a good mate, so might the other ones, my Tirian said inside my head. *An animal does not pick, pick, pick at the edges of a meal, looking for advice on whether to eat. An animal swallows it down and then sees how it sits. If he is poison to us, he goes, if he is pleasing, he stays. It does not require the mental work you are expending.*

Yeah, but the rituals I would normally use to identify whether he's good for me or not don't work here.

They are mealy-mouthed and not worthy of you, she replied. *Human women know not if a man is lover or danger, or both. You have constructed convoluted customs to try and ascertain this before, yet even with them, so many women are killed or harmed. You are stronger than this man, than any of these men. There is no risk here. He cannot force you, cannot obligate you to do anything, not unless you allow it.*

So how do I figure out what I want, without those familiar tools?

Experience, whim. Touch this man. You wanted to beforehand. See if he pleases you. I will remove him if he doesn't.

And suddenly, I was back in the moment. I had a big, hot looking guy under me and he was smiling slightly, his eyes dropping to my lips and lingering. I spread my legs further, feeling the tension in my thighs pull at my swollen folds. I could feel the cool air over my over-heated skin, a precursor of the caresses that were sure to come.

He took a deep breath in and smiled, reaching up to cup my head, looking into my eyes. I nodded, my breath starting to come in fast now, watching his mouth as I drew closer and closer. He groaned as our lips touched, opening his mouth to pant slightly before pushing mine open with a persistent tongue. He yanked my hips down, hard against him, forcing a wiggle from me as the stretch deepened. His hands went to my hair, grasping great hand-fuls of it as he caught my lip in between his, sucking on it. I whimpered into his mouth as his hand went up my shirt, yelping as those fingers closed around a nipple. I thrust against him without meaning to as he rolled the sensitive point between his fingers, his grip shifting from gentle to a slight pinch that left me gasping. Finally, I pulled away, pushing his hand down and fighting to catch my breath. "I don't know what this means, what it will lead to, but right now, I want you to come into the house and fuck me. That cool with you?"

He smiled, "I thought you'd never ask."

I wasn't 100% sure this was the right thing to do, but I walked up the steps with Aaron's hand in mine. Brandon and Shaun looked up from where they sat at the kitchen table, but I brushed past. I looked down the hallway, not wanting to go into the big bedroom we all slept in. In my gut, I felt that that space needed to be kept for those I knew I wanted to stay around. I opened the door of a room I'd never gone into and found a slightly musty smelling bedroom with a large bed in the middle. I walked in, standing by it, running my hand over the nubby white raw cotton and heard the door click behind me.

He moved in against me, his body a wall of warm muscle at my back, and ran his fingers lightly up my arm. I shivered under the slightly ticklish caress, but felt an almost painful tightening in my nipples in response. I leaned harder into him, Aaron wrapping an arm around my waist, and arched as the caress wound its way up my neck and into my hair before floating past my collarbone. My heart rate began to pick up as his hand slid down the centre of my body, and I moved to try and direct the caress where I needed it. The arm at my waist tightened, holding me still as his teasing, slow hand curled across my ribcage, coming closer and closer to my aching breasts, but then veered off. I growled in frustration, and he laughed.

"Take it off," I said, pulling free of him and turning around. "All of it, I want to see you."

"What about you?" Aaron asked.

"What about me?" I snapped, though my clothes chafed at my skin. I stared him down, not letting my gaze fall, until he chuckled and began to yank his t-shirt off.

I felt no such ambivalence now. My nipples were tight and begging to be touched, my shorts damp from my weeping pussy. I wanted to throw myself on the bed and be attended to, have the desire coiling in my groin teased and provoked until I came around something unrelenting. I stepped closer as he unbuckled his belt, pushing his hands away and taking over. I unsnapped his pants and shoved them down, easing his underwear over his rigid length, pausing to watch it snap back hard against his belly. His cock jerked under my inspection.

I looked over that which I had only felt before. As I'd imagined, he had a thick shaft, and I wondered if I'd be able to close my hand around it. Veins stood out proud against the surface, snaking up to a bulbous head. I dropped down lower, not sure if I'd be able to fit it into my mouth, flicking out my tongue and laving it over the shining head. "No," he gasped, "I won't last."

"There's four other guys down the hall who can pick up the slack," I said.

"Want to be inside you," he said, eyes closed, groaning as my fingers gripped the base of his dick, hands dropping away as I ran my tongue along his length. I opened my mouth as wide as possible and took the head into my mouth. "I..." His voice trailed away as I pumped it and swirled my tongue. His words became incoherent as I began to suck him down deep.

He sounded vulnerable as his breath caught in his chest, his fingers tangling in my hair, and his moans coming in rapid pants. I increased my pace, my tongue shifting like a snake along the underside of his dick. I waited until he was grunting, thrusting into my mouth, his movements starting to come fast and irregular... and then let his cock go with a pop.

"Get on the bed," he growled, pulling my shirt off with one hand and shoving down my pants with another. One closed over my breast, sending a lightning bolt of pleasure through my body as he roughly plucked at my nipple. "God, yes..." he hissed when the other hand slid up my thigh, trailing through the fluid there and then slipping between my folds. "Little girl, I'm gonna eat you all up."

I lay down, reaching up with my foot to hook it behind his head as he crouched on the end of the bed, pulling him closer as he slunk along the covers. "You're so wet, you glisten in the light," he said with a groan.

"I'm hoping you're going to make it a whole lot... unh!" He didn't fuck around with preliminaries, forcing his tongue in along my seam, parting my folds before moving up to circle my clit. I jerked my hips upwards when he pulled away. I growled, I was done with teasing, I just wanted to quell this goddam fire that had been building in my groin all day. I wanted to come, several times if possible. I told him as much as he ran kisses down my inner thigh, and he laughed.

"Oh, you'll get yours, honey, and if that isn't enough, as you said, you've got a team on standby down the hall. I just want this first time to last, make an impression."

"I'm gonna make an impression, with my foot up your... ah!"

He buried his face into my crotch, no more glancing, teasing caresses. My hips jerked up when he pushed his tongue inside me, wriggling like a fish, before pulling away to close his lips around my clit. I tried to scrabble back, the pressure so intense it was almost painful, but his hands closed like iron on my thighs, jerking me closer. I had no sooner accustomed myself to that vacuum like pressure then he pulled away, licking my now painfully throbbing clit. His tongue moved slowly and surely, but not hard enough, not fast enough. I was so damn close. I felt his chuckle against my skin as I began to whine, my hips lifting, trying to move closer, force the delicious friction to intensify.

"What do you need, love?" he asked, his voice somewhat muffled by his position. "Jules? What do you need?"

"I need you to fuck me," I said, getting up on my elbows and trying to pull him up with my feet, but he resisted with ease. "Your dick looks like it's going to make me ache so good when it goes in. I want to find out if I'm right. Now."

His grin gleamed in the low light of the room, and he crawled over me, slow and predatory, just like I imagined his beast did. I heard the low, rumbling growl in his chest, but I wasn't afraid. I had the big bad wolf right where I wanted him, well, almost. He pushed me back flat on the bed and then positioned himself between my thighs, holding me down when I tried to hasten the process. He smiled as he rubbed that big head across my wet cunt, moving slower, circling my aching centre and only dipping in slightly as I growled and whined. It worked though, nothing that had happened before or since could wriggle its way into my mind. My focus was completely and utterly narrowed down onto the point where my body and his met.

I let out the most horrendous groan as he pushed his way inside me. I probably sounded like a cow giving birth, but I just didn't care. Part of me was trying to scrabble back, the slight pinch as he stretched me wide growing more and more pronounced as he moved, until I was sure my eyes were bigger than my vagina. I panted like a woman in childbirth when he stopped, having moved as far as he could go. "You OK?" He sounded genuinely concerned.

"Bit bigger than I'm used to," I said, breathing hard as I willed my body to adjust. I patted his shoulder and smiled weakly, but his face fell, and he tried to pull away. "No, no, no," I said, the drag of his cock moving a bit much to cope with. "Don't move, please don't move."

"I'm hurting you. I don't want to hurt you."

"No, not hurting exactly." I didn't sound convincing, my voice was all high and breathy. "This is just a challenge. Like climbing Everest."

"We can try again later, maybe work up to this with one of the other guys," he said, a terrible finality in his voice. He began to pull away but my loud yelp was enough to stop him. "Fuck, what do we do?"

"Just, just move a little bit," I said, my hand hovering over his shoulder as I felt him shift his hips slightly. He was barely shifting inside me, yet somehow that was more than enough. Just tiny, tiny thrusts that had my muscles beginning to relax and my nails digging into his shoulders.

"We've got to stop," he gasped. "I'm going to hurt you."

"Hey." We both turned to see the door had opened a little, and Brandon had stuck his head in. "Everything OK in here?"

"I gotta stop," Aaron said, shifting as if he would yank himself away from me, only stopped by my high-pitched scream and sharp nails.

"No, no moving!" I said.

Brandon shut the door and came over to the bed. "What's up, love?"

"Too much of a good thing," I said through gritted teeth. "It felt so hot going in, but now I feel like I've bitten off more than I can chew."

His eyes dropped down to our groins. "I'm just going to take a look, that OK with you two?"

"No need, I'll just think of my dead grandmother or something, and go soft," Aaron growled.

"If it felt that good going in, it will probably feel really good when she comes," Brandon said. "Do you want to try for that?" Aaron nodded. "What about you, love?" I nodded. "Well, OK then. I think you've just tightened up a bit, tensing because you expect it to hurt, and then it hurts because you've tensed. I just need to relax her a bit, that OK?"

Aaron gave a quick nod, "I don't want to hurt her."

"I know, and you won't. Women have remarkably elastic bodies. She can take you, can't you, love?" I wasn't 100% sure of that, but I wanted to. Brandon's calm voice and long, slow caresses down my body reminded me just how I got here. Aaron's head jerked up as my cunt twitched around him, my back arching as Brandon's fingers slipped to my clit.

"She'll need near constant clit stimulation if you want to fuck her," Brandon said, sliding two fingers up and down the sides of it. "All those endorphins will both relax her and make her more able to cope with your size. Try and move now and see how it feels."

Rather than feeling like my insides were being yanked out by his cock, there was that heavy, pleasurable stretch, feeling like my clit was being massaged from the inside as well as the outside. My legs curled around Aaron's hips, not letting him pull back so far, not wanting to stop that amazing pressure now. Brandon's fingers grew bolder, flicking at my aching clit, pulling the hood so it rubbed back and forth. His mouth dropped to mine as my head fell backwards. "Get your clothes off," I gasped as Aaron grew bolder, thrusting harder, faster.

"You OK with that, mate?" he asked, hands going to his pants.

Aaron didn't even look up, just nodded briefly before focusing on us. My hand wrapped around Brandon's hard cock as soon as he lay back down, the welcome feel of his fingers on my clit working me higher and higher. I shifted my legs so that my ankles rested on Aaron's shoulders, him groaning as he sunk deeper into me. "She's getting close," Brandon said with a gasp, his other hand closing over mine as he thrust into it.

"Can you take it?" Aaron said, slamming harder into me now, his strokes growing faster, as if against his will.

"Hang on," I said, pulling free of the both of them, feeling the horrible emptiness that came with this. I pushed Brandon up by the bedhead and then flipped over onto all fours. "Gimme all that you've got," I said, spreading my legs. Aaron bit back a snarl, positioning himself between my thighs in one moment, and forcing himself inside me in the next. Brandon's cock went between my lips as I gasped, my hand going around the base. He bucked against my mouth, my groans of pleasure sending vibrations up and down his length.

"Get her there!" Brandon panted. Aaron's hand snuck around and flicked at my clit.

I was nothing other than formless flesh, caught on the spikes of two opposing forces. For all my sexual aggression this morning, I now felt helpless, flung about wildly on the rough waves of the men, feeling almost like the impending orgasm was being forced from my body. I was completely at their mercy, swallowing down Brandon, being opened up by Aaron, over and over and over again, until...

I yanked my head back from Brandon's cock to scream out my pleasure, his dick spurting wildly not a moment later. Aaron's fingers dug into my hips as he jerked to a stop, momentarily paralysed as his body spasmed. I felt him empty inside me, felt each violent pulse. We collapsed onto the bed in a messy pile. New guy, old guy, it didn't seem to matter, only sucking in oxygen was a priority, though I was glad when Brandon pulled me into his arms. I felt sheltered for a moment, protected. From what? I knew what my Tirian would say. I looked over at Aaron who gave me a shaky smile. From my own desires. I reached out and smoothed a short curl back from his forehead. His mouth closed, his eyes following the gesture, somehow curiously more vulnerable than when we were fucking. Brandon let out a happy hum when I pulled the strange man closer, willingly caging myself between their bodies. It was weird and awkward, I think we both knew that. We'd said a total of twenty words to each other, so it had to be, but there was potential there. Aaron laid a gentle kiss on my forehead, not seeming to care when his and Brandon's limbs got tangled in each other's as they held me. Nothing in my life had prepared me for relaxing into the embrace of two hot men, but right now, I was dealing with it.

We dozed for a while in the quiet of the afternoon, not fully asleep, the strangeness of each other's bodies too much for complete relaxation. When my eyes flicked open, I found Aaron looking into mine, his hazel ones soft. He ran a hand across my cheek, and I turned my face into it, kissing the palm and something flared behind his eyes. I felt it too, deep inside, an ache for another round, but it sat cheek by jowl with a more immediate tenderness. He'd been slamming into me when we were both racing towards orgasm and now, I was feeling the after effects.

"I don't think I've got another in me, though god knows I want to," I whispered.

"S'OK," he said with a grin. "I've had sex one more time than I expected today, so it's a good day by my definition."

I pulled myself gently from Brandon's grasp, straddling Aaron again. His smile widened, his eyes trailing down my body, lingering on my breasts. "You're so big, all over," I said, running a hand over his impressive chest. His muscles popped under my caress, and I wasn't sure if that was deliberate or not. I swivelled around and saw the heavy length of him had risen to the occasion. "Big is part of the problem though," I said with a sigh. He just chuckled, bunching his abs as he grabbed my legs and flipped me around, so I straddled his face and now looked down on his dick.

"Fucking's only part of the fun," he said, rubbing his slightly stubbly chin along my thigh.

"God, Aaron, I'm not sure if I can take... oh!" His tongue flicked out and licked my seam with the lightest of caresses. The feel of his breath on my skin was almost stronger. Taking my silence as permission, he traced his tongue on the most sensitive part of my anatomy, just letting the tip glide along my slick skin, twirling and circling, drawing my attention to each and every aching inch of it. I groaned, feeling my cunt twitch in anticipation. I looked down at his rigid dick. I could take it, with a bit of help from Brandon, surely I could. I started to move down towards it but his fingers dug in for a moment, forcing me to stay put. *Two can play at this game*, I thought, and I reached out, trailing my fingers along his length.

There's a weird electrical sensation that comes from letting your fingertips glide very, very lightly over another person's skin. I let the pads of my fingers only just skim over his hardness, watching them shift as they scudded over rigid veins, spreading when they encountered his swollen head. "Fuck," he mumbled into my thigh, and I could feel the tension in his body, trying to force me to increase the pressure of my caresses. The weird thing was, his cock felt even harder, as if wanting to thrust into my palm and not being able to get himself there.

His revenge came in the form of a flurry of feather-light touches to my clit. Its sensitive throbbing due to all the attention it'd been getting, and the heat running through my body. "God, please..." I murmured. His tongue flicked faster, not harder and not firmer and not what I needed, but while my other hand began to claw at the sheets, I kept the other around him, just as delicate. My fingers twirled and twisted, my thumb resting in that sweet spot just under the flare of his head. His hand went around mine, forcing my fingers closed and then thrusting into the tight space, but I wrenched my hand away, moving so my thighs encased his face. I ground down, the sudden rush of sensation feeling just glorious. My arms reached up, for what I didn't know, my hips undulating against his mouth for a moment before he grabbed me and threw me backwards, into Brandon's vice-like arms. Apparently, he was awake now.

"There's a pleasure that comes from not having what you want," Brandon whispered in my ear.

"I'm not feeling it," I said as Aaron pinned my ankles to the bed, using his body to hold them there as he bent down to begin again.

"Sure you are," Brandon said as my body jerked at the first ghost-like caress, then he began to pinch my nipples between his fingers. "It's all you can think about, isn't it?"

When Aaron moved in closer, cock in hand, I thought, *Finally, finally he's going to give me what I need.* I curled one leg around him to drag him over. "Nuh uh, princess. You won't be able to walk tomorrow if we do."

"Well, Brandon can fuck me, and I'll suck you off."

Brandon chuckled. "I like the way your mind works, but let's see what he has in store for you."

That big, thick cock slid through my folds like a hot knife through butter, the hard shaft shoving my clit hood back and forth. It wasn't satisfying, my legs flailed and I began to shift within the cage of Brandon's arms, struggling, fighting to take what I needed. Aaron chuckled, avoiding my attempts to catch him and pull him closer, that big head of his grazing the entrance of my aching cunt without going any deeper.

"Makes you want it so much more, doesn't it?" Brandon asked.

"Yes." I wriggled out of his grip and then rolled free, standing naked at the end of the bed, both of their eyes on me. "You," I said to Aaron, "get on the bed."

He moved to do as I said, and I watched that big body spread out like a welcome feast, right when I was feeling the ache of need deep within me.

"Jules..." Brandon said, coming to stand beside me, then he grabbed my arm, something that made me see red. My lips peeled away from my gums as I snarled at him, which made him fall back instinctively, but he came closer again, much to my disgust. He took in my expression, listened to the rising sound of threat coming from my throat, but he reached out for me, even as a look of resignation washed over his face. "Jules, the heat is riding you, making you think your body can do things it's not ready for, love. Aaron will do whatever you want, but its gonna kill him to see you in pain tomorrow. And the heat will still be burning inside you, even if you are bruised up from today. Fuck, Jules, we can satisfy you in so many ways, but we're trying to make sure you get through this in one piece."

"How do you know what my body can and can't do?"

I watched Brandon's eyes slide to meet Aaron's and something, something I didn't understand passed between them. I noted the shift of Brandon's throat as he swallowed, then cleared it. "We experience our own heat, when a new female comes into season. It drives all single men into overdrive, but there's only so many female outlets for that."

"You..." The word hung in the air, unfinished. I didn't need to ask, I could see it in their body language. "You've fucked each other."

"Maybe. I don't tend to remember faces," Aaron said, sitting up. If it wasn't for his straining erection, I'd have thought him almost ashamed. "It seriously becomes any means to get off. It's not about your partner, it's just a need. Some do form partnerships after the heat wears off. That's what Doc reckons it's for, to throw potential partners together in more and more combinations until they stick. If you're still in the arms of someone or several someones when the heat dies down, you know that's probably where you need to stay. We've been through it, we know what's happening to you."

"And you know how much pain I'll be in, don't you?" I said to Brandon.

Those grey eyes slid over Aaron's form, lingering on all the parts that were hard and aching. His tongue flicked out for a moment, swiping along those plush lips. "I do."

"And that's what you're trying to protect me from? Or is it something else?"

My Tirian shifted inside me, looking at Brandon in a whole new light. Was he potential pack mate or competition for my men? I could feel her whuffing, stretching out her muzzle to scent the man, looking for signs of a possible threat.

"Fuck, Jules..." Those eyes met mine and didn't waver. "I've fucked guys, guys have fucked me. If that's what you needed to hear, then there, that's the truth of it. But if you want me in your pack, and the condition is that I never look at another bloke, then done. Hand on my heart, I'll occasionally miss the novelty of it, but that's about it. You don't get it, love. Girls from the outside don't. This is about you. Everything in me wants to make you happy, keep you safe, fuck you senseless." He moved in closer, slowly, until he was saying the words against my lips. He trailed kisses along my jawline, then buried his face in my hair when he pulled me against him. "Biological instinct or real feeling, I'll never know, but you've gotta forgive me if I want you to avoid some of my mistakes."

I stayed still, not letting myself soften in his arms. I wanted to. Outsider me heard a calm, sweet voice and felt a warm, hot body and just wanted to surrender, but I wasn't her anymore. That was disorientating, because that meant I didn't know who had replaced her. So that was perhaps why the next thing I said was a surprise to all of us.

"So, what would you do?"

"What?" Brandon pulled back, frowning for a second before searching my face for further clarification.

"What would you do with him? If you were me?"

I looked down and saw the slight twitch of his hand, the throb of his cock, pre-cum pearling on the tip as he considered what to say. When I looked up, the two men remained where they were, hadn't moved an inch, but the air was thick with a tension that had come from nowhere. Their eyes bore into each other's, before Brandon shot a look back at me, eyes hooded.

"You want to see that, princess?"

"Don't call me that."

"Slade does."

"And if I wanted Slade in here, I'd call him. I want you and him, to show me what this heat was like before me. What it would be like if you'd never stepped inside this building, never laid a finger on me. If you were in the barracks or the mess hall, what would you be doing when the heat rose?"

"You want me to see if he can take me?" Aaron rasped.

"Is that what would happen?" I asked. "Would he be on his knees in front of you?"

At my words, Brandon moved like a puppet on a string, falling to the carpet, but still maintaining a distance between him and Aaron. He turned to me, something that seemed to cost him some effort, if the shake of his muscles were anything to go by. "We're doing this for you. Remember that. If this gets too much or too weird, you say so, and we'll stop."

"I won't," I replied.

"So, you gonna have a taste of this?" Aaron asked, stroking his cock.

"You think I'm the bottom because I'm not as burly," Brandon said with a grumble, though I watched him shuffle closer. "I'm gonna fuck you until you see stars after this."

"That right, little man? Well, let's see what you've got."

Aaron is all of a sudden mouthy and pushy, perhaps who he really was when my Tirian's dominance isn't beating down on him. But despite the arrogant smirk on his face, he cupped Brandon's cheek gently as the other man moved into his space, drawing his chin up and placing a careful kiss on the lips he must have been imagining wrapped around his cock. It was a slow, almost polite thing initially. They explored each other's mouths like humans would shake hands, getting to know each other, testing each other's measure. Then I heard Aaron's breath hitch in his chest. Those big hands buried themselves in the raven's wings of Brandon's hair, the smaller man cradling Aaron's head. Those hands began to draw each other closer, until the kiss was an open-mouthed, desperate thing. It was Brandon who pulled away first, grinning when the other man followed him, his lips like magnets, tugging Aaron's along. He got to his feet, and for a moment I thought he was going to end things. For some reason, my breath caught, unwilling to breathe in or out, until I knew if he would. Instead, he wrapped his hand around the base of his cock, and he moved forward, thrusting slightly into the small gap between its head and Aaron's mouth.

"You want to taste it, don't you? Feel my hard length in your mouth, feel me thrust it down your throat." The bigger man nodded, completely transfixed by Brandon's dick, watching every slight shift of his hips. "Are we going to put on a pretty show for my girl? Are you going to swallow me down, tears streaming down your face, grateful for a mouthful of my dick?"

Aaron nodded, then surged forward, dropping to his knees and then running a long lick up the length of the other man's dick. I watched Brandon's head drop back for a moment, and then he let out a heartfelt sigh, just lost in the sensations created by the other man's swirling tongue. When he opened them a slit, he looked over to me and grinned, a wild, careless thing I'd never seen on him. *Do I squash this down somehow?* I think. *Stop them from being who they really are?*

"Stop overthinking, outsider girl, and enjoy," he said, grabbing a fistful of Aaron's very short curls and thrusting his cock past Aaron's lips, which had been rubbing themselves all over his head. He shivered when Aaron's muffled groan sent vibrations down his shaft, then looked down. "Don't touch," he said when he spied Aaron thrusting his dick through the tight grip of his hand. "After we've got our ladyship's juices running, I'm going to lie you down on that bed and fuck the cum out of you while she rides your face. That all right, love?"

He looked to me for an answer, and I quickly nodded. There was something in his tone that made the Tirian within shift restively, but I didn't fucking care. I could feel the damp slick on my thighs, the twitch of my clit, and remembered exactly what that stubbled face felt like when it was between them. Dominance can get fucked, this is hot.

My approval was all he needed, Brandon now applying himself to the task. I watched the tears run down Aaron's face as Brandon fucked his mouth, but his hands dug into the smaller man's buttocks, as if to stop him from pulling back so far. I shifted closer, sitting down on the bed and feeling the two of them move, watching Brandon hiss as his thrusts got faster, deeper, his fingers digging into the other man's scalp, and all I heard was the rattling rasp of his breath. Then he jerked back, cock twitching in the cool air, the skin angry and red and slick with saliva. Aaron reached for him, trying to draw him back in but Brandon batted him away.

"Get on the bed," he ordered and Aaron moved to do so, glancing over at me and then grabbing my hand.

"You OK with this?" he rasped, but then his eyes fell closed as Brandon pushed his legs up to his chest. "Gods, just fuck me," he said as I heard the pop of a bottle top.

"Nah, only cunts go in dry," Brandon said, and any complaints were lost as soon as he started spreading a clear liquid around the other guy's arse. Brandon winked at me as I peered over, watching those nimble fingers slip up and down over Aaron's pulsing hole, my mouth dry from hanging open by the time he pushed the first in.

"Gotta go for the prostate," he said to me, almost conversationally. "Helps open him up, and brings all sorts of pleasure."

"I don't really have the right equipment for that," I stuttered.

"Oh, I don't know. Scarlett Du Jour wrote this really hot scene where the MC rode her man's arse with a strap on, but even if you're not into that..." he pulled his finger away and then applied more lube before pushing another in, Aaron's cock jerking at the intrusion. "You've got two hands. Just feel around for a hard lump just inside. You'll know when you hit it."

Aaron's legs fell limp, and a full body shudder went through him. He let out a long, low moan followed by some kind of disbelieving chuckle as he rode the waves of pleasure Brandon was wringing from him.

"A lot more sensitive when we're in heat," he said. "Now, that mouth of his is empty. 'Bout time you did something about that."

"You're awfully bossy," I said, but I crawled along the bed, eyes on Brandon when I threw a leg over Aaron's face. His eyes bore into mine as he continued to saw his fingers in and out of the man, and when he added a third, I swear I felt it inside me. Aaron's hands went around my hips, and he jerked me down unceremoniously, eating me like he was a starving man. My eyes fluttered as desire roared through my veins. I'd been all in my head, watching, learning. Any intellectual interest was shouldered aside as the man's tongue and fingers thrust inside me, as my clit was rubbed roughly, dragging me higher and higher. We both paused for a moment when Brandon pulled away, and I watched him oil up his dick, a singularly male look of satisfaction on his face as he caught me watching, then he moved between Aaron's legs.

"Better get yours quick," he said in a hoarse rasp as he pushed his dick into Aaron. They were just gentle thrusts initially, but Aaron redoubled his ministrations, grinding me down so hard, I worried about his ability to breathe. Not too much, as I found my back swaying in the air as I rode his face, just as Brandon bottomed out.

211

Aaron was tight as a bowstring between us, his cock a massive, aching thing, twitching in the air, his hips searching for some kind of friction to get him where he needed to be. One hand slipped free of me, his fingers glistening as he reached for his cock, but Brandon smacked him away, the slap pulling a gasp and a throb from Aaron. "Hands in cunt," he ordered. "You'll get yours. Just feel me inside you, rubbing against the spot that aches the most." Brandon changed his angle slightly, something that pulled another groan from Aaron.

His fingers, his tongue felt possessed now. He was a cyclone of sucking, thrusting, licking, and I was just caught in the middle of it. A deep ache began to develop in my pelvis, one that was only assuaged and made worse as my hips shifted. I couldn't watch Brandon anymore, but I could hear the harsh sound of his breath, the slap of his body as he pounded into Aaron. Then a slick finger slid backward, circling my arse before pushing in.

I jerked, my eyes going wide open at the strange sensation, and then I saw the arc of cum jetting out of Aaron's cock, splattering all over his belly and chest. His groans reverberated throughout my whole body, and I followed him into ecstasy, only seeing hazily the moment Brandon slammed inside him one last time.

I'm not sure how long it took for everyone to disengage, clean up and collapse into each other's arms, but it felt like only moments later when a quick knock at the door came. Slade opened the door, popping his head in before being given permission to enter. He took in our various states of exhaustion and repletion with a grin, and said, "Time to clean up, lovers. Looks like we're about to have a family dinner."

26

"Hi, Jules."

I stepped out into the living area, still damp from the shower, unable to look away from the screen door where Brandon's mum and some other strange woman stood. The guys were all seated around the dining table or busy at the bench, brewing something up.

"It's OK, Jules," Brandon said, but I flinched when he put a hand on my shoulder. I bit back a warning growl. This man had done much to ease the ache of my heat and showed promise in his domination of the bigger Aaron, who had entered the kitchen, rubbing his hair with a towel. "They don't have to come in if you don't want them to. They just want to talk. They'll stay outside if it makes you more comfortable."

I looked around the room, everyone looking at me, but not meeting my eyes. Finn and Slade were preparing tea, Finn carrying all the implements in on a tray once the kettle boiled and the hot water was poured. "Jules?"

"You can come in," I said finally, moving to take my place at the head of the table. I watched my men shuffle down, each making sure to leave at least a chair between them and the interlopers. The distance eased something inside me, even though it placed them farther away from me.

"Here, love," Slade said, coming and placing a cup full of steaming tea before me. He paused by my side as I breathed in the aroma. English breakfast with a splash of milk, my favourite. The two women didn't move to pour themselves a drink until I'd taken my first sip.

"So," Janice said, her name coming back to me now, "this is Carissa. She was the friend I mentioned beforehand." I looked over at the petite blonde woman who didn't meet my gaze. "She came from the outside as well. There's always talk when a new female starts putting her pack together, but she reminded me just how jarring this process can be for someone who's not from here. That's why we came by." She smiled, a fragile thing. "Right when you don't want any visitors, to see how you are finding the transition."

"It's strange." The words were out of my mouth before I could even think. "Right now, I feel kind of embarrassed by your question, because I'm thinking of what I've just been doing with your son and Aaron. That's my human side. It wants to ingratiate myself, get in your good books. You are my potential partner's mother. By human traditions, I should try to earn your respect. Your disapproval of me could make or break my relationship."

"And your Tirian side?" the newcomer, Carissa asked.

"Wants to drive you all as far away as possible from my men, from all my partners."

My teeth were bared as the words came out, the sounds beginning to be distorted by the growl that rose unbidden. What Carissa did next, shocked me.

"I understand," she said, and placed her hand over mine.

For a moment, I fought the urge to slash out at her, to let the nails of my fingers transform into claws, to punish her hard for daring to lay hands on me. She didn't look scared. Janice did, I could smell the acrid, enticing scent of the spike of fear as she watched my muscles tremble with the effort of stopping myself from lashing out. Carissa just smiled, the peaceful gentle smile of a saint and waited.

"It's OK, what you're feeling. It's what we all felt when we created our packs. Girls who grow up here like Janice, they've been collecting little harems of friends since preschool, where we would play with dolls, having the princess wait to be rescued by the prince. One of the many differences between humans and animals is the amount of the brain hard-wired with instinct. Yours has shifted from the malleable pure human one, to one that's all of a sudden dominated by strong instincts that probably seem completely alien to you."

My eyes bored into the table-top as I listened. She paused, waiting for a response, and all I could do was nod.

"You have desires you've never had before. Impulses you'd never even consider are now second nature. You're having to develop self-control in new ways. All of the little parts of your identity that you had painstakingly created over your twenty odd years of life have been thrown into disarray. You don't know who you are some days..." My fingers closed tighter around the strange woman's, encouraging. I needed her to keep telling this story.

"We expect to go through the heat. We school our sons and daughters, teach them how to get through it without hurting other people," Janice said, "But Carissa made me see outsiders don't get any of that. Kelly's damn rules about newcomers prevent us from helping you with that adjustment before it happens."

"Why is that?" I growled.

"Because not all of you will. We had some outsider girls come, get built up, expecting to turn, expecting to take a harem, and then..."

"And then they didn't. It's why Doc takes those iris photos, right? To see who's most likely to turn," I said.

Janice nodded.

"Our ways are different. What's best for the family trumps what's best for the individual. We had girls turn and run when the moon came and went, and nothing happened. There was even one who returned, letting humans into the Sanctuary. They brought weapons."

I watched Janice's fingers worry at a cloth napkin.

"People died, kids died. That's when things changed."

215

"So now, we come and try to help once the change has happened, try to assist you to make the mental as well as physical transition. This is hard, Jules, but you're not alone."

I looked down the table and saw every eye trained on me. Every one broadcasted what their owners felt, concern, worry, empathy. My Tirian snarled at this, she didn't like any sign of weakness being shared with the group, but I had little choice. I was stunned to find tears burning in my eye sockets. What on earth did I have to cry about? I was an all-powerful supernatural creature, had legions of hot guys throwing themselves at me. It appeared any and all sexual fantasies I'd had in my life could be explored. I was safe, had a home, food, a job. Me and Buddy would be OK.

Buddy.

My eyes jerked up, belatedly searching the room, the yard outside for signs of the Husky.

"Guys, where's my dog?"

The first thing I saw on the guy's faces was wariness. My guts turned to ice as I scanned them. "Buddy?"

"He's with the doc, Jules," Finn said.

"Why? He's my dog." I felt my hackles began to rise, my voice deepening. "Why isn't he here!"

"We thought it better that—"

"You're a risk to the dog right now, and we know you'd hate yourself if you hurt him," Slade said.

"Hurt him? He's mine! He should be here!"

His eyes dropped down to where my nails, no, my claws dug into the table. Splinters had exploded around the puncture marks.

"You're not stable yet, Jules. Of course, you aren't. We didn't want to bring your dog here until the change has settled and the heat is finished. You've gone through such a massive transition. The fucking bastard from the other side hurting you..."

I sat back down, focussing on just breathing for a moment. Buddy. The minute I'd said his name, it was as if a whole part of my brain had been unlocked, a rush of memories and feelings hitting me. The velvety-soft surface of his ears, his woo woo greeting whenever I got home, the little dance he performed when I was putting out his food, the leap up onto the bed and circling, always three times, before settling down in a tight ball. I rubbed at my sternum, feeling the ache now.

But they had a point. I glanced down the table and saw a big group of strong paranormal creatures all on tenterhooks, waiting to see how I'd react. I took a long shuddering breath and then settled back against my chair.

"What happened to it. Him. It's a him, isn't it?"

"The fuckhead that came through to take you?" Slade said. "He--"

"All unfriendlies are locked up in a secure facility. It's an underground, fully reinforced concrete bunker. It has several lock fail-safes, is patrolled by a platoon of our best men, each one of them armed with high powered rifles," Aaron said. "You've got nothing to worry about."

"I'm not worried. I want to see him."

Well, that put the cat amongst the pigeons. Everyone started talking at once, everyone but Carissa. She just squeezed my hand.

"She can do what she wants," Carissa said with a snarl that cut through the cacophony. "If she wants to see this man, you'll show her, Aaron, son of Maureen." She turned back to me. "That's what I wanted to tell you. We aren't taught to trust ourselves in the outside world. You grow up questioning your clothes, the way you look, how loud you are, and how much of your real self you're 'allowed' to show. You question if it's OK to come across as smart or struggling, who you're with, what message you're 'putting out' when talking to men. There are huge industries all constructed around women's doubt. Don't doubt yourself here."

"It's probably a bit soon for it, but we believe the Great Wolf's hand is behind our instincts," Janice said. "The men, their first instinct is to protect you. That's how it should be, but don't let it stop you from doing what you need to. Whenever you are wondering what to do, remember, your instincts are there for a reason."

We had a nice meal afterwards. The guys had evidently been working on it while I was in the bedroom, getting laid. I knew, in theory, there were human women that allowed men to treat them like queens, but I'd never met any. I felt restless as the dishes were brought to the table, like I should be up and doing something. It took me a little to see the pride on the men's faces as they organised the impressive spread of food, but then everyone was seated and turned to look at me. Um... did they say grace or something here? I pulled the closest dish towards me, and said, "This looks amazing. Thanks, guys! Let's eat."

And with that, the silence was broken. First, it was the sound of utensils scraping, of dishes being requested and passed, then the small talk returned. I watched these beautiful men and women have a meal, just like families did across the country, and shook my head. A month ago, I'd been serving dickheads in a diner, and now this. *Don't doubt yourself*, echoed in my mind as I dug in.

27

"No one's saying no," Slade said.

"Sure sounds like it."

"Jules," Aaron said with a sigh, "just give me a little time to talk to my brothers. Taking an unmated woman into a compound of men..."

"Maybe I want that," I snapped.

All of the guys went still around me for a moment. When I looked them over, each face was carefully blank.

"What? Does that get you hot or something?"

"Well, yeah. To see you drowning in—"

"Enough, Slade," Finn said. "What we think is beside the point. The question is, does it make you hot?"

My Tirian had all sorts of thoughts on that. For her, this was a simple, sexual survival of the fittest test. Who could get us off, and keep getting us off until we didn't want to anymore, would make for suitable potential mates. Of course, other characteristics such as the ability to work with the rest of the team, being good with children, being able to fulfil their responsibilities were all important, but not to be considered until sexual compatibility had been established. I felt my cunt slicken at the thought of it. The men who had been with Aaron at the matching hall, their faces were hazy right now, but their bodies. They were all built like him, huge broad frames packed with muscle. My eyes dropped involuntarily to Aaron's pants.

"That's got nothing to do with it. I want to see the... thing that attacked me. He tried to kill me."

"And it's gonna happen, I just want to give the CO some time to get the facility in order. He can pull in married men to look after the place while you're visiting." I stared at Aaron. He came closer, reaching out a hand with a question in his eyes, placing it on my waist and drawing me closer when I didn't say no. "We're not trying to stop you from doing what you need to, just making sure you're safe."

I nodded stiffly, something that softened when he bent down to brush his lips against mine. Yesterday's disorientation seemed to have vanished. Aaron had proved himself worthy, he was in until I decided otherwise.

"And I need to alert Kelly to what we're doing. Not to stop you," Finn said, sliding in on my other side. "But she's going to have thoughts about this. If we want to prevent her from marching down there in protest, I need to have a conversation."

"I can't understand why he would have attacked me like that. Everything I saw showed the black wolves raping and capturing women, not trying to kill them. I nearly died. If I'm going to move on, I just want to see him."

"And I'll tell Kelly that, I promise. Aaron will alert the prison facility. Slade's going to pick up some supplies with Brandon, so Shaun will be here if you need anyone, OK? We'll be back soon."

I nodded.

Finn deposited a kiss on my forehead and then pulled away. Aaron was a little slower, holding me close for a second and then kissing me goodbye.

"Do I get one?" Slade said with a grin, hugging me close.

"So you can imagine me drowning in dick?"

"C'mon, Slade, I don't want to spend any more time away from here than we have to," Brandon said, pulling him towards the door.

"You've gotten so bossy lately," Slade said with narrowed eyes. "What's gotten into you?"

"It's more what he got into Aaron," I said. "Actually, I agree with your little fantasy. It'd be totally hot to see you drowning in dick. One in each hand and every hole."

"Now, sweetheart..."

"Covered in other men's cum like the slut you are."

"Honey, let's talk this through."

"No time for that, no matter how I might wish otherwise." Brandon shifted his dick in his pants. "Best food comes in the morning, so we need to be there before all the queens start making their demands. So c'mon, hot stuff, wiggle those buns."

Slade shot him a shocked look when the other man slapped him on the arse.

"Are you sure we need Brandon in the group?" Slade said. "The joint blow job was one thing, but the man's starting to take liberties."

"Jack and Hawk will be by to look over the fence. I don't think there's an issue with it, but it's not a bad thing to check it." Brandon caught Slade's side-eye and glared at him. "We'll all be back in a few hours."

"You good, Shaunie?" Slade called out as the blond man emerged, drying his hair with a towel. He nodded.

"I know where the guns are, but we're not likely to have an incursion, not with what she said at the matching hall."

"Right then, anything in particular you want us to pick up, love?"

I let my eyes rake over the men, imagining for real the various ways we could waste the morning, if they weren't so damn certain we needed food to survive. Slade saw the heat there and grinned, slow and sexy.

"Wear some of that out with Shaun, love, but save some for me."

An awkward silence settled over the lounge room as the door shut. Shaun grabbed his cigarettes from the dining room table and said, "Wanna come sit on the porch for a bit?"

"OK."

I blinked when we emerged out into the morning light. With the exception of going to the matching hall, I'd been closeted in the house since I'd turned. There was always someone dragging me down to the bedrooms the moment I was up and about, the only sun I saw was when we had a meal together or filtered through the bedroom curtains. There were several chairs set up on the broad deck, empty cans of beer and an ashtray covered the small coffee table. I took a seat.

"We haven't talked...well, at all," he said. He lit a cigarette, then came to a squat beside me, rubbing my arm. "I'm sorry about before. There just wasn't much point pursuing things further until the change happened."

"I obviously felt differently about that. So, what? You didn't want to get to know me unless you knew there was an opportunity to become part of my harem?" My Tirian shifted inside me, eyeing the man closely.

"I really did have to work that night."

"And the next night?"

"You got snapped up, just like I thought you would. Then you got...sick. When you turned, I figured I'd try to prove my worth when you went through the change."

"And so here we are."

I looked Shaun over. His hand dropped lower, to rub along my thigh, something that had me stirring despite myself. I didn't know Shaun, didn't know if I liked him, hated him or just didn't care. I did know right now that I liked the feel of his hand against my skin, that fall of his ragged blonde hair, the dramatic bone structure, the flex of the muscles in his forearms all had an effect. His blue eyes stared into mine as his hand worked slowly higher. I licked my lips as I hooked my leg over one of the arms of the chair. His eyes dropped down, his hand had slid up and under the hem of my shorts. His fingers grazed along the seam where my thigh met my groin. They weren't where I wanted them to be, which had me wriggling on the seat, something that made him grin.

I heard the crunch of tires on gravel as it came up the drive, but Shaun didn't look away or move his hand. Rather, his fingers brushed over my mound, edging closer and closer to where I ached the most. If you'd asked if I'd let a guy stick his hand up my shorts and brush my pussy as strangers drove up to my place a couple of weeks ago, I'd have thought you were mad. If you'd said I'd be moving in my seat as the driver's eyes bored into mine through the dirty windshield, gasping when Shaun's fingers slid through my folds, smearing my dampness across my clit to give it a few flicks, I'd have been aghast. Probably as horrified as I was when he waited until the doors of the truck were slammed shut, and I could see the men walking towards us, to withdraw them.

Superficially, you'd think Jack and Shaun were similar. They both had long blond hair and lean muscular bodies. But Shaun's eyes just burned into mine as he licked my leftovers from his fingers, whereas Jack was a picture of arrogant swagger, strolling on over, Hawk a dark shadow at his shoulder. His smile was sly as he took everything in, Shaun adjusting his cock, moving away from me to sit down, me dropping my leg, aiming for a semblance of modesty.

"Hey, baby," he said, green eyes glittering as he looked down at the two of us. "Just here to see to the fence. Make sure you're secure in your little castle."

Hawk's eyes scanned the lot of us, his nostrils flaring as he took in my skimpy clothes and Shaun's fingers, before coming to rest on my mouth.

"Yeah?"

Jack was trying to bait me, I could feel the shift of my Tirian inside me, unhappy at such a blatant display of disrespect. She wanted him flat on his back, neck bared to our teeth, and then she wanted to explore all the many ways he could make up for his previous show of insolence.

He flicked a look over at Shaun. "How's it going, Shaun. Missed you on the worksite."

"Had my hands full."

"Have you indeed?" His eyes slid down my body, taking an inordinate amount of time in the process.

I noted Jack's unbuttoned work shirt, casually putting on display a tantalising glimpse of his lean chest, something I was willing to bet he'd planned. His pants hung low on his hips, a dark blonde happy trail leading the eye. He chuckled when I took in the sizeable hard-on there.

"Sorry, baby," he purred, "you smell so damn fucking hot. Me and Hawk, we'd lick every damn inch of you. Shaunie as well, if that's what you want."

Of course, my mind then supplied a very detailed visual of just that. It felt like my thighs were drenched as I watched my mental images of Jack, Hawk and Shaun do amazing things to my body and theirs. *Fuck*, I stiffened in my chair, *I had no idea guy on guy got me so hot.*

"I'm not your baby," I said, getting to my feet. He was standing so close it meant our bodies were almost touching. I'd intended to say something snarky, put him and his ambitions down, but standing here, I could fucking smell it.

The guys said they knew when I was receptive by my scent. I never got it before, but perhaps due to the situation, due to Jack's obvious frustration, I was flooded with the warm, spicy smell of aroused male. I could feel the slight tremor in his body as he held himself back from doing anything, and I lifted my head, so my mouth was only inches away from his. I watched his nostrils work, his tongue flicking out to swipe across his bottom lip.

"No?"

"No. I said no one was to approach me outside of the matching hall, and I meant it. You're all hot, you all have big dicks, you all fuck like demons. The thing that differentiates one from another isn't hair colour or the breadth of your chests." I pushed one finger into Jack's. The silk of his skin, his smell had me wanting to slide my palm all over that rigid surface, sliding further and further down. "It's your ability to fucking listen when I talk. I said I didn't want anyone approaching me sexually, that I would chase you. You never gave me that chance."

"But—"

I slapped my hand over his mouth, feeling those soft lips underneath it, and wanted to deploy them somewhere else. The scent got stronger, somehow what I was doing was turning him on further, which just made this all hotter. But if I didn't do this, I was going to have half the single guys in the compound at the gate, and I didn't think either of them could build a barrier strong enough to keep the lot out.

"Fix my fence, then get the fuck out."

"C'mon," Shaun said, grabbing my hand and drawing me inside.

Jack watched me go, an expression between lust and anger burning in his eyes, Hawk already turning towards the truck in defeat.

"Try not to think about me when he fucks you."

I WAS SURPRISED to see I was shaking when I got inside, something I noticed when Shaun's hand landed on my arm.

"It's OK," he said, stroking me slowly.

I turned to look at him, to ask him what he meant, hoping he'd know, that someone would know what the hell was going on. But that's not how the heat works, apparently. I looked into his blue eyes, saw the desire there, smelled that same tempting scent of arousal. We stepped into each other's arms, because of course, we did. When a mouth descended on mine, kissing, sucking at my lips, was it Jack's or Shaun's? My beast didn't care. She just wanted that hand that was sliding up my thigh to force them open and settle between them. It was only featherlight touches initially, his fingers gliding across my drenched skin, forcing moans from me. I wanted it harder, deeper. I wanted the stretch that comes from—

He chuckled, pulling away and then picking me up before depositing me onto the kitchen table. I was hit by the bright light pouring in through the sliding door and turned, concerned at just what we were showing the world. "Don't worry about them," he said as he drew my shirt up, the cold air pulling my nipples even tighter. I gasped as his fingers circled and then pulled gently on them, something that made both guys outside stop in their tracks. They were standing on the gravel path, next to the truck. Tools dropped from bloodless hands, and Hawk took a step forward before mastering himself. They were talking, I could see that, but about what, I didn't care.

"We call this a dominance fuck," Shaun said, removing the last of my clothes and placing a kiss on my ankle. "When the males get a little too feisty, start to try to push the female around," another kiss, by my knee, "trying to get her attention, she'll often take her pick of the men she's considering and fuck them, right in front of the contenders." I was only half listening now, as his mouth trailed along my inner thigh. "They can't look away, the heat riding them too hard, so they're forced to watch her take her pleasure." Thumbs slid down the edges of my cunt, separating me slightly, and I felt the brush of cool air. "They watch her come..." a quick flick of his tongue over my clit, "and come with her chosen, and learn their lesson. You want that?"

I could barely make out what he was asking as he pushed two fingers into me. I fucking needed it, the burn inside me had roared to life. All these available men and their stink of desire had me throbbing. I arched my back at the intrusion, loving the stretch, particularly as I knew a greater one was coming. He'd positioned me perfectly, I realised, so I had a clear view of the guys as he got me off, just as they would of me. I watched Hawk slam a hand into the side of the truck as Jack watched me, eyes wide. Eyes that followed as Shaun's hand slid up my ribcage to cover my breast, eyes that took in my gasps as he tugged at my nipple, that saw my legs fall open as Shaun's mouth covered my cunt, noting every single shove of that blond head as he worked his tongue inside me. Hawk's hand went to Jack's fly as Shaun's mouth closed around my clit, and he jerked it open as Shaun began to suck. I was crying out now, feeling that long, galloping roll towards orgasm, my toes curling as I watched Jack push Hawk's head down. His gaze never wavered as the other man took his cock in his mouth, not even when a shiver ran through him as he felt Hawk suck him down.

It was almost alienating, this desire. It had little to do with me and what I wanted, it was only hormones flooding my body. I hissed when his hands cupped my breasts, and wriggled against him. I didn't need the foreplay. He could stick his dick in me, and I would ride him to a quick, hard climax. Actually, I wanted just that.

"God, fuck me."

I didn't give a shit about any of them now as Shaun clambered over me, hooking my legs around him as he lined his dick up, and then I felt it at my opening. His thumb rubbed the hood of my clit as he worked himself into me. It was always a slow process, even if I was dripping, but somehow that steady pressure just made it better. We were both gasping, me digging my hands into his hair until he finally bottomed out.

"So good, Jules..."

I dug my fingers into his scalp.

"Fuck me hard, Shaun. Make it brutal."

I was jerked back as his legs dropped down to the floor, his fingers digging into my hips. "Tell me if it gets too much."

It wouldn't, I could feel that in the first punishing stroke. I'd had every damn part of my body worshipped since I got here. Gentle kisses, sweet strokes, my clit traced so lovingly, it was almost remade anew. But sometimes it was just friction that got you off. My fingers dropped down to take over clit duty as he slammed into me, the rapid drag of his cock inside me making the burn flare hotter. I felt limp, lost amongst sensation, the steady build of arousal coming completely outside of me. I couldn't think about my life, what we'd make for dinner later, or what the fuck I was doing having exhibitionist sex on the table we had breakfast on. I could only feel.

I was crying and screaming as we got there, Shaun never missing a beat, powering through as the pleasure that smouldered sulkily inside me suddenly exploded. Like the drop of ashes on my skin, prickles washed throughout my whole body. I sobbed as the bliss became almost an ache, so intensely sweet. And then it happened.

He thrust through my body's response, my cunt clasping, tugging at him but, to no avail. He ignored my orgasm as he chased his with all the power of predator. It pushed me higher, somehow. And then I opened my eyes. Jack's and my face were identical, as that terrible pleasure wracked us. I didn't know if I was the one on the kitchen table, feeling Shaun empty himself inside me, or with my fingers buried into Hawk's hair, forcing my cum down his throat. I was gasping when Jack pushed him away, tucking himself into his pants and stomping around to the other side of the truck, when Shaun collapsed on me. I ran my hand through his hair, stroking him as he regained his breath.

28

"What do we have here?"

Slade walked in not long afterwards with a box in hand. He dumped it on the kitchen bench and checked the two of us out.

"You been putting on a show for the boys, princess? That's just mean."

"Jack got pushy, she pushed back," Shaun said, doing up his jeans.

"Did you, princess?" His grin was shockingly bright. "Darlin', I love dominance displays on a woman. Did ya get all hot and bothered when those boys watched Shaunie do you right?"

I was about ready to do the same thing to him, but his tone softened as he came over, his words no longer so mocking when he caught my scent. "You sure the damage is done?" he said, tracing my nipple with his finger. "I, for one, would be more than happy to make sure the job was done properly." He murmured the words, coming closer and closer, until I could feel his breath fanning across my lips. Fuck, I wanted him again. "What do you think, princess? Another round while you're still sopping from Shaun?"

His words broke me out of my haze for a minute. "That turns you on? Fucking me while I'm full of another guy's cum?"

He shrugged, shooting me a crooked smile. "It's all part of life for us, so may as well get a bit of a charge from it. The thought of your hungry little cunt full of cum and ready for more is fucking hot."

"What are you doing, Slade? We've got to get...oh!"

I looked over Slade's shoulder where Brandon had dropped another box on the bench. He took in me and everyone else, both inside and outside the house, with a quick glance, then inclined his head with a little smile. Slade's hand went between my legs, his fingers burying themselves in me with ease.

"Your cunt's all swollen and wet and pouty, your clit's sensitive." He smiled when I shuddered as his thumb grazed it. "I'll slide in so damn easy."

His mouth brushed mine, the stubble scraping against my skin when my hand went around his neck, pulling him down to deepen the kiss.

"How long will this madness continue?" I asked as I undid his fly.

"Only a couple more days, babe, then the tough stuff begins."

"The tough stuff?" I frowned, my brain sure I should be finding out what that was rather than wrapping my hand around his dick. I didn't, I just watched the flare of his pupils as I stroked his hard length.

"Who can you live with? Who do you like?" He grabbed me at the waist and lifted me up, backing us up until I hit the wall. "Mmm..." he groaned as he pushed himself in. "So fucking wet." He began to thrust, rocking me in his arms. "But the deal breaker? Who you can love."

29

"Are you sure I really need this?"

I'd had a shower, and Aaron and some of his army buddies had arrived. I was currently standing in a pair of jeans and a long-sleeved shirt, getting a bulletproof vest fitted.

"It's what I wear when I go down there," Aaron said, checking all the straps. My skin crawled. The pressure and rub of the clothes felt so wrong, and I was starting to drip with sweat.

"Are we done?"

"Never," Slade said with a shake of his head, pushing himself away from the wall.

"It's been all cleared. Kelly will be standing by, at a distance," Finn said, sticking his head in the door.

"Why at a distance? It's him I want to see, not her."

"Right now, you're one little ball of dominance displays, topped off with a very healthy sex drive," Slade said.

"New Tirians have gotten caught up in battles with the alpha before, and it hasn't ended well. She keeps as far away as she can, to avoid any unnecessary pain." Finn smiled when he saw my bald stare. "You think you can take her? Try once the heat's settled down and you've selected your pack."

"Don't." I looked over my shoulder to see Brandon had drawn closer.

"What?"

"Don't...don't go getting caught up in power struggles."

I took in his frown, the arm's crossed firmly across his chest.

"Are we good?" I pointed to the bulletproof vest. Aaron nodded.

It was bulky and uncomfortable, even more so when I reached out and gave Brandon a hug, but it was worth it when those arms loosened and went around me.

"I just want to see this guy."

"I know." He buried his head in my hair, breathing in my scent. "It worries me."

"We'll take care of her," Finn said. "Not that she needs it. She's near-indestructible now, you know that. With Aaron and the guns..."

"Worries aren't rational, but they feel like they are," Brandon said, stepping back. "I'll be here when you get back. Be safe, and I hope you get what you need."

Finn was the only one apart from Aaron that would come with me. A couple of big burly guys nodded as soon as we came outside and climbed into the front of the truck, leaving me to get in the back, Finn on one side and Aaron on the other.

Finn smiled at me as the truck started rumbling down the road. My body was sure this was going to be just like the matching hall incident, which had me wriggling in my seat. He noted this, his eyes growing hooded. I reached out and placed a hand on his leg, something he captured quickly. He tangled his fingers in mine, rubbing a thumb over my knuckle.

"It's been too long," he said when I cocked an eyebrow.

"It was only last night."

"I know, but it never feels like it's enough. I'm either in you, or watching one of the guys in you. I'm lucky Kelly put me on indefinite leave, because I am a fucking mess right now."

"First order of business when we get home," Aaron said. "Him first, then me. Sound good, Jules?"

They both watched me shift in my seat, my legs crossing and

uncrossing. What the fuck was I doing, leaving the house? All I could see, think, feel was exactly that. We'd worked out a Goldilocks protocol for sex, where I went from one to the next until everyone was 'just right'. I hadn't had any more pain with Aaron, something he knew damn well from that smile on his face, only the pleasure that came from having more cock than I would have ever thought possible.

"You OK, Jules?" Finn asked, his smile unwavering. "Something you need? Because we can turn this truck around. You just say the word."

"No," I said, reaching out for both of them, one for each hand. I pressed the palm into each straining groin, letting them slide up and down, up and down to the musical sound of their groans.

30

It wasn't what I expected. I guess I'd not had a lot of experience with underground bunker or prisons, so I didn't have much to compare it with. While I knew the guys were aching, it was all business when we pulled up. The guy in the front got out first, checking out the area. Not sure why. It was flat and dusty and empty here, a large fence running around the compound. There was only one other car there, and a hole in the ground.

That wasn't totally accurate. When we piled out, I could see concrete steps leading down into the bunker, and a large, reinforced steel door blocking the entrance. Kelly stood leaning against the other car, waving a hand when we walked over to the compound.

The men Aaron brought with him went first, guns held with a casual competence. One walked up to a scanner in the side of the stairwell, and upon inspection, the door clicked open. Finn took my hand as we walked inside.

It was all grey cinder blocks and steel reinforcement down here. There was a small waiting area with bench seats bolted to the wall and a reception desk, cordoned off by metal screens. One of the men walked up and pressed a button. Another man arrived, stopping when he saw us, nostrils working, before schooling his face into a neutral expression. "So, we're going through with this?"

"She says she needs it, to get over what happened," Aaron said.

"Well, you've got the clearance. Steer away from the mess room. We couldn't find enough married guys to cover everything, and some of those that are...well, they're questioning their vows right now. She's a bomb waiting to go off, and so's he. Get her in, and get her out."

"Got it."

The metal door swung open and we walked in, moving down a long hallway until we reached another set of gates, and another. We continued through, the only thing that changed was the man standing at the doors. One took an involuntary step towards me, something that had the men's guns whipping up and a growl coming from Aaron, but he seemed to master himself, moving back to his position. Then we came to the final door, a huge portal that looked much like an old bank vault door. The men nodded, and then keyed in the numbers to open it.

"May as well take the fucker's food in for him while you're in there," a big burly guy said, shoving a tray at Finn. "Don't you worry, love. We'll keep you safe. Take a look, get your fill, and then you turn around and pretend like this fuck never existed, yeah?"

I found myself agreeing just from the heavy weight of his gaze. Seemingly happy with that, he gestured for us to precede him.

The cells looked a lot like the ones in human prisons that you see on TV, though the bars were much, much thicker. It took me a little while to register him, curled up in a corner as he was. There was no bed, no blankets, just a tap and a small reinforced hole in the ground.

"Well, well, what do we have here?"

The voice sounded rusty, corroded from disuse. He uncoiled himself, forcing me to look up and up as he stood. He grinned through the smears of dried blood across his face, through the matted fall of his long black hair. Those ice blue eyes burned into mine as he slowly inspected every inch of me. "I knew you'd come. Closer, little queen, closer."

I took a step towards the cage before I'd even thought about it, only the hands of Finn and Aaron stopping me from fulfilling his order. I blinked and frowned, looking down at where their fingers dug into my skin. When I glanced at Finn, he gritted his teeth, putting everything into keeping me where I was. I brushed them aside, something that made the black wolf laugh, but stayed put. *What was that?*

You wear my mark, little queen.

My gaze jerked up, and I met those blue eyes head on, my hand straying automatically to the place where he had bitten me.

"What did you do?"

His teeth were bright against the grime of his skin. He smiled with all the light-heartedness of a child, tossing his snarled mane over his shoulder.

"That's the question, isn't it? All I know is," his hands went to the bars, something that had the soldiers stepping forward, "biting is an intimate thing, y'know. The feel of their flesh in your mouth, swallowing down their blood. I'll be seeing you, little queen, a whole lot more now."

The guys started to growl, but I held up a hand.

"How? You're locked up in a cage. You piss and shit in a hole. You won't be seeing anyone but these fellas for the rest of your life."

He shrugged nonchalantly, pushing away from the bars before shivering and turning into his Tirian form, the wolf looking like it was only just contained by the room. Those red eyes stared into mine for a moment, before bolts of electricity arced out from the roof, walls and floor, forcing the wolf back into his human form. He lay on the ground, laughing between rasps of breath before rolling to his feet, standing short of the bars again, but now he was in a much better condition. His skin was now clear, pale as the moon, his hair a long fall of black feathers. He crossed his arms, smiled down at me with a cruel twist, as my eyes compared the well-muscled form in front of me with the black wolf of my fevered visions. The men started to curse when his hand went to his dick, but the shouted threats didn't stop him, and neither did the pulled out tasers.

"Sweet dreams," he said as the electrical bolts zapped out again, and he fell to the floor.

31

The drive back home was a quiet one. I'm sure the guys wanted to say they'd told me so, but they thankfully kept their mouths shut.

He was posturing, I tried to tell myself, *trying to look like a big man while being locked in a cage.*

That one is a threat, my Tirian replied, *one I don't know if I can protect you from.*

Well, that sure put a downer on my mood. When we rolled in, Jack and Hawk were still working on the fence, but I just glanced at them. I had bigger fish to fry. I sat down at the dining table when we got in, trying to process. A cup of tea and some biscuits appeared in front of me, then a warm hand on my shoulder. I looked up to see Finn standing there, along with Aaron.

"He can't touch you," Finn said.

"Who can't touch her?" Brandon asked, striding out of the kitchen and over to the table. "I thought she was just looking at the dickhead in his cage? What the fuck happened?"

That threw the cat among the pigeons, and I sat there quietly as the guys filled each other in.

"You said she'd be safe," Slade snapped.

238

"She was, is. He got electrocuted a few times while pronouncing vague threats."

"What fucking threats?" Shaun said.

"He said he'd see me again. He's locked up behind metal bars and concrete, and there was a metric fuck tonne of men with guns there. It was just empty threats. Don't let it worry you, I'm not going to."

I picked up the cup and took a big sip of tea, feeling the need for something to ground me as much as anything.

"I'm talking to the boys, see if we can't beef up security along the fence," Shaun said, opening the sliding door and stomping outside.

"What're you thinking, Aaron?" Slade said. "We get some munitions up here, set up some defences?"

"You clear that with the alpha?" he asked.

"I can't see her refusing the request. She's already distraught the prick got through in the first place," Finn said. "We should have anticipated this, built the house security up before we even brought her here."

"And what do you want?"

Brandon sat down at the table, watching me closely, the only person who was. He smiled when I noticed him, but it wasn't necessarily a happy thing.

"What I've always wanted," I said, putting the cup down on the saucer. "What's going on? Who are the black wolves? Why did he bite me? Why did he fight to get to me? What's behind the 'Sanctuary' fence? You know, all the usual questions one might ask when transformed from human to something else when not drunk on dick."

Slade shot a look at Finn and then sat back down, nodding. "The heat's abating. The 'ole pre-frontal cortex is coming back online. Of course, you have questions, love, and we'll answer every single one of them. As soon as we feel like you're safe. Finn, get Kelly on the line."

"No."

Slade frowned then looked at me. "No?"

"No, tell me first. Something always gets in the way. Kelly, the heat, the matching hall. I want to know, Slade, now. I want my dog, my stuff, my fucking life back..." Silence reigned as my voice cracked.

"And if not that, then I want to know what the fuck is going on. Who are the black wolves? I've had visions of them."

"What?" Finn stiffened. "You've never told us that."

"Sucks, not being given all the information, doesn't it?"

"What did you see?"

"I saw the...white Tirians, how they came from the women who were raped by the men. I saw those crystal spearheads and the gate and the first alpha..." My voice trailed away as I saw the guys looking at each other. "What?"

"None of us have ever seen or heard what you just described. It could be a women's thing. Not all knowledge is shared with the men," Brandon said. "I could get my mum to come over."

"Sounds good. Tell her I'll be a lot more hospitable this time."

"She understood, but sure."

"Jules, from what you're saying, you know more about him than we do," Aaron said. "The only intel we get is the dark wolves are the unfriendlies. The gate, that's locked away in the Sanctuary," Aaron said. "We stop all creatures that can pass through from coming into this realm. Most come for dubious reasons. There are resources here that they can't get back home, there's land, minerals and human wrought goods. Incursion rates always spike around the full moon, but we've been given no intel about them wanting women. That was why we were so ill-equipped to deal with your attack. We only bite other Tirians in dominance displays and sex, never anyone that can't turn. Doc had no idea how to deal with a human infected with our venom."

"So who would know?" Everyone's eyes slid around to Finn.

"I'll get Kelly on the phone, organise a meet. Who do you want sitting around the table?"

This was the first time anyone had asked me a question like that. Before this, people were invited into the house, and just stayed until I said otherwise. I hadn't said otherwise, hadn't even considered it. My body was calling the shots, and it wasn't ready to disregard any warm form that might bring it pleasure, except for rude pricks like Jack. Brandon, I wanted him there. His hand was on my arm, his grey eyes taking in every one of my micro-expressions. He was good for me, I realised. Things felt right when he was around, he seemed to get what I needed to adjust to being a part of the Sanctuary. I reached over and squeezed his hand, and a small smile appeared on his face.

Slade sat next to him. He was trying to stay calm, but his eyes were slightly too wide, his face a little pale. My straight talker, he'd tell me what he thought, whether I wanted it or not. In some ways, it was reassuring to see someone as confident as him as shaken by the black wolf as I was.

Finn was pulling out his phone, and I watched the play of sinews in his forearm as he brought up Kelly's contact, guessing it was only me that saw the slight shake there. His shoulders had started to tighten. I got up before I even thought about it, placing a hand on either side and pressing my fingers into the big muscles there. His eyes darted up and over his shoulder. For someone who was so confident and ready for action, there was something almost shy in his gaze. Finn had looked after us, managing my transition, the house, the mating hall. He was always level headed and prepared, which was why, as my hand slid down and into the front of his shirt, I liked watching his fingers go limp, dropping the phone to the table-top, and feeling him lean back against me. My fingers circled his nipple, I heard his breath hitch as the door opened and Shaun returned. While I stroked Finn, he and Aaron discussed what they would do to fortify our place, to keep us all safe, geared up to make calls, get equipment, take action.

This is what he'd wanted, the black wolf. He was locked up, caged and constrained. He had no power, so he'd taken what he could, our peace of mind. He'd ruffled feathers, sowed seeds of fear and doubt. I straightened up, letting my fingers trail along the muscular column of Finn's neck.

I wasn't in Melville anymore, not working at the diner, I wasn't even human. That Julie had died when she was bitten by the black wolf. So who was I now?

I looked around the table at the guys, only Finn quiet under my hands. They all talked to and over each other, sharing ideas, trying desperately to work out how to keep us safe. These very different, very beautiful men cared for me and each other, would do anything to protect us. I felt a hard lump rise in my chest, something I would never swallow down.

"C'mon, let's go," I said.

Heads turned, fingers paused in the process of making calls, conversations stopped. For a moment, old Julie quailed in the face of all that undivided male attention, but Jules shouldered her aside quickly, accepting their regard as her due.

These are your mates, my Tirian said.

Maybe. I don't know yet, but I want to.

They look upon you with hunger. You can smell their desire. They strive to protect and care for you. For now, these are your mates. Enjoy it, relish it, surrender to it, for now. When you know you care enough to do the same for them, you will know they are your pack.

Perhaps it was this advice that prompted what came next.

"All of you. In the bedroom, naked, now."

We'd had plenty of group sex, but usually with no more than two of the guys involved. The heat had definitely abated. I could think a whole lot clearer, but somehow, that just made the idea hotter. There was no foggy cloud of instinctual lust directing my actions. My eyes skipped over every single one of them, my gaze tugged hither and thither by their individual beauty. There was a brief pause, as my order hung in the air, then everyone moved as one. Shaun locked the sliding door and drew the curtains, and Finn swept me up into his arms, provoking a yelp as he carried me down the hall. The light in our room flared bright as we stepped inside, the others following hot on Finn's heels, pulling off clothes, revealing acres of hard-muscled flesh.

By the time Finn put me down, there was an honour guard of naked male bodies leading to the bed, erect cocks straining as they waited. I turned to see Finn was half the way to the same place. He paused, hand on his fly, grey eyes searching mine until I reached out and placed a palm on his cheek. I heard the rustle of the others moving when I kissed him, and put out a hand to stop them from coming any closer as I focused just on the feel of Finn's lips against mine, soft, slow, nipping. It deepened as I undid his jeans and pushed them down his hips, him groaning as his hard cock slapped against his belly.

"Jules..."

He reached for me but I pulled back, letting my fingers trail down his body as I went. His brows creased, then smoothed, his smile twisted with frustration as he watched me move over to Slade.

"You liking this little display, love?" he asked as I placed my arms around his neck. He moved to turn me, so I did so, facing the group. "Look at them, aching to touch you." As if to prove his point, his fingers trailed up my ribs and cupped my breasts.

"And each other."

"Some of them. You want to see that, love? When I push my cock into you, you want to see one of them take another? Hear them groan as one of them settles in deep while I swallow yours when I fuck you?"

"If they want it." I wanted to sound cool and open-minded, but instead sounded all breathy. "That's what I want, for people to be able to tell me what they want, and if everyone's cool, to go for it." I turned to face him, glad to see that twinkle in his eyes was back. "And what do you want?"

"Let me go first." His voice came out as a hoarse rumble. He was trying to play it cool, fixing that sly grin of his on his face, but I could see the need plainly. "Let me be the one that works his cock into that tight little cunt of yours, watches you squirm around on the bed as you try to push me clear and pull me closer. Let me send you into the arms of one of the others with my cum dripping down your legs."

It was hot, what he described, but there was something else there. His eyes bore into mine, his smile fading, as if somehow his gaze could communicate what he dared not. My kiss was light, gentle, trying to reassure him, but he wasn't having it. He yanked me to him, forcing his tongue between my lips, pouring everything he had into it before pulling away again. I blinked, feeling dazed by sensation and the sudden absence of it, and then he smiled, quick and brilliant as the sun. "C'mon, you better get to the others before they burst."

"Let's get these clothes off," Shaun said when I moved to him. I tangled my hands in his hair as he removed them, neat as a maid. He struggled to meet my eyes as I leaned in to kiss him, but his fingers dug into my waist as his lips brushed mine. The lightness of his touch seemed to belie what he was feeling. I could hear the desperate rasp of his breath as we touched, something that only got more intense when he turned me around and pushed me dazed towards Aaron.

I should have felt self-conscious, standing there naked in front of five guys, but I didn't get a chance to. Aaron's lips were on mine the moment I was close enough, his hands everywhere. I found myself clinging to his chest, our tongues twining as his hand slid up my thigh. "Jules, you're so wet."

He said it like I gave him the greatest gift, like it was steak and blow job day, and he was getting a double suck while eating a 400gm, grain-fed, Scotch filet. The rumble of his voice and the press of his mouth was one part reverent, one part ravenous. I panted against his lips as those fingers slid across my seam, the V rubbing on either side of my clit. My thighs widened instinctively, my hips thrusting along with his caresses, the pleasure building and building...

"Time for Brandon, Jules."

The man in question's face swum into focus as I blinked. He took in my dazed expression with a heavy-lidded smile and drew me into his arms. For some reason, resting my head against the hard expanse of his chest and breathing in his scent was just what I needed. He chuckled a little, then brushed my hair back from my face.

"It's a bit overwhelming, yeah?"

He said it quietly, as if only for us.

"Yeah."

"We're gonna make you feel so good." He spun me around to face the group. "Look at them. They're aching to be inside you, just like I am." He flattened his hand against my pelvis, grinding me back against his rigid length. "Ask them to touch those hard dicks."

I glanced over my shoulder, but then turned back to the rest of them. "Do it."

Big square hands, knotted with muscle, grasped each thick cock. Some, like Slade, made a show of the act. He moved his hand so, so slowly up and down his dick, as if remaking every inch of it with his movements. Veins stood out on Finn's neck and temple. He did what I asked, but it looked like it hurt him to do so. I remembered how long it had been for him, longer than the others.

"We shouldn't do this to Finn. He needs it too much."

"He does, doesn't he? Look at that cock, those veins standing so proud. It's so red and angry." We watched Finn shudder with the effort of holding back. "You can ease his suffering, if you want."

A memory of Brandon working his dick into Aaron flashed into my mind, so I looked back at him.

"What do you want?"

His smile was perfect, bright and beautiful, and he knew exactly what I was and wasn't asking.

"Me? I want to push Slade out of the way, drop you on the bed and bury myself in you." His smile widened when he heard my sharp intake of breath. "I want to be selfish and just fuck you until we both come. But really, I want to see you let go, really let go. I want to see you spread out and wanton, with us sucking, licking, biting, fucking every bloody inch of you. I want you to come until you can't anymore and then I want you to come just once more. I want you covered in our cum, marked by any and all that smell you as ours."

A growl went around the room that sounded like one of agreement.

"And you? Do you want to experience that too?"

"Being on the receiving end?" His eyes roamed my face, as if looking for clues. "If that's something you want to see, I'd do that for you. But not with these guys. There's only a couple here that'd be into that. But it's not what I need, Jules. I need what everyone here needs. You."

I kissed him then, because it was all so intense and overwhelming and confusing. And because despite my protestations, the geeky guy who quoted comic books and gave me romance novel recs, who also was a little bit of a dominant, was getting under my skin. They all were. And right now, I wanted to celebrate that. What we had, it was fragile. I wasn't sure if all of our bonds would deepen enough to be made permanent, but I wanted to find out.

I was brought back to the here and now when Brandon's hands cupped my breasts, and his fingers tweaked my nipples hard.

"Don't get too caught up in your head, love."

I smiled, then gasped as I felt that tug on my clit each time he rolled my nipple with his fingers. "I'm not."

I pulled away, something I didn't want and neither did he, if his clinging caresses were anything to go by. I moved clear of him and went to Finn, stilling his hand and then drawing his head down to mine. He fell upon me like the hungry wolf he was, his kisses open mouthed and brutal, his hands cupping my butt and jerking me close, his dick grinding into me. He tried to claw me back when I drew away, a low growl indicating his need. That stilled when I dropped down to my knees in front of him.

He needed this, to take the edge off, so he could regain some control and be the man I knew him to be. One who focussed on what had to be done for the good of the group, not his own needs. I was gratified to hear his gasp as my hand wrapped around the base of his cock, his long drawn out groan was music to my ears as I licked the underside with my tongue. I traced the angry head, placing teasing kisses on the crown. He thrust instinctively, trying to force me to stop playing and swallow him whole. But I held him still, forced him to endure it when my lips parted so, so slowly over the head, stopping to twist and shift, rubbing them all over it. He was panting hard as I worked him in deeper, my tongue flickering like a snake along his rigid length. His hands came to rest so, so softly on my skull, almost a benediction.

"Oh, fuck, Jules...."

"Take pity on the man."

I felt a hand on my hips, drawing me up to standing, but not dislodging me from Finn's dick. I glanced back and saw it was Slade.

"Let's work together, for the benefit of the pack," he said with a wink, then spread my legs before dropping down between them. I yelped at the first lick along my seam, but he stopped too soon. "You stop, I stop."

Finn began to hum as I buried his dick in my throat, his fingers a little firmer. "Oh, fuck. Oh, fuck," he started to chant as I worked my mouth up and down his length. He was so hard, so ready, I could almost feel him flex. I gasped as Slade's lips fastened themselves to my clit, something that had Finn pushing even further still. I gagged a little, tears streaming down my face, but closed my hand tighter around the base so I could control how much I was taking. It all started to blur, Finn's pleasure, my pleasure, Slade spearing his fingers inside me as he licked furiously until...

Finn's hips jerked forward as he emptied into my mouth, rope after rope of cum spurting as he sobbed his ecstasy. Slade disengaged, leaving my clit throbbing in the cool air, and he slapped me on the butt.

"Come on, princess. Time to get on your throne and be worshipped."

"I hate it when you call me princess."

"I know," he said, sidling in close, then trailing his fingers through my wetness before licking it off his fingers. "It makes you fuck that much harder."

"C'mon," Finn said, taking my hand and then falling down onto the bed, dragging me with him. He shifted until he was half lying against the headboard and I was on him. "We'd all rather fuck, than fight."

"Speak for yourself," Slade said, but he dropped down between my open thighs, a hungry look on his face.

As he started to lay kisses against my inner thigh, the others crawled onto the bed. Finn tilted my head back, swallowing down my moans as I felt hands trail all over my body. His lips were like roughened satin, slow and sensuous, as hands traced the sensitive skin of my groin, raked across my ribs, then circled my breasts in ever decreasing circles until closing on my aching nipples.

SAM HALL

God, this was less like sex, and more like being swept along on a tide. The sensory overload was intense. Sometimes during sex before I'd come to Sanctuary, I'd wished my boyfriends had had another set of hands. Like my nipples were aching for attention as he went down on me, or I wanted fingers inside me and rubbing either side of my clit. Well, this was something altogether different. Sensations warred, the soft tugging on my clit, the fingers working their way into me, the stinging suction on my nipples, the open mouthed and deep kisses. Pleasure was painstakingly drawn from every square inch of my flesh. I shivered as my mind fought to process each bit individually, but I couldn't. It was a symphony of sensation, and I was being dragged along with it.

Surrender.

As soon as the word appeared in my mind, I felt myself go limp. This wasn't about my pleasure or theirs, it was ours. Every single one of my lovers worked together as a team to give me this most amazing experience, and it was my job to enjoy it. My ribs rose up from the bed as the tension grew. Sharp stabs of pleasure flared hard inside me as my skin hummed with the gentler pleasure of touch. When Slade stood, positioning himself between my legs, I moaned, "Yes..."

"Hungry, love?" he said, rubbing his cock along my cunt.

I nodded.

"Open your eyes," he said. "That's right, look at me, stay with me."

Heat warred with something painfully naked as he pushed his cock into me. His brows creased and smoothed, the skin tightening around his eyes, as if somehow that would protect him from what was being said wordlessly.

I could try to dismiss it as just a physical thing, his body intersecting mine, moving faster and faster, increasing that delicious friction we both craved. And yet, as intense as that was, there was so much more. He was giving me all he had. The flex of his jaw as he struggled to keep himself in check, the gorgeous shift and play of muscles in his torso as he moved, the shuddering rasp of his breath, the way he fought to give me his best. I struggled to hold onto his gaze. I wanted to throw myself into the dark, close my eyes where there was only the delicious ache of my clit and the hard thrust of his cock, but I couldn't. It felt so good, he watched my teeth worry my lip, saw my squirms and thrust harder, pushing us closer and closer...

Until I reached up and pulled him down with me. He was no longer thrusting into me, we were moving together, a multilimbed organism, reaching out for something that was bigger than we were, until we caught it.

I felt his throbs inside me as he came, my own orgasm spiralling along with it. We swallowed each other's gasps, unable to pull apart even to catch breath, the swell in my chest part emotional, part oxygen deprivation. I didn't care. It was as if I sought annihilation, as if continuing to operate as a separate organism was somehow an affront to the natural order of things. I cried out when he was pulled from my arms, but it was Brandon who took his place.

I didn't need to be told this time, I kept my eyes on him as we moved, the sexual act now a series of tiny separations and rejoinings that shook something inside me. "Beautiful girl," he said, tilting his head, and I saw the glitter in his eyes. The second orgasm caught us both by surprise. It was as if this suspended state of bliss was our natural one, and for it to come to some kind of crescendo was unheard of. He slid regretfully from my arms but then Shaun was next.

He reached out for Brandon, pushing him down between us, so the other man's tongue flickered over my clit as Shaun shoved himself inside me. His hands went to Brandon's head and my hand, linking us all. He wore an expression of tormented bliss, his eyes falling almost closed as he moved, but he drew the three of us along with him. A tug on my nipple drew my gaze away, and I saw Aaron bend down and suck it into his mouth. My fingers restively roamed across his close shorn skull. He released it with a pop and growled, "I can't wait to get inside you."

He got his chance not long afterwards. Shaun collapsed further down the bed, Brandon pulling away, but not too far when I put my hand on his arm. He smiled and flopped down beside me, placing a couple of quick kisses on my lips.

"You OK, love?" Aaron said.

I turned back to see that mountain of a man place a hand on my hip before moving any closer. I couldn't miss the tension in his body, his abdomen a wall of rigid muscle, but he paused, checking if I was alright to proceed. I rolled up onto my knees and wound my arms around his neck. For some reason, that sheer mass of muscles made me smile. While he was gentle and considerate, the illusion that he could snap me in two with little effort was kind of sexy. This made the gentleness with which he cupped my face and kissed me all the more special.

I turned when I felt a weight shift behind me, and saw that Finn had joined us. He drew my head back, kissing me before releasing me to Aaron. The two worked together, passing me to and fro until I was half drunk from it all. It began to blur, was I looking into Aaron's eyes or Finn's? Who exactly didn't seem to matter. A warmth rose as I was stroked, growing hotter and hotter until one of them slid inside me. I had given up on eye contact, lying with my head thrown back as they dragged cries from me, ragged and torn from my chest, filling the air. *This is it, the end, the last one I have in me*, I thought. And as if in recognition of that, the pleasure built and built. Past the point of simple bliss, past intensity and ecstasy to something altogether foreign. I should have come a million times by now, and I kind of did. My cunt spasmed, my clit throbbed, but it didn't end. Nothing resolved, fell away. Rather, my nerve endings laboured on and on, sending wave after wave of heartbreakingly beautiful sensation through me, until this felt less like sex and more like a natural wonder or disaster, completely alien and devastating .

"Mmm..."

The purr was an unfamiliar one so my eyes snapped open. Instead of Aaron or Finn or any of my lovers, the black wolf pumped between my legs, his smile a cruel twist, but his eyes were heavy lidded with lust.

"Oh, no," he said when I tried to scrabble back. All my new found Tirian strength deserted me as his fingers dug in like iron, holding me in place. The place his fangs had bitten into in my shoulder throbbed in time with my cunt.

I'd like to say that all the lovely feelings brought about by our group lovemaking dissipated, but perhaps in the final betrayal, my body kept responding, now a foreign sensation that ignored my mental and actual screams. Orgasm struck like a million knives, hitting me harder and harder, forcing cries from me until I came no more.

32

The women filed into the meeting room. They were all adults, only women who had experienced their first change were admitted to the council room, though some carried babies on their hips. They took their seats as Kelly moved to take the alpha's chair.

She waited for quiet, something that came automatically, with the exception of one fussy baby. The alpha smiled as the mother tried to hush the child with a series of jiggles and pats.

"You know why we're all here. We'll need to admit the outsider soon, so things need to be clear before Julie takes her place within our numbers. I need to reiterate that it is expected that we all adhere to the agreed path of action."

Not entirely agreed upon, which became evident. Kelly watched many of the women shift in their seats, turn to those next to them to pass comment. This was the lot of the alpha, to witness the concern and dissension, and then lead the group.

"More outsiders are coming. The scattering times are drawing to an end. One way or another, our peoples are going to become one." The noise only grew louder, shriller at that. She heard their anger and their fear, and nodded, not speaking until it settled. "This is what our mothers and our mothers' mothers have prepared us for, since time immemorial. We can do this. We are strong. We can reclaim our ancestral lands, and defeat those who would enslave us, once and for all."

"Isn't this a lot to put on one outsider girl?" Janice asked.

Kelly acknowledged that and leaned back against her chair. "It won't be just one girl. We will all have our role to play, but in the new outsiders, there will be others who'll play key roles."

"Who will remain ignorant of their path."

"I wish there was another way, really I do. But in the end, all we can do is trust the messages the seers left us. May the line remain unbroken."

"May the line remain unbroken," the women all repeated.

ACKNOWLEDGMENTS

As always, love and appreciation to my partner, Matt. He had to back away from this one, especially when I was writing M/M and multiple partner scenes, but as always, he wholeheartedly supports my creative endeavours, encouraging me to get this out earlier rather than later and asks no questions about why I'm writing pervy stuff.

Editing was done by the lovely Meghan Leigh Daigle. She was able to wrangle my bloody tense shifting habit into a much more readable, grammatically correct form.
   https://www.facebook.com/Bookish-Dreams-Editing-105567517555119/

Cover was created by the amazing team at Mibl Art
   https://miblart.com/

Thanks to Katie for reading what I thought was a rubbish story and believing in it. Also to Andrea, Amber and Bekah who took over alpha duties, pointing out errors with an eagle eye. All of your feedback was heartening and invaluable.

Andrea pulled double duty, also beta reading the book, along with Kathryn, Charlotte and Teresa. We've had a ton of hysterical, blunt, saucy, intense and incredibly inspiring conversations over the development of this book. All of you are the lifeline this author needs to keep on keeping on!

ABOUT THE AUTHOR

I grew up in that bit of Australia you saw in Crocodile Dundee. Yup, I have seen saltwater crocs in the wild, have held a koala (the 70s, when stressing wildlife for the kiddies was still cool) and have swatted an insane number of hand sized spiders (they think I am their queen and are always wherever I am!). I have a gorgeous child with ASD, a super supportive, truly awesome partner and so, so many animals. Seriously, there are double the pets to people.

Being a little baby writer, trying to make her way in the big, crowded, world of self-publishing, reviews are our lifeblood. Seriously, we're sitting in isolated rooms wondering what the hell we are doing with our lives, so chuck a review on Amazon or Goodreads and I will loooove you!

Stalk me!

Facebook author group: Sam's Hall of Heroines
https://www.facebook.com/groups/2356697491274667/
Come and see teasers and me explain what the hell was going on in my head when I was writing that.

Instagram:

https://www.instagram.com/samhallauthor/
Teasers, WIPs and pictures of my animals here!

ALSO BY SAM HALL

Book Lover 1: Not My Fantasy

When Ash and her sister inherited their grandmother's magic shop, they figured they'd be selling crystals and smudge sticks to ageing hippies. Instead, they find themselves dealing with a failing business and a revolving door of tinsel-haired elves and fairy-tale princes.

And that's not even the weird part.

Cursed in some sort of freakish loop, Ash wakes up every morning next to her sister's latest book boyfriend, or fangirl crush. Frazzled by her unwanted nocturnal visitors, Ash fights for the focus needed to save the shop from bankruptcy. Then, in walks Gabe. Looking like a biker wet dream, Ash immediately dismisses him as another of her sister's lusty manifestations. But this hottie is real and may hold the key to saving their business.

Things appear to be looking up, until an inter-dimensional gateway is discovered in the store that allows characters from every multiverse imaginable to cross over. Can the sisters learn how to control the portal before it destroys the line between fact and fiction?

If you love paranormal romance and urban fantasy tropes, but want to have a bit of fun with them sometimes, this is your book. If you watched a lot of bad 80s fantasy with papier-mâché props, noticed all romance guys have massive wangs or checked the back of a wardrobe to see if there was a portal to another realm, this is your book. If you like snarky, sex-positive female characters, this is your book. If you still have a total soft spot for talking animals and really wish you could have one of your own, this is your book.

Book Lover 2: As You Wish

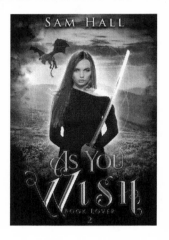

Tess is over being a sidekick.

After experiencing life as a dragon rider, doing inventory at the shop is a mundane nightmare. Unfortunately, Ash continues to insist she live a normal life, staying safe on their side of the inter-dimensional portal.

Of course, Flea could be a welcome distraction... if he would speak to her. They shared one truly amazing night and then dark-haired hottie popped through an inter-dimensional portal to save her, but now, he barely manages a hello when he comes into the shop.

As if responding to her unspoken need for a little action, dragon riders suddenly appear and demand her presence before their court. What she thought was going to equate to a traffic fine for having an unregistered dragon quickly morphs into a life-or-death journey.

Join Tess and the gang as they rampage through the land of Aravisia, on a quest to discover the truth behind Nan's curse!

Book Lover prequel: Read You Like a Book

Everyone wants to wake up next to a hot book boyfriend, right? Well, not Ash.

Her grandmother has just died and she knows the service tomorrow is going to be a hard one. She has to say goodbye to the one member of her family who always had her back and her mother's perfumed steamroller tendencies seem to get out of control each time there's some kind of family emergency.

The last thing she expected was to wake her was the Big Bad Wolf, particularly one as hot as Fenrir Vanguard. Big, muscular and ready to eat her all up, it becomes very difficult for Ash to focus on the fact he thinks she's his fated mate and a woman called Red. Oh, and the fact he's the lead character in her sister's favourite paranormal romance.

What will Ash do with a sexy beast who's ready to bond with her, promising an eternity of hot paranormal sex and his whole heart? How will Ash break it to those she loves that she has a fictional character who can't bear to be more then two feet away from her in her life? How will she deal with her own fear of being hurt, by him and by the passing of someone she loved?

In the Lap of the Gods 1: The Bottom Rung

I may have been born in the Quarter, but I refuse to die here.

I live in the Quarter, the societal cage where all of Cremorne's paranormals have been locked up, but I'm neither vampire, werewolf nor witch. I'm the lowest of the low, doomed to be one of two things: junkie or vampire's pet.

Desperate to escape, I'll do whatever it takes to get out, to get all of us out, even if that means shaking my country and the gods themselves to the core to restore the balance. I'm collecting allies so I can start a revolution and finding power my kind would never dream of, but this game has been in play for a lot longer than I've been breathing and there's a chance I'm just another pawn.

That's OK, because I am determined to win.

Author's note: This book is an RH tale, so the MC does not choose one partner, but the romance angle is definitely pretty low key in some instances and is a bit more complex than girl meets multiple boys and falls in love. It takes a lot of its inspiration from 80s urban decay films like The Warriors and Blade Runner, so is kind of dystopian in tone. Politics and how power is used to control is a big theme, though hopefully the reader isn't bashed over the head by it!

In the Lap of the Gods 2: Rise to the Bait

I've got the powers of a goddess and I'm not afraid to use them.

Being the avatar of Lyra should have made my life easier. Instead, it painted a target on my back. Thrust into a werewolf camp, I was forced to run in a brutal ritual, for the gods themselves to decide who my mate should be. Never one to take things lying down, I refused to let that decision be made for me.

But my troubles didn't end there.

Hesse has set aside his casual brutalisation of the captive anomalous population. His focus has become far more personal when he realised exactly who has been stripping him of his assets. It wasn't blood banks or wolves he wanted. It was me.

Now, to stay out of his clutches, I must face my greatest fear and learn... to trust. Only with the help of allies do I hold any hope of defeating Hesse. Will it be enough to free our people? Or are we doomed to crumble beneath his tyrannical reign?

Upcoming Releases

In the Lap of the Gods 3: Fight to the Top

To be released early 2020

The Wolf At My Door 2

To be released in 2020

From the desk of the amazing Belle Harper!

Rescuing Harlow: A Post Apocalyptic Reverse Harem Romance (Seeking Eden Book 3)

Rescuing Harlow is part of the Seeking Eden world, but can be read as a STANDALONE

"In 2041 the world experienced the largest solar flare in history. It took out all the world's satellites and caused the power grid to overload. Causing a worldwide blackout. With no power to contain it, a virus was accidentally unleashed. The release of the NEX virus spread rapidly. Many people died within the first month. Most of the female population was wiped out. Those who survived the virus had fled to make shift cities, but even then, no one was safe."

Harlow had survived years of torture at the hands of the Red Raiders.

Jake and Lucas had won her heart, but her past had been keeping her from ever telling them those three words.

Will the three of them, together with help from Kade, be able to find and rescue her son?

Will she fall for the witty and humorous Kade? The shy but sweet Knox. Or will love prevail or hate win out between Harlow and Asher..

*** Rescuing Harlow is book 3 in the Seeking Eden series and part of a duet. Book 4 Claiming Harlow coming December 2019. Trigger Warning: this book contains references of abuse, there are no scenes of abuse***

Made in the USA
Columbia, SC
07 April 2020